Published by Acoustical Books, LLC

KenLozito.com

If you would like to be notified when my next book is released visit

WWW.KENLOZITO.COM

Paperback ISBN: 978-1-945223-78-5

Hardback ISBN: 978-1-945223-79-2

PATHFINDER

KEN LOZITO

CHAPTER 1

THE *PATHFINDER'S* bridge jerked to the side, and Connor tumbled to the deck. His head hit the side of the workstation and a white bolt of lightning lanced across his vision. The ship then lurched upward, shoving him into the air, and some unseen force slammed him back to the deck, hard. The breath rushed from his lungs and he gasped. He blindly reached out for the edge of the workstation, hearing others cry out.

Connor rolled onto his knees, shaking his head a little, trying to clear it. Alarms blared from the speakers overhead as he coughed, trying to regain his breath. He saw Noah looking disoriented as he lay sprawled against the wall. They locked gazes with a confused frown. Then, everything lurched to the side. Centrifugal force pushed Connor to the side, and Noah rolled out of sight.

Connor held onto the edge of the workstation with a vice-like grip, but his legs lifted and he grunted with the effort, gritting his teeth. He heard someone else cry out as they fell over a chair, and he glimpsed Glen Rhodes's shoes as they disappeared from view.

The lighting on the bridge became dark for a long moment before the red glow of emergency lighting took over. Amber holoscreens flickered around the bridge as if something was interfering with the power.

"General Gates, are you okay?" Sergeant Brent Seger asked, rushing toward him. Seger extended a dark-skinned hand, helping Connor regain his feet.

"Thanks," Connor replied, looking around, almost expecting another shift. "Check on Rhodes." He gestured toward where he'd last seen the Director of Colonial Requisitions.

"Yes, sir," Seger replied.

Connor looked around and saw the top of Noah's head behind a workstation in the corner. He hastened over, calling out to him. His friend had a trickle of blood flowing down his cheek from a shallow gash within the hairline near his left eye.

Connor squatted down and snapped his fingers in front of his friend's face. "Noah, look at me."

Noah blinked, as if being roused, and winced a little. "My head," he said and looked up at Connor.

"Are you alright?" Connor asked.

Noah looked down at his body in a quick assessment and leaned away from the wall. Connor helped him to his feet.

"Took a blow to the head, but I think I'm alright." Noah looked around at the bridge, noticing the flashing alarms. "I thought the earthquakes were done."

"They're supposed to be," Connor replied.

He had seen the same report. The *Pathfinder* was dry-docked at the Whitehall R&D facility on New Earth. The area had been experiencing a buildup of seismic activity that had gone quiet.

Noah frowned in thought as he moved to the nearest holoscreen.

Glen Rhodes let out a muffled curse when Seger pulled a chair off him. Rhodes stood and let out a growling hiss, limping to the side and barely making it to another chair.

Seger helped him.

"No, I'm not okay, dammit," Rhodes snapped at Seger.

The CDF sergeant assigned to Connor's protective detail looked slightly amused.

Rhodes leaned down, rubbing his ankle for a few seconds. He blew out a breath and looked at Connor. "What the heck happened? I thought this facility was safe."

They hadn't gotten off on the best of terms before the inspection. Glen Rhodes represented an oversight committee whose job it was to review materials requisitions for joint R&D projects. He was a glorified accountant who wielded enough influence to become a thorn in Connor's side. Noah had warned Connor before the meeting, describing Rhodes as having a prickly demeanor.

"We're trying to figure that out," Connor said and glanced at Rhodes's ankle. "I'll get someone from medical to come take a look at that foot.

Rhodes shifted in his seat and flexed his foot with a slight wince. He shook his head. "I don't know why the CDF insisted on building a research facility way out here, hundreds of kilometers away from the nearest city."

"It was a risk-based decision, considering the kind of work that goes on here." Connor regarded him for a moment. "The briefing you received would've covered that information."

He glanced over at Noah, who stared intently at the holoscreen while his hands flew through the interface, navigating a stack of sub-windows.

"I'm quite familiar with the project briefing," Rhodes replied. "I found that part in section thirteen, sub-section 3-B, where it states that surveys of the area showed fault lines that could lead to significant seismic activity."

"It said *possible* seismic activity, and they couldn't be sure whether it would be significant," Connor said. He brought up his wrist computer, opening a comlink. "Major Burkhardt, what's the status from Whitehall Central?" Connor frowned at the comlink, which hadn't been established. He checked the configuration, and the settings for short-range were correct. He tried it again, and it failed.

"I can't reach Major Burkhardt either, General Gates," Sergeant Seger said.

Connor nodded and tried to reach central but failed. Burkhardt was leading Connor's protective detail and was in charge of coordinating the schedule with Whitehall Central.

"I can't reach anyone from central on any frequency, sir," Sergeant Seger said.

Rhodes looked as if he were about to speak and then lifted his wrist computer. "Mine says out of range. That can't be possible. No doubt one of the many security measures for blocking communication signals has been enabled."

Connor frowned and checked general data communications to the facility's network. The status was unavailable.

"Can't you just disable it?" Rhodes asked.

"Not from here."

Rhodes rolled his eyes a little. "The security measures are a bit excessive, and now we're cut off."

Connor glanced at Noah. "Has there been an attack?"

Rhodes became still.

"I can't tell," Noah replied. "The computer system is a huge tangle of errors. I'm trying to sort it out."

"An attack? Who would attack us?" Rhodes asked. He shook his head, eyes widening. "Oh no! Cassidy, my daughter... she was. I don't know where she is." He scowled at his wrist computer. "I can't get a location. Everything is offline." He began to stand.

"Easy," Connor said. "Let me figure out what's going on."

Rhodes shook his head. "I'm not going to sit by while my daughter could be hurt."

"You're in no shape to go look for her. We'll find her," Connor assured him. "You have to trust me."

Rhodes stared at him intently.

"Glen," Connor said, "I'm a father, too. Okay? I understand. Believe me, I understand. Let us do our jobs and sort this out. We'll get the rescue team in here with medical support to search for everyone on the ship."

Rhodes clamped his mouth shut and nodded, then scowled toward his leg as if his body had failed him somehow.

Connor went to Noah, and Sergeant Seger came to his side.

"I've got a ping-back from Kincaid. He's near the robotics lab," Seger said.

Connor nodded and looked at Noah's holoscreen. "You've got to give me something."

"I can give you something, but none of it makes any sense," Noah replied irritably.

Connor stared at the data feeds and frowned. "That can't be right."

"I know," Noah said.

Rhodes limped over to them and looked at the holoscreen. "What is it?"

"It's the I-Drive. It's drawing power," Connor said.

"What?!" Rhodes said. "How's that even possible? It's supposed to be offline while in dry-dock."

A flash of alerts burst onto the holoscreen like fireworks, and Connor felt himself float up from the deck. His stomach quailed at the sudden loss of gravity.

Rhodes flailed his arms helplessly, and Sergeant Seger tried to steady him.

Noah grabbed the workstation and managed to stay in the chair. Automatic restraints burst from the back of the chair and secured him to it.

"Oh my God!" Noah exclaimed. "We're going to enter hyperspace."

Connor's eyes widened, and he looked helplessly at the holoscreen as he floated toward the ceiling. Several truths became apparent to him in that moment: They were in serious trouble; the I-Drive was online, taking them who knew where; and none of it made any sense. The computer systems had been offline. Could the seismic activity have triggered some kind of restart?

"Why are the artificial gravity systems online?" Rhodes shouted.

Since they were on New Earth, there was no need for artificial gravity.

Connor glanced at a wallscreen, and his mouth went dry. "They're not," he replied, and looked down at Noah. "What's the status of the umbilical?"

Noah frowned and looked at the holoscreen.

The *Pathfinder* had been connected to the R&D facility's power and computing cores. Noah looked up at him, his mouth partially agape, confirming their situation without saying anything.

The lack of gravity could only mean one thing. They were no longer on New Earth. They were somewhere in space on a ship that had been dry-docked on the planet for over a year.

Connor forced his mind to focus and glanced up. He raised

his hands over his head as he came to the ceiling, then pushed off and sank back to the deck.

"Sergeant, get Rhodes to a chair, now!"

"Yes, sir," Seger replied, grabbing Rhodes and pulling him toward the nearest workstation. The older man moved awkwardly, having never been in zero-gravity before.

Years of training kicked in as Connor reached for the chair. Moving in zero-gravity sometimes looked as if you were moving very slowly, but that was a misconception of the untrained. Oftentimes, you were moving quite fast, which became apparent when he reached the floor. He'd just managed to grab onto the chair and strapped in when the I-Drive engaged.

CHAPTER 2

THE LIGHTING on the bridge dimmed as the power draw from the I-Drive pilfered power from all other systems. Connor managed to spin into the chair, and emergency straps burst from the sides and top to hold him in place.

A warbled groan came from outside the bridge, and Connor felt as if something were squeezing his head. He gritted his teeth, the muscles in his neck and shoulders becoming tight. This sensation spread to the rest of his body, making him feel like something was stretching and compressing everything. Then, as if an invisible field had passed, the pressure subsided and emergency lighting returned to normal.

Connor exhaled forcefully as he turned toward Noah. "What happened? Are we in n-space?"

Noah's eyes darted across the data, looking as if he couldn't believe what he was seeing. Then he nodded. "We're out of the initial field from the I-Drive, but the readings are strange—" He stopped speaking and frowned. "The I-Drive is spooling up again."

Connor felt his body press into the seat as artificial gravity came online. That would make things easier and much less dangerous.

"Shut it down," he said.

"I'm trying. The system is not confirming the command," Noah replied.

A comlink chimed on Noah's workstation, and a woman's face appeared. She had piercing emerald eyes, and her auburn and gold hair was tied back into a practical bun.

"Naya, thank God. Are you near engineering?" Noah asked.

"I'm heading there now. Got tumbled about. This is going to sound strange, but I don't think we're on the planet anymore. There are several sections that show decompression," Naya said.

Connor recognized Naya Corman's voice. She was a lead engineer working on the retrofit that was upgrading the ship's systems. He shared a look with Noah, both of them wondering if anyone had been in those sections at the time of decompression.

"Are you able to get systems access?" Noah asked.

She shook her head. "We were in the middle of the system upgrade, about sixty percent through it. It's like the computing core doesn't know what to do with itself."

Connor knew enough about computing cores to understand that a system was at its most vulnerable during an upgrade, and that Noah's team had been planning the upgrade for over two months, the process of which required instability. A failure in the middle of such a complex undertaking would leave any system unstable. They were in real trouble.

"The I-Drive is drawing power from the core," Noah said.

She frowned. "That can't be right. The power core was in maintenance mode because we were running off the facility's power system."

"It's right. We can figure out the hows and whys later. I can't shut it down from here. The system won't accept the commands I'm giving it," Noah said.

"Understood," Naya replied and licked her lips, a worried frown appearing on her face before she looked at the camera of her wrist computer. "It's a two-person operation and I'm all alone down here."

Noah glanced at Connor for a second. "What about Tripp? Isn't he there?"

She shook her head. "I don't know where he is."

Noah blew out a breath as he unstrapped his restraints and stood. "I'm coming down. I'll meet you there."

"Roger that," she replied and severed the comlink.

Connor stood. "I'm coming with you."

"You're not leaving me behind," Rhodes said, beginning to stand.

Noah shook his head. "Connor, I need you to stay here on the bridge."

"On the bridge? What for?"

Noah looked away for a second. "Right now, this is one of the safest areas on the ship. I can only do so much from engineering. Internal comms systems should come back online. The bridge has a direct connection to the computing core. I have several diagnostic routines running, trying to stabilize the system. They will require manual input when they're finished."

Connor didn't like being relegated to the bridge, but Noah was right. He would be able to help and coordinate from here once the comms systems came back online. They needed to focus on finding the people who'd been aboard.

He looked at Seger. "Go with him, Sergeant. Make sure he gets to engineering."

Sergeant Seger was short and muscular, with a no-nonsense attitude that Connor liked, but the same quality could also make him stubbornly adherent to his primary mandate of protecting Connor.

Seger sighed. "Burkhardt is going to have my ass for leaving you alone, sir."

Connor smiled. "*I'll* have it if you don't do as I say. The situation has changed. Get Noah to engineering and assist him however you can."

Noah was already heading to the door, and Seger quickly caught up with him.

Rhodes stared at Connor with pure exasperation. "Recklessness. An I-Drive engaged while dry-docked at the facility? Do you know how many people have lost their lives from this?"

Connor gritted his teeth, his patience stretching thin. "No, and neither do you. We don't have time to sit here and point fingers. You can either help me or sit down and be quiet."

Rhodes glared at him and then shook his head. "No way am I gonna just sit by."

"Good, take this seat right there," Connor said, gesturing to the seat next to him. He turned back to the holoscreen. "Let's figure out what kind of shape we're in."

He activated the main holoscreen, and a long list of alerts dominated the screen. Just about every system had been affected. At least they had life support, but only for the areas of the ship where bulkhead doors had closed.

Rhodes looked at Connor. "How do I clear these alerts on my screen so I can use the comms system?"

There was only a slight edge to his voice, which Connor was going to assume was because he was concerned about finding his daughter.

Connor showed him how to minimize the alerts and brought up a new data window. "There's the comms system," he said. "Actually, wait. I'll try a broadcast first."

He initiated the broadcast, which took almost a full minute to become active. Not a good sign, but he kept that thought to himself.

"Attention everyone aboard the ship. This is General Gates. We're still trying to figure out what happened. The danger has not passed. Comms appear to be spotty. If you have access to standard comlink, use it to contact the bridge with your current status. We need a headcount of everyone aboard and whether anyone is injured. It's not safe to roam the ship. Stay in the section you're in, as long as you can secure yourself. Repeat, the danger has not passed. Report in with your current status. If you're unable to contact the bridge, sit tight. We'll be making a sweep of the ship shortly. General Gates, out."

Rhodes regarded him with a thoughtful frown. "Who's going to make a sweep of the ship?"

"I have people aboard who are qualified for search and rescue."

Rhodes arched an eyebrow. "You mean your protective detail?"

Connor nodded.

"Isn't one of them missing? How many people are assigned to your protective detail?"

"It varies, but I had three people here today. You've already met Sergeant Seger. There's also Major Lance Burkhardt and Captain Tyler Kincaid. All good men."

Rhodes narrowed his gaze a little at the mention of Kincaid, and Connor decided to ignore it.

"You brought your daughter and another inspector?" Connor said.

Rhodes nodded. "Jorath."

Connor knew the names of everyone Rhodes had brought on

the ship. Jorath was an Ovarrow, who had joined the colony from a nation known as the Konus. "Your protection."

Rhodes frowned in surprise.

"We vetted everyone in your party before allowing them to come to the facility. Standard field evaluations for colonial officials require at least one protector assigned, although with Jorath's background he also has the credentials required for his evaluation duties."

Rhodes sighed. "I see you know a lot more about us than I gave you credit for."

Connor looked at the holoscreen, checking the status of the diagnostic subroutines that Noah was using to fix the computer systems.

"Still doesn't excuse the recklessness of this whole operation. This situation is a direct result of it."

Connor gave a slight shake of his head. "Rushing to conclusions without all the facts is foolish, Director Rhodes."

Rhodes inhaled explosively, and his face reddened. He looked toward the door for a second. "How you can be so calm? How can you be okay just sitting here?"

Connor resisted the urge to make assumptions about Rhodes's character and life experience. Instead, he replied. "I'm not calm. I'm focused. When you've faced the things I have, you quickly learn the futility of giving in to your emotions. It doesn't change anything. All those questions you probably have, I have as well. I want to know what happened, too, but there are more important things to worry about. Higher priorities, like getting an accurate headcount."

To himself, he added, "And can this ship hold together long enough for a rescue mission?"

Rhodes seemed to consider this for a few moments. "I'm

surprised you don't already know how many people were aboard."

"Special circumstances."

"Because of the inspection?"

He nodded a little. "Partly, but mainly it was because of the planned computing core upgrade. Staff had to be reduced because of limited access required for the work that needed to be done."

"I see."

"Work on the ship was ramping up," Connor said as the ship status updated. Many sections with airlocks showed a red status, and he didn't know whether they were damaged or merely offline.

"How come we're not able to see people's status via their implants or wrist computers?"

"Not sure. Probably has to do with all those errors. Systems are offline or not working properly. We're in the dark."

"Yes, but personal comms are still available."

"Entering and exiting hyperspace temporarily interferes with personal comms. I don't know why they're still working—" Connor said, and several comlinks registered throughout the ship.

"Time to work," Connor said. "I need you to note the names of the people reporting in, as well as if there are any injuries."

Rhodes nodded and brought up a blank sub-window, then waited.

As people were able to contact them, they learned that either there weren't as many people aboard the ship as they thought, or there were more people missing than they anticipated. Among those who were missing was Rhodes's daughter, and Connor tried to remember the last thing that Burkhardt had said to him.

He'd been going to check something at the facility, but had he made it off the ship? Burkhardt was an outstanding officer.

Connor glanced at his wrist computer, thinking about his protective detail. Captain Tyler Kincaid was the wild card of the bunch. His record indicated a certain number of questionable decisions, but he had also demonstrated a dedication and discipline that was a cut above the rest.

He glanced at the ship's status. External sensors were offline. They were no longer on the planet, and the problem was that without sensors, they couldn't figure out where they were. Without comms, they couldn't call for help. The *Pathfinder* hadn't been in space in over a year. The ship was a recommissioned frigate that had a twenty-plus-year career in the CDF. It had been retrofitted twice but was eventually outclassed by the newer warships. The ship was much too small to be considered for long-term exploration, which made it a prime candidate for the experimental I-Drive that he and Noah had been working on for the past eighteen months.

Connor kept going over what had happened in his mind, and none of it made any sense. None whatsoever. What should've been impossible had happened, and now they had to figure out how to stay alive so they could call for help.

He recalled seeing the exposed bulkheads as they entered the docking area. The ship looked like a skeleton of its former self, and now it had to keep them alive. Rhodes thought he was calm; he wasn't calm. He knew better than Rhodes the desperate situation they were in. He was just better at masking it. Only his decades of military training allowed him to push the fear and confusion to the side so he could still function, focusing his attention on what was important. Maybe they could stay alive a little while longer.

CHAPTER 3

Captain Tyler Kincaid stared out the armorplast windshield of an old Abrams troop transport rover that was decades older than he was. He had no idea how it had gotten to be on the Falcon class CDF frigate, which was also older than he was, but the old rover had become his own personal life pod.

The rover didn't have a charged life support system, and when the alarms blared, it wasn't like he'd had a lot of time. He'd been in the vehicle bay and had barely cleared the door as it shut between the vehicle bay and the repair shop. He kept thinking about the maintenance tech who'd been walking through the airlock when the alarms sounded. They'd been on the other side of the vehicle bay, and the door control panel indicated that the area had decompressed.

When the deck had shifted under his feet, he'd climbed into the rover, believing it to be the safest place for him. The rover still had its long storage-locking clamps attached to the frame. He'd shut the hatch and had barely strapped himself in when the whole world took a tumultuous nosedive. If he hadn't acted so quickly, he would've been banged up pretty badly, or worse.

Tyler sighed and leaned forward to look at the lockers in the corner. Their doors were open and their contents strewn across the maintenance area. Tools had clattered onto the deck as the ship… He couldn't guess as to what had happened. The ship had moved with enough force to make those tools deadly weapons as they flew by the rover, with more than a few banging against the armored body.

Tyler looked at his wrist computer with a frown. He'd been speaking to Burkhardt when the alarms began to go off and they were disconnected. The network access indicator spun, as if waiting to be allowed to connect again. He was disconnected from everything. The repair center only had emergency lighting enabled. He couldn't see the other two doors to the room, just the wide doors to the vehicle bay.

Decompressed…

"That's gotta be a mistake."

No way could the bay be decompressed. Did that mean the repair center was also decompressed? Was he sealed inside the rover with only the air that was available when he'd gotten in?

He gave the vehicle controls a tap, hoping the old rover had power, but it was futile. "Worth a shot, regardless."

He stared at the warning light above the vehicle bay doors. The doors were sealed to the bay area, which meant that the decompression had only occurred in that room and not the repair center. He glanced at the hatch above him. With no access to any computer system, the only way for him to confirm whether the repair center had somehow lost life support was to pop open the hatch and hope for the best.

Tyler wasn't averse to risking his life, but the circumstances he found himself in were stranger than what he was used to. His instincts kept telling him that the R&D facility had been attacked. Nothing else made sense to him. It was either that they'd been attacked or a massive earthquake had opened a huge fissure that the ship happened to fall into.

He frowned in thought. They were right side up, so regardless of what had happened, they'd ended up in the direction that made it easier to navigate the ship.

The red light above the bay door seemed to taunt him. Those sensors never malfunctioned, so even if there was an attack or some crazy, destructive earthquake, he felt he could trust the sensors.

"Focus, Tyler," he said and looked around the sparse inside of the rover. The vehicle had been stripped of its equipment.

Staying in the rover wasn't an option because he was going to run out of air. There were two other doors to the repair center, and he closed his eyes, trying to remember the layout of the room. The door behind the rover was closer.

He considered his options. Over ten minutes had passed since the ship became somewhat stabilized. They'd lost gravity before. It was either that or they'd experienced a very long fall into a deep fissure that had miraculously appeared on New Earth. How the heck could they be in space? But artificial gravity was working, so that had to mean they *were* in space. Burkhardt had warned him when he'd recruited him for General Gates's protective detail that he had to be ready for the unexpected. The famous CDF general had a long history of having the most peculiar events occur wherever he was. However, having a ship somehow teleport into space had to be a new one, even for him.

Tyler sighed. "I can't just stay here."

He unbuckled his safety straps and grasped the release for the hatch above him. "Here goes nothing."

His muscles tightened in anticipation, but then he sank back into the seat. Space and decompression would kill him. The lack of oxygen had to be affecting his brain.

He leaned down and felt under the dashboard, found and opened a small covered auxiliary port, and connected it to his wrist computer. He couldn't jumpstart the rover, but he could access its emergency systems, including the vehicle's sensors.

A small holoscreen appeared above his wrist computer and showed that there was an atmosphere outside the rover. He could breathe, but the room was sealed off from the ship's life support system for some reason.

He glanced at the temperature. It was cold but bearable, at least for the time he needed to leave the area.

Kincaid opened the hatch and frigid air rushed inside. He quickly climbed out of the vehicle, trying to ignore the shock of cold on his face. He hated cold weather. Even serving a few rotations off-world on veritable ice worlds hadn't lessened his dislike of the cold in the slightest.

He climbed down the footholds on the side of the rover and landed on the deck, looking at the door behind the rover. He knew it led to the interior corridors of the ship. Hopefully, those areas were not damaged.

Tyler gave the rover an appreciative bang with his fist and hastened toward the door. He palmed the controls and the door opened to a corridor with pulsing amber lights. The door to the repair center closed behind him as he entered the hallway, and he noticed that the air was much warmer. He heaved a sigh of relief.

He was in a short, L-shaped corridor with doors closed at both ends. The doors must've shut as part of an emergency response. Tyler brought up his wrist computer and accessed an offline map of the ship. He also tried to reach Burkhardt on his personal comlink, but the connection wouldn't establish. He needed to get to the bridge.

The nearby door to this left led to a much longer corridor, and he began jogging. About halfway down, he heard faint knocking sounds. He stopped and tilted his head to the side a little as he listened. It seemed that the sound was coming from a wall on the far side of a darkened room.

Tyler went inside the room and turned on the lights. The room was some kind of lab that contained small animal pens along the left wall. A long, dark table was along the other side of the lab.

The knocking stopped.

Tyler quickly crossed to the far wall and banged it with his fist. "Hello!" he called out. "Is there anyone there?"

He banged his fist on the metallic wall three more times and waited for a response.

An answering knock came back, along with a very muffled response that he couldn't quite make out. It sounded like a woman's voice, but he couldn't be sure.

"I hear you, but I don't understand you. Just give me a second to figure out where you are," he replied.

Whoever they were banged on the wall insistently. They needed help and must be starting to panic.

Tyler brought up the schematic of the area. The room on the other side of the wall was a large, round, holodisplay dome used for stellar cartography. He couldn't access the room from the lab.

Tyler pounded on the wall. "Listen to me." The knocking stopped. "There is a maintenance access way on the other side of the dome. There should be a door there. I'll meet you over there."

A muffled reply came back, and he was pretty sure they'd said the door was locked. He didn't have anything that could cut through the wall of the lab, but the maintenance corridor was his best option.

"I'm heading to the maintenance door now," he said and hoped they could understand him.

Tyler raced out of the lab and ran to the end of the corridor, making another left. He passed by several small offices, then came to a small engineering room. A pair of workstations off to the side showed active holoscreens with a long list of alerts. He went by a small workbench with storage underneath and tapped the door controls to the maintenance corridor. The indicator light flashed red as access was denied.

Tyler tapped his wrist computer on the panel and the light became green as the door opened. He raced down the narrow corridor, having to go sideways to accommodate his large frame. He wound his way past equipment and found the door to the holodome.

There were scorch marks near the door control panels, and it was dark. That explained why they couldn't use the door.

He banged on the door and tried to find the manual override. He found the panel but couldn't open it. Some kind of corrosive material covered the seams of the panel.

"Hello!" Tyler called out.

An answering knock came, as well as a deep-sounding guttural response. Then the translator on his wrist computer became active. "I hear you," said a deep voice. "We're trapped."

Tyler recognized the voice. It was the Ovarrow who was part of the inspection team. "Jorath, is that you?"

"It is I. Who am I speaking with?"

Jorath had a serious air about him, even for an Ovarrow.

"This is Captain Kincaid. The controls on this side are fried."

"To be expected. One of the technicians with us attempted

to override the door controls to free us, but his efforts triggered some kind of overload," Jorath replied.

"Are they hurt?"

"He is stable."

Jorath had all the warmth and compassion of a rock.

"Is anyone else hurt?"

"Captain Kincaid, there are several people who need medical attention. None appear to be life-threatening. Are you able to get the door open? The door we used is locked and will not allow us to override it."

Tyler glanced at the schematics of the area. The adjacent corridor to the holodome observatory was near the vehicle bay, which was decompressed. The door to the observatory was the only thing keeping them alive.

"Okay, give me a minute. I need to go get something to help me open the door. I'll be right back," Tyler replied.

He went back to the engineering closet and opened the storage lockers where he found a patch repair kit with a small plasma cutter. This should get him through the panel for the manual override. He grabbed a few other tools he thought he might need and headed back to the other door.

Tyler fired up the plasma cutter and held it near the panel for the override. Bright, high-heat plasma made short work of the corrosive substance. He killed the torch and used an age-old pry bar found in most standard engineering kits. He shoved the business end of the tool into the seam of the panel and forced it open. Inside, the panel was a mess. A black sludge looked to have leaked in from the top and covered the handle for manual override. He leaned away from the foul-smelling stuff and used his trusty pry bar to knock the handle down and force the release of the door. It popped open a little, and Tyler used his new favorite tool to force the door open the rest of the way.

A tall Ovarrow stood on the other side and regarded him for a moment.

"Come on. It's kinda narrow. One at a time," Tyler said, gesturing for the big Ovarrow to move past.

Tyler went into the observatory and saw a young man lying on the floor. He had unruly red hair and pale skin, and he was so thin that Tyler thought a strong wind could've knocked him over. He had several scratches on his face and neck. The name Tripp Krin appeared on Tyler's internal HUD.

A woman with her back to Tyler was leaning over the man, speaking softly. Tripp blinked a few times.

Tyler cleared his throat. "We've got to get him out of here. Tripp, I'm Captain Kincaid with protective services for General Gates. Can you stand?"

The woman leaned back, and the shape of her body tugged a memory from his past.

"It took you long enough to get in here, Tyler," she said.

He blinked. "Cass?"

Cassidy Rhodes helped Tripp to his feet without looking at Tyler. Her buttery blonde hair was cut to a thick bob that complimented her perfectly tan skin. Bright blue eyes regarded him cooly.

Tyler tilted his head to the side, resigned. "Hello, Cass."

Years of cold resentment emanated from her gaze. "Hello, Captain," she replied waspishly.

Tyler rolled his eyes. "Tripp, are you alright?"

The young man was hunched over more than normal, and he grimaced. "Got my wires crossed."

"I see that," Tyler said and grabbed his arm as he teetered on his feet. "Come on, we've got to get out of here. It's not safe."

Cass blew out a breath, muttering something about understatements. Then she walked away.

Tripp looked at him. "I don't think she likes you."

Tyler chuckled a little. "Yeah, well, she's got good reasons. Come on."

A young woman followed them. "Captain Kincaid. Hi, I'm Grace."

Tyler peered at her, and his HUD updated with her identification. Civilian Specialist Grace Mendel. Her honey skin was a few shades lighter than brown, and she had dark-brown eyes and puffy cheeks.

"Hello, Grace. Why don't you go ahead and I'll make sure Tripp stays upright," Tyler said.

He glanced around the observatory, looking for anyone else, then followed the others.

Cass helped Tripp through the door, and Grace took over as his escort.

Cass gave him a stern look that softened a little. "I'm sorry about before."

"It's fine," Tyler said, waving the comment off.

"Do you know what happened?"

He shook his head. "No idea."

She frowned. "How could that be? I thought you were part of security for General Gates."

Jorath lingered in the doorway to the corridor, watching them.

"I'm cut off. No network access," Tyler said and lifted his chin toward the workstations. "Those are unresponsive. I was heading to the bridge when I heard the knocking, and here we are."

Tyler looked at Jorath, gesturing for him to move out into the corridor. The others looked at him expectantly.

"Tripp needs medical attention," Cass said.

He nodded. "You're right. There's a medical station near the galley." They looked at him blankly. Civilians. "The dining area. You know… food?"

They nodded, and Jorath simply stared at him.

"I'll head to the bridge," Jorath said.

Tyler shook his head. "No, we need to stick together. I don't know what happened, but I don't think we're out of danger just yet."

Jorath looked as if he was going to protest, and Cass spoke. "He's right. We should stick together. We don't know if there are other damaged areas of the ship. The earthquake could've done more damage than we think it did."

They didn't realize it wasn't an earthquake, or that the ship was in space. He decided not to tell them. No need to scare them any more than they already were. He checked his wrist computer. "Come on, this way. There's an emergency comms terminal on the way," Tyler said and led the way.

Part of him was still shocked to see Cass here. He hadn't seen her since before he'd left to join the CDF. He pushed those old thoughts and maybe a few regrets from his mind. He needed to report in and find out what was really going on.

CHAPTER 4

Connor resisted the urge to leave the bridge for the hundredth time in the past few minutes. His broadcast wasn't making it to the entire ship. Glen Rhodes bounced his leg in a release of nervous energy. Connor doubted that Rhodes realized he was using his injured ankle. Perhaps it was only a slight sprain, and a little bit of rest was all he needed.

"There must be more than eight survivors. There had to be at least thirty people on the ship," Rhodes said.

There had been some check-ins and several injuries reported, with some of them being quite serious. Rhodes was worried about his daughter, who was among the missing.

Connor stared at the comms system, waiting for Noah to finally give him a status. When the comlink registered, it still came as a shock as he acknowledged the call.

"Took us longer than we thought to reach engineering," Noah said. "It's bad out there. There are entire sections that are completely cut off, which forced us to take a more circuitous route here."

"Did you encounter anyone?" Connor asked, hoping for some good news.

Noah gave a slight shake of his head and sighed, looking guilty. However, this passed in a moment as his friend refocused himself.

"Understood. What's the status of the I-Drive?"

Noah looked away from the comlink. "Naya, any luck over there?"

"No joy. I've never seen a system this messed up. Computing resources are all pinned to the max. It's like there aren't enough cycles to allow for our commands. And that's only from the systems I can get a status on," Naya replied, her voice tight with frustration.

Noah pinched his eyebrows together in a scowl, then looked at Connor, gritting his teeth.

"How can we fix it?" Connor asked.

"We *can't* fix it. Not like this. The I-Drive is still counting down, readying to do another jaunt through hyperspace, although *that's* not even right. It's not behaving like it should. I don't know what it's doing."

Rhodes was about to chime in, and Connor silenced him with a withering look. The older man blinked in surprise and was silent.

Connor looked at Noah. "There has to be a way to safely power it down."

"Normally, yes, but we had multiple systems routing power through the umbilical to the facility. The only way I think we can stop it is by bringing down the computing core to reset it."

Connor's mind raced with the implications of Noah's solution. The computing core of a ship was the brain that kept the ship operating. A full reset would also include resetting the ship's power core, effectively cutting off every system on the ship. Life support could run on emergency power, but the ship wasn't flight ready. They'd be dead in space with no guarantees that they could restore power or the computing core.

"I know it's crazy, but we're not going to survive if the I-Drive engages again while the ship is in this state," Noah said.

"Why not? The I-Drive engaged before and we survived." Rhodes asked.

Noah looked over at him. "Each time the I-Drive cycles, it's more debilitating to the ship. We're losing entire sections because it's a shock to the whole system. Remember how we lost gravity before and there was a delay in artificial gravity coming back? It'd be like that but worse, or it might not comeback at all. It's because of the draw on a malfunctioning power core. With the computer system non-functional, it can't manage the containment field for the energy core. If those systems fail, we'll lose power, but it's also anyone's guess as to whether the containment field failure would shut down gracefully."

Rhodes was about to ask another question, but Connor cut him off. "He's saying there is a chance the ship could explode. The power core would become unstable because the computing core can't manage it. Noah's right: we don't have a choice."

"But we need to find the missing people. Cutting the power will affect all ship's systems, right?" Rhodes asked.

Connor nodded. "We need time to do a sweep. How much time do we have?"

Noah looked as if he'd swallowed something foul.

Connor continued. "We need to give people time to get strapped in and maybe into an EVA suit for individual life support."

"I'll give you as much time as I can. Making the countdown available," Noah said.

Connor put it up on the main holoscreen.

"General Gates," Sergeant Seger said, "I'm not much use here. Permission to make a sweep of the ship on my way back to the bridge."

"Granted," Connor said, then added. "Set individual comlinks to short-range broadcast mode. They can be used to form a patch network in case comms go out again."

"Got it, General," Seger replied and left.

Connor looked at Noah. He could only imagine what was going on in his friend's mind. He felt guilty for what had happened.

"Noah," Connor said quietly, "stay focused. You can do this."

Noah blinked as if being roused from his thoughts and nodded. "I'll keep you posted."

The comlink went on standby.

Rhodes cleared his throat, and Connor wasn't sure how he'd react if Rhodes continued with his belligerent behavior.

"Are there any emergency EVA suits here on the bridge?" Rhodes asked.

Connor thought about it and couldn't remember. "I'm not sure," he said as he stood and began looking. He checked various storage compartments hidden on the bridge, but they were empty.

"Do you have any children, General Gates?" Rhodes asked.

"You can call me Connor. Yes, I do. Two. They're grown. I have one grandson, Jacob," Connor said with a smile. "He just turned a year old. You, Glen?"

Rhodes smiled a little. "Seven of my own. Cass is my youngest, and we have fifteen grandchildren." He frowned a little. "I'm surprised you don't have more kids."

"We're working on it," Connor replied as he checked another storage compartment. It was empty.

His wife wanted more kids, a lot more, and so did he. His

old friend Juan Diaz had many kids of his own and a tribe of grandchildren. But he had to stop thinking about his family because those thoughts sometimes spiraled out of control, and he needed to stay focused. They needed to fix the ship so they could contact home and wait for a rescue mission.

He heard Rhodes speaking to someone.

"Yes, General Gates is here," Rhodes said and looked at Connor.

Connor hastened to his workstation and saw Captain Tyler Kincaid on vidcom. He gave Connor a quick status update.

"Five people with you. That's good news," Connor said, increasing the count to fourteen.

"We're making our way to the medbay, but we keep encountering sections of the ship that are cut off," Kincaid said.

A woman spoke next to him and Kincaid nodded. "Sir," he said and then waved the other person over. "Sir, this is Cassidy Rhodes. She wants to know if her father is with you."

A beautiful young woman looked at Connor.

Rhodes nearly leaped out of his chair. "Cass! Are you okay?"

She smiled. "I'm fine. Are you hurt?"

Rhodes shook his head, looking relieved. "Never mind that now. You've got to get somewhere safe. Can you make it to the bridge?"

She glanced at Kincaid for a second. "I don't think we can."

Connor cleared his throat, and Rhodes looked at him. "We don't have much time."

Rhodes nodded and reluctantly went back to his chair.

"Captain," Connor said, "you don't have much time. You've got to get those people someplace safe and secure."

"Understood, sir," Kincaid said. "General, I haven't had any contact with Major Burkhardt since the event."

"Neither have I," Connor said.

Major Burkhardt had a family of his own. After a certain age, most colonists had families.

"Focus on keeping those people safe and send me a status update when you reach the medbay," Connor said.

"Yes, General."

CHAPTER 5

The others in the corridor looked at Tyler when he closed the comlink. Jorath looked as relaxed as the stiff Ovarrow could be expected to look.

"We stick together and head to the medbay," Tyler said.

"What's the countdown timer?" Cass asked, gesturing above the control panel near the door.

"They need to bring down both the power systems and the computing core to stop the Infinity Drive from engaging and taking us out of n-space."

Jorath let out a guttural huff. "That is inadvisable."

"I'm sure it wasn't their first choice," Tyler said and started walking, gesturing for the others to follow.

The ship had two medical bays on the main deck. The primary medbay was centrally located and the one he intended to take the others to. Then, he'd make his own sweep of the ship to look for Burkhardt. He had to be on the ship, likely unconscious somewhere.

No matter what route he took to reach the primary medbay,

the corridors were locked down. They had to backtrack a few times, and he eventually led them down a maintenance shaft that took them near the backup fuel-processing area.

"Tyler," Cass said with less of an edge to her voice, "what about the robotics lab? I saw a sign for it. Could there be EVA suits stored there as well?"

He shook his head. "No, there are just charging stations for the drones, with some replacement-parts storage."

The route they were taking was leading them to the mess hall. "The secondary medbay is located near the mess h—dining hall."

Cass glanced at her wrist computer where a small countdown timer was on display.

They made quick progress through the ship that led them right to the mess hall, and Tyler heard several people speaking. Finally hearing other people was both reassuring and worrisome. There were three people inside.

An older bald man knelt on the floor and had two of his fingers pressed against the carotid artery of an unconscious, olive-skinned man. He looked up without taking his fingers away and raised his chin in greeting. "Hey," he said while glancing at the others and then focusing on Tyler. "Captain Kincaid."

The man's name appeared on Tyler's HUD. "Louis Maclean," he said and frowned. "Aren't you the cook?"

The man stopped, feeling the unconscious man's pulse. "Name's Mac, and yes."

Grace helped Tripp sit down at one of the nearby tables.

Tyler looked at the man on the deck. "What happened to him?"

"He took a nasty fall. Stubborn fool wouldn't listen to me and got banged up pretty good. His pulse is steady. He'll probably have a mother of all headaches when he wakes. Not to mention a broken arm, at that."

Tyler frowned in thought. Mac had the bearing of someone who'd served in the CDF.

Mac arched a dark-gray eyebrow. "I wasn't always a cook, Captain."

"Medic?" Tyler asked.

Mac's usual enigmatic smile appeared. "Among other things."

Jorath cleared his throat. "We should not stay here. This area isn't safe."

Mac chuckled. "Says who? You? What do you know about it?"

Jorath blinked, stumped by Mac's response.

"Ovarrow," Mac said teasingly. "So, by the book."

Cass glanced at Tyler for a second. "We were going to the medbay."

Mac frowned.

"Primary medbay was cut off, so we had to cut through the backup fuel-processing area."

A young man came out of the kitchen. He had blond hair and looked at them all in surprise.

"Hopper, it's about time. Help me get Husker here into the chair. We need to secure him good and tight before the countdown finishes up," Mac said.

"Right," Hopper said and hastened over.

Mac looked up at Tyler. "We could use some help."

Tyler nodded and helped them move the unconscious man. He was tall, willowy, and solid, much heavier than he looked.

Mac shook his head. "Geez, Rabsaris, I should've stopped giving you that extra pie."

They eased Rabsaris Husker into a chair near the wall, and

Hopper wrapped several towels around his neck to help stabilize his head.

Tyler looked at the others as if noticing them for the first time, and what he saw made his insides clench.

Louis Maclean—Mac—regarded him for a moment, giving him a knowing look. "Keep your head in the game, son."

Tyler blinked. Had he been *that* transparent?

Cass looked at him in confusion, but Tyler looked away and checked the countdown timer.

Cass looked at hers and gasped. "We lost time. It just changed."

Mac nodded. "Captain, this is the safest place for these people."

"A dining hall?" Cass asked in disbelief.

"Trust me," Mac replied.

Cass shook her head. "Thank you, no." She turned toward Tyler.

He shrugged. "He's not wrong. All ships, especially military vessels, have safety zones. The designers try to account for where people have a tendency to be. Crew quarters, which are on the upper level, are one area. Medical bays are another location, and," he said, gesturing around them, "mess halls."

Tyler clapped his hands, getting everyone's attention. "We need to hole up here. Find a seat."

No one moved except Mac and Hopper.

"Now!" Tyler said sternly.

Cass flinched and narrowed her gaze. Tyler walked over to a control panel by the door. He opened the holoscreen and selected the option for emergency lockdown protocols. Flashing lights appeared overhead and automatic straps came out of the bottoms of the chairs, securing people to them.

Tyler checked the timer and looked out into the corridor.

Burkhardt could still be out there. He stepped toward the door and someone grabbed his arm.

"Where are you going?" Cass asked, her bright blue eyes wide.

"There are still people missing. I'm going to check as many places as I can with the time we've got left," he replied.

Cass held onto his arm. "Are you crazy? There *is* no time."

Tyler gritted his teeth.

Cass gave him a knowing look. "Who's out there? Who are you looking for?"

Tyler blew out a breath and closed his eyes. "A friend. A really good friend."

He started to leave, but Cass held onto him.

Jorath called over to them, but Tyler ignored him.

"I know that look," Cass said. "It's the one you get right before you do something foolish."

"Like you care now," he snapped, and shook his head with instant regret. Cass let go of his arm. "I'm sorry, Cass. I didn't mean that, but he'd do the same for me."

She shook her head. "Go. Leaving is what you're best at."

Tyler's jaw clenched for a second. The words stung, and no truer words had been spoken.

"You should go sit down," Tyler said.

Cass turned away from him. Her shoulders were drawn up tight, her hands clenched into fists. She took a few steps and stopped. "Tyler, please."

There was a tender note in her voice that gave him pause. The last time he'd heard it was when he'd walked away from her the last time they'd spoken. A part of him regretted it, and it was that part of him that reacted strongly now. Tyler slowly turned toward her with a tightening of his teeth. He felt as if he were abandoning Burkhardt, who'd mentored him into becoming the soldier he was. It stung, and he felt ashamed, as if he were disappointing him. But Burkhardt had taught him to always weigh the facts. He didn't have to like them, but they couldn't be ignored. Cassidy was right. He needed to be here. Burkhardt was on his own.

He sat next to Cassidy, and together they watched the countdown as it drew inevitably down. A few seconds before it ran out, he held Cassidy's hand. She stiffened for a moment but then leaned a shoulder toward him.

CHAPTER 6

Emergency lighting on the *Pathfinder*'s bridge gave Connor plenty of light to see with because of his neural implants, but Glen Rhodes commented on how dim the light was.

Both men stared at the main holoscreen as the countdown timer whittled down to the inevitable. Connor listened to both Noah and Naya coordinate the emergency shutdown procedure of the computing and power core, a task he knew should take at least a dozen people, but they were the only qualified people to do the actual work.

Connor glanced at Rhodes, who listened intently to the comlink to main engineering.

Rhodes met his gaze. "You'd never know they hadn't done this before."

Connor nodded. "Noah is the absolute best at what he does. He picked his team based on their merits. I trust him with my life."

Rhodes frowned a little. "I know there's a long history between the two of you, but there have been serious missteps here. Please, hear me out. If everything was running smoothly with all the safety measures in place, then how do you explain this situation? There will be a thorough investigation into this. With so many people missing—or worse—there has to be. This isn't a personal attack on you or the great Noah Barker."

"We push the envelope here. That's what we do. This research is dangerous."

Rhodes lifted his palm. "That's exactly my point. Exactly. If you push too far and too fast, you could get burned."

"It's a balance. There is no way to alleviate the danger completely. And we haven't pieced together what caused this. I'm not afraid of an investigation, and you can wager that Noah isn't either. He'll go over every possible detail until he understands exactly how all this happened. I've known him since he was little more than a kid. He's never hidden from responsibility. He's among the most humble and courageous people I've ever met."

Rhodes regarded him for a long moment. "That's really saying something, coming from you." He paused for a moment. "There is a bias here. Can you be objective?"

A soft, bitter chuckle bubbled up from his chest as he stared at Rhodes for a second. "To a fault, but I think we're getting ahead of ourselves."

Rhodes became quiet as he stared at the main holoscreen.

There was more going on than the emergency shutdown of both the computing and power cores. They had to time the actual shutdown to coincide with the I-Drive as it made its final power draw to put them into hyperspace. It was going to function as a forced failsafe step that would compel the I-Drive to cease its operation. With the state of the computing core, Connor equated it to performing complex maneuvers with a weighted suit hindering every movement you made. Nothing responded as quickly as they were used to, so Noah was essentially setting up a complex house of cards that a series of well-placed dominos needed to knock over at precisely the right moment.

Connor's mathematical capabilities only went so far. He was out of his element and had to rely on both Noah and Naya, both engineers, with Noah being among the most famous geniuses of any generation.

"Here we go," Connor said as the first of the timers reached its end.

The holoscreens on the bridge went out, and the screens blanked out before going off altogether. The same was occurring on all systems across the ship. The computing core was being cut off. The lighting on the bridge dimmed, leaving only two emergency lights near the door to the bridge. A reddish, hazy glow penetrated the darkness.

"I never took the option to upgrade my implants," Rhodes said.

"They should still help you see in the dim light."

"Not as much as I would like. How often does anyone find themselves in such darkness?"

Connor had seen many dark places during his military career. Darkness was subtle and sometimes eroded people's calm. Born of necessity, he was no longer one of those people. He didn't seek out dark places, but had found himself in them more times than he could count.

The screens went off, along with all the low-sounding hums that were barely noticed until absolute silence settled on the bridge. In Connor's experience, there was nothing more unsettling than a ship that was completely silent.

"I feel like I should hold my breath," Rhodes said.

The comlink to engineering went offline with the rest of the other systems on the bridge.

Connor felt his body rise a little as the artificial gravity emitters lost power.

"I understand," Connor said, trying to ease the other man's growing anxiety. "We've got plenty of oxygen in here."

Rhodes turned toward him. "Not your first time in a situation like this either?"

Connor shook his head. "No."

"Tell me about it."

Connor considered it for a few seconds. "I doubt it would set your mind at ease."

There was a banging sound that seemed to originate from outside the bridge.

"What is that?" Rhodes asked.

"Loss of power triggers the automatic bulkhead doors to shut. It happens fast."

They were both quiet for a few moments.

Rhodes blew out a breath. "I keep trying to think of something to say, and I can't think of anything."

"When the power comes back online, we'll do a damage assessment of the ship and all its systems. Then we'll try to figure out where we are and call for help," Connor said.

"You make it sound so matter of fact."

"It is."

"You don't happen to have a personal subspace comms available?"

Connor chuckled. "No. If I did, I would've told you. I'm relying on the ship's comms system just like everyone else."

"Shouldn't the power have been restored by now?"

Connor glanced at his wrist computer. "Not according to the timeline. We've got a few minutes yet."

He watched as Rhodes looked down at his own wrist computer.

"Look, Rhodes, I'm going to do everything that I can to get you home safe. The same goes for everyone else here."

Rhodes shook his head and looked as if he were participating in a conversation with himself. "Thanks. I know you're trying to reassure me, but I've never felt this cut off before."

Connor looked at him. "Seriously? Don't you ever leave the cities?"

"Well, yeah, of course I do. But I don't leave the planet. New Earth suits me just fine."

Connor remembered the early days after their war with the Vemus. Most of their satellite communications had been taken out and they could barely keep the comlinks online. Rhodes was definitely old enough to remember those times.

"I guess I just take those things for granted," Rhodes said, sounding almost regretful.

The lights came back on, followed by workstation consoles across the bridge. Connor blinked as his eyes adjusted to the normal light. A comlink registered from engineering.

"Power systems are coming back online. Sorry, it took a bit longer than I thought it would," Noah said.

"No worries, Noah," Connor replied.

Artificial gravity came back, and he felt it slowly return to the normal 1 g.

"What is the status of the I-Drive?" Connor asked.

"It's offline. I've isolated those systems, and it'll remain offline until we've run diagnostics of the all the other critical systems," Noah said and paused as a ship status window appeared on the main holoscreen. "Are you seeing this?"

Forty percent of the ship showed a red status.

"Is that right?" Rhodes asked. "Forty percent of the ship is inaccessible?"

Connor studied the screen, then blew out a breath. "It's

right. Look at the locations. There are maintenance locks on those airlocks, forcing them to stay open." Rhodes gave him a confused look. "It's standard procedure while in dry-dock. It makes moving equipment easier and quicker if you don't have to cycle through the airlock every time you need to enter the ship."

"You're right," Noah said. "I forgot all about that."

"The good news is that it's easily fixed."

Rhodes smiled, looking relieved to hear it.

"We'll have to go out there and disable the locks," Connor said.

The smile vanished from Rhodes's face. "Go out there? You mean you can't do it from here?"

Connor shook his head. "Not possible. We just need to find some EVA suits, and a standard tool kit ought to work."

"But does it require going out there? Can't you just access those areas from inside the ship? Seal off the area, rather than going on the hull to access those places?" Rhodes asked.

"Too much risk," Connor replied. "See these areas here that are red? They are two or three sections beyond the airlock because the bulkhead doors failed to close properly to seal off those sections."

Rhodes blinked, finally understanding just how dangerous their situation actually was.

Connor brought up the workstation holoscreen. "Still no comms system?"

Noah frowned and looked offscreen for a second. "It's offline. Diagnostic can't even do an eval because the array is disconnected."

Disconnected or damaged? Connor thought. "We'll need to check it. At least shipboard comms are working now. We just can't contact home."

Noah heaved a sigh. "Or see where we are. Sensor array is offline as well."

"First things first. Are critical systems stable enough for us to make a sweep of the ship?" Connor asked.

Noah considered the question for a moment before replying. "We're not in danger of the I-Drive causing further instability. Life support systems are working, but diagnostics are still evaluating the critical systems. I can't guarantee we won't see further degradation from those systems."

"What the heck kind of answer is that?" Rhodes asked.

Connor turned toward him. "It means this ship wasn't ready to be in space. Atmospheric scrubbers need filters renewed so we don't have toxicity in the air we breathe. That reminds me." He looked at Noah. "We'll need the water reclamation systems working and a current count of our supplies."

Noah nodded. "Right. We won't know what shape we're in until we can access those other areas of the ship. Naya and I will find some EVA suits and check there."

Connor laughed and shook his head. "Not this time, Noah."

His friend frowned. "Why not? I'm still EVA certified."

"I know, but we need you here, either on the bridge or in engineering. Wherever you think is best. I'll take a team outside to remove the maintenance locks and check both the comms and sensor arrays," Connor said.

Noah pinched the bridge of his nose. "So, you're going to fix them if they're broken?"

"No, I'll turn my camera on and you can walk me through it, or Ms. Corman will fix it," Connor said.

He watched as Noah looked over at Naya, who gave him a sympathetic smile. He looked back at Connor. "Fine. Have it your way. I'll stay here in Engineering. The computing core is only partially functional. I'll see to swapping out some components."

"General Gates," Naya said, "my team is missing. They could help Noah with those components." She gave him the names of her team.

"Tripp Krin is injured, so there might be a delay with him helping. Grace Mendel is in the mess hall," Connor replied and looked at Rhodes. "Are you able to walk?"

"The ankle is a little stiff, but I'll be alright."

Connor conferenced in Kincaid and Seger.

"Sir," Kincaid said, "we were moving the injured people to the secondary medical bay. I hope the autodoc is up and running."

Connor glanced at Noah, who shook his head. "It's one of the damaged sections. I'll get started on that one first."

Connor looked at Kincaid. "After you get them to medical, we need volunteers to help do a sweep of the ship. Just observe and report only."

"Understood, General. There are people here who can help." Kincaid paused and looked away. "I'm sorry, sir, but Jorath is insisting on speaking with Director Rhodes." The young CDF captain looked a little irritated.

"Inform him that personal comms are working now. He's free to contact whoever he wants."

Kincaid chuckled and bobbed his head once. "Understood, sir."

Connor looked at Seger.

"I'm just about to reach the bridge, General," Sergeant Seger said.

Connor spent the next few minutes coordinating with the other survivors as they split into teams of two to explore the ship.

Their current headcount was fourteen, and he hoped there were more survivors than that. There had been more than thirty people on the ship when the event occurred.

CHAPTER 7

Connor didn't have access to service records, so he had no idea what skills the survivors had that could help them. He had to rely on people being forthright with their abilities, as well as accurate about how well they could perform certain tasks. In his experience, sometimes people had a wonky sense of what they could and couldn't do, even in an emergency situation.

He'd just finished one of the sandwiches that Mac had insisted they all eat. The mess hall had become the unofficial coordination area for them to gather in after they searched the ship for survivors.

There were fourteen people accounted for on the ship, and over sixteen were missing. He didn't know if they were dead because there was no way to confirm it. It was a point he kept having to make to Glen Rhodes and some of the others. They wanted to assume that all the missing people were dead. Connor had to admit that, given the circumstances, there was a good chance they were right, but the door couldn't be shut on the fates of those missing people. Too many times he'd witnessed people surviving things that should have been impossible, himself included. But luck could only take them so far.

Connor kept looking for Major Lance Burkhardt. Lance had been leading Connor's protective detail for the past eighteen months, ever since he'd returned to New Earth. Lance had a calm but firm manner with carrying out his duties that Connor approved of and had come to rely on. Lance had been a good balance to Captain Tyler Kincaid and Sergeant Brent Seger. Kincaid was full of the vigor that came with men in their early twenties. He was dedicated, disciplined, and needed more time in grade to fully mature into his current rank. Whereas Seger had a no-nonsense attitude, but the way he accomplished his tasks was narrow in scope. Both soldiers were hardworking, and they were what he had to work with. They were good men; he just needed more of them here.

"Excuse me, General Gates, but may I ask you a few questions?" Jorath asked.

Connor looked at the Ovarrow. Most of New Earth's native inhabitants were long-limbed, with sharp protrusions at their elbows and shoulders. It gave their facial features a somewhat severe look. He'd long gotten used to Ovarrows, as most colonists had. They'd been integrating into colonial society for over thirty years. The Ovarrow who had joined the colony had chosen to abandon many of the self-destructive ways that had nearly ended their civilization and decided to emulate the moral foundation of humanity instead. They'd taught the Ovarrow human history to avoid falsely elevating themselves to that of a deity. Common sense could traverse intelligent species, and the Ovarrow were smart. They recognized that the colonists overall lived better and more satisfying lives, and they'd chosen to merge those qualities with the traditions they'd kept from their own society.

Connor looked at Jorath. "I have a few minutes."

"Thank you," Jorath said and rested his hands on the table. "I thought internal ship sensors tracked the whereabouts of people on the ship. Why is it that with the computing core restored, we can't bring up those records?"

"It's because those systems were disabled as part of the core upgrade that was going on."

"That means we might not have an accurate accounting of those who are missing."

Connor nodded. "That's true. Security checkpoints for Whitehall R&D facility will be able to reconcile who is missing, and we'll be able to account for those missing people after we return home."

Jorath considered this. "I see. Yes, that makes sense to me. One other question regarding the computing core upgrade: If the computing core was essentially offline during the upgrade, how could the I-Drive become active? My understanding is that it requires coordinates from the navigation system to work."

"The computing core was offline while its systems were being upgraded. The way it works is that the core becomes subservient to Whitehall's R&D systems. Further investigation is required to figure out what exactly happened. In theory, somehow the I-Drive systems became active during the upgrade, leveraged the umbilical that connected the two computing cores, and used that to plot a course."

Jorath nodded as he followed along. "Yes, but what course could it have used? Did it pick a course at random from the navigation system?"

"These are all good questions. Any answer I give you at this point would be pure speculation, and I don't particularly enjoy guessing when I don't have to." Connor stood. "I do have to go. We've got to restore communications so we can get help."

"Thank you for your time, General Gates," Jorath replied.

Connor returned his tray and finished his water. Kincaid and Seger did the same.

"Excuse me, General Gates."

Connor turned and saw Cassidy Rhodes looking up at him. He thought he saw Kincaid shake his head from the corner of his eye. Cassidy's gaze narrowed a little in response.

"What can I do for you?" Connor asked.

"Actually, General Gates, I was hoping there was something I could do for you. You're about to go into an EVA to remove the maintenance locks and check the arrays for communications and sensors. I'd really like to help."

Kincaid came over. "Sorry about this, General," he said and looked at her. "Cass, I already told you that you don't have the qualifications to do this."

"You're wrong," she replied and looked up at Connor.

Connor felt a flash of irritation at being caught in the middle of some kind of lover's quarrel. He didn't have time for that. However, he didn't want to dismiss Rhodes's daughter's offer of help out of hand.

"What EVA experience have you had?" Connor asked.

"I've been to the lunar bases many times and have EVA experience there. I've also been to Atticus Way Station and Research Center," she replied.

She looked sincere and more than a little agitated with nervous energy.

"I see. While you do have some EVA experience, it's limited to guided tours in relatively safe environments. I don't mean to discount your experience. If it comes down to it, I might have to take you up on it in the future, but this isn't one of those times."

She stared at him. "I can help."

Raising a daughter had taught him a few things about dealing with women, which essentially made him a little more sensitive to their requests. "You can, just not with this. It's too dangerous." He lifted his chin toward Kincaid and Seger. "We have the training for this, and it's still going to be high risk. We're blind to what's out there, and I won't needlessly put anyone's life in danger."

Her eyes sank to the floor. "I understand, General."

Connor walked away. Kincaid and Seger caught up to him in the corridor.

"Sorry, sir, I tried to tell her. She just won't listen to me," Kincaid said.

They went to the robotics work area and began putting on their EVA suits. The suits hadn't been in service for a while, but they'd passed the integrity checks that cleared them for service.

Connor glanced at Kincaid. "How long have you known her?"

The young officer frowned in confusion for a second. "Oh, Cass. Since before I joined the CDF."

Sometimes the things people *didn't* tell you said a lot more than what they *did* tell you.

"I take it she didn't want you to join?" Connor asked.

Seger went to help Naya retrieve some equipment they would need.

Kincaid shook his head. "No," he replied. "We had different career goals. Mine was to one day work with you, sir."

That explained Cassidy's regard for Connor.

"She's very capable but stubborn beyond belief," Kincaid said.

Connor smiled a little. "And blames me for you joining the CDF?"

Kincaid shrugged. "I'm sure she's gotten over it. How did you know, sir?"

Connor chuckled. "Not the first time this has happened, but we can't get distracted."

His expression became serious. "I won't, sir."

Connor eyed him for a moment. "Did you get along with her father?"

Kincaid met his gaze. "Not after he learned of my career choice."

Connor had never had to deal with a disapproving father, although he'd been one once or twice. Lenora had left everyone behind on Earth. She'd been part of a large family, and Connor had only seen the recordings of them that she'd kept.

"Sir," Kincaid said, "this won't be a problem."

"Only if you let it become a problem, Captain."

"Understood, sir."

They met Naya and Seger at the airlock.

"These are for both of you," Naya said, gesturing toward two small storage containers. "I've identified the airlock doors that we know are propped open. The release process is simple. Disengage the locking mechanism to remove the entire wedge. Then, push them inside to be retrieved later, once those areas are depressurized. We'll make our way to the front of the ship where we'll check both the sensor and communications array." She paused for a moment, eyeing them. "Sergeant Seger has advised me that to keep the teams equal, he's to be my partner. General, you'll be partnered with Captain Kincaid."

Connor nodded. "Neither one of them can bear the thought of not being near me."

Nora blinked for a second and then grinned. "That's right. Protective detail. I keep forgetting. Noah told me about that. If you see something you're not sure what to do with, please don't hesitate to show me or Noah."

Engineers were experts in many things that were technological and mechanical, so Connor understood the attitude. It still amused him, because he'd been conducting missions in space longer than any of them had been alive, which was a stark reminder of just how old he was becoming, even in his own thoughts. He wasn't about to become the crotchety old man who snapped at everyone younger than he was, insisting that he knew what he was doing. He chuckled inwardly.

They entered the airlock and were soon standing on the *Pathfinder*'s hull. They engaged their magboots so they'd stay put.

Connor looked around at the vast starscape. It was best just to take in the sight for a few moments before focusing on the task at hand.

"I thought it might've looked a little familiar, but it doesn't at all," Kincaid said.

"Agreed," Connor replied. He enabled the camera on his EVA suit.

"How far away from New Earth could we possibly be?" Seger asked.

"Impossible to determine without the sensor array back online. Then it will be up to the nav computer to figure out where we are," Naya replied.

"We can't be that far from New Earth. The I-Drive was engaging only in short bursts," Kincaid said, then looked at Connor. "Sir?"

Connor had been hoping he would recognize the region of space they were in, but he hadn't. "It's all speculation at this point, but if I absolutely had to guess, then I'd say we're probably less than two lightyears away from New Earth. We'll know for certain once we get the arrays back online."

They split into two groups and, over the next few hours, visited the other airlocks. It was just as they'd surmised. The airlocks were forced open with a maintenance boot. Once they removed the boot, the doors shut without incident. Then he had Noah initiate a full diagnostic of those areas before restoring life support to them.

The upper decks had been completely exposed. Retrofit efforts had been focused on berthing areas and reconfiguring cargo areas. There'd formerly been a weapons depot, but that hadn't been used since the ship was last in service. As they closed the airlock doors, Noah was able to restore life support to those upper decks. Mac insisted on leading several teams to make a sweep of those areas. Connor had made a mental note to ask Louis Maclean about his military record. There was no way he'd been just a cook and former medic.

They crossed the top of the ship, and Connor still couldn't spot New Earth, making him doubt his earlier estimation of being within two lightyears of home. He'd thought that having spent so much time in the New Earth star system would've meant he should be able to spot it easily, but the stars here appeared to be so much more distant. This was an alien starscape. It was either that, or he was so disoriented that it affected his ability to figure out where they were.

A private comlink registered with this EVA suit.

"Hey, Connor," Noah said, sounding tired. "I figured I'd contact you with some good news. The autodoc is up and running, and treatments for the injured people have begun."

"That *is* good news," Connor replied.

As he walked toward the bow of the ship, he looked over at the four-mag cannon turrets. He knew their capacity. They were light-defensive turrets, meant for small attack-craft deterrence.

"I thought so," Noah said. "Diagnostics are still ongoing."

"Do you know how many times the I-Drive engaged?"

"Three times. We stopped it before the fourth one was about to happen. Why?"

Kincaid turned back toward him, and Connor gave him a small wave.

"I can't figure out where we are."

"That's not surprising. It doesn't take much, or you don't have to go far for things to look unfamiliar," Noah replied.

"I know that, but there is more to it than that."

"Well, we'll know more once the arrays are back online."

The arrays were nestled in the center of the hull, near the bow of the ship. Connor headed for the communication array. There weren't any damaged areas.

"Looks like they'd replaced the transceivers and just hadn't taken it out of maintenance mode," Kincaid said.

Connor studied the array for a few seconds. "Looks right."

"It looks intact," Noah said, observing through Connor's video feed.

"The control panel is over there. Go over and take it out of maintenance mode," Connor said.

Kincaid walked over to the control panel and navigated the options. "Done."

Connor nodded. "Over to you, Noah."

"Right, I've got it," he said, and Connor waited for him to continue. Noah sighed. "Sorry, it's being treated as new equipment, so it's running first-time use checks."

"The computing core is the gift that keeps on giving," Connor replied.

Noah chuckled. "It's a feature."

Connor smiled.

Kincaid joined him. "Why do I get the feeling this isn't the first time you've had this conversation?"

"You're right about that," Connor said and heard Noah blew out a frustrated breath. "What's going on, Noah?"

"Comms isn't working."

"What's wrong?"

"According to the ship's systems, nothing. It says everything is functioning normally. We're green across the board for communications. However, I can't establish contact with COMCENT, and I can't detect comms signals of any kind."

Connor looked at the array. "What do you need me to do?"

"I'd tell you to kick the darn thing if I really thought it would do any good," Noah said, sounding like he was multitasking. "Diagnostics returns the same. The comms array is fine."

Several comlinks registered with Connor's EVA suit. They were across different signal types, and all came from the ship. "See, the comms system is working."

Connor's thoughts flatlined for a second and then started racing.

"That can't be right," Kincaid said. "I thought subspace comms had a range of thirty lightyears. Is the array underpowered?"

With the new data connections, Connor was able to check for himself rather than asking Noah.

"Power level for the array is fine."

Kincaid blinked and looked at the vast starscape with renewed awe. "How did we get more than thirty lightyears from home?"

Connor allowed his gaze to drift across the view of the distant stars. "It's more than that. We have outposts surrounding the New Earth star systems."

"How far do they go?"

"Many of them are for maintaining communications with Old Earth, but we've also begun expanding out to support the exploratory missions. Those are at least ten to twenty lightyears out."

"So that means we'd have to be something like forty to fifty lightyears away from New Earth," Kincaid said, his voice dripping with shock.

Connor felt as if something were pulling him toward the ship, but it was gone in a few moments. "Let's check the array again. Maybe we missed something."

It couldn't be possible. There was no way the I-Drive could've taken them so far in such a short amount of time.

The communication array was in perfect working order, and Connor had to admit that they were a lot farther from home than he'd initially thought.

CHAPTER 8

The hours seemed to go by like minutes. Determined to check every meter of the hull, Connor had lost track of them both. They couldn't be sure that the alerts for the hull integrity checks were reliable, so Connor had insisted on performing visual inspections of those areas. Sometimes the ship's internal sensors were correct in their alerts that there was a problem, and other times they weren't. He couldn't remember what the ratio was between the two, but it was enough to warrant them staying outside.

Connor looked up from the hull, noting the spot on the holo-interface. The ship was in terrible shape. Each issue they found with the ship was yet another reminder that the ship—their life-pod—would only give them refuge for so long.

A new comlink chimed, and Connor acknowledged it.

Louis Maclean looked at him, his gray eyes pushed forward in concern. "General Gates, it's fallen to me to urge you to come back inside."

Connor frowned. "Fallen to you?"

"Incumbent upon?" Mac shook his head. "I'm not good with formalities. Since I have the most medical experience here, the ship has started hassling me about all kinds of things that an actual medical doctor would normally be concerned with. I guess the computer had to settle for the next best thing." The older man smiled a little, probably trying to soften the message. "Anyway, sir. You've been on that EVA of yours for nearly thirteen hours. I must insist that you come back inside to rest. You and the others," Mac said.

Connor glanced over at Kincaid, who was about fifty meters away from him. He was beginning to make his way over.

"I see," Connor said. "Message received."

Mac blinked and rubbed his hand over his bald head. He lowered his voice. "Sir, I've been around long enough to know when a man is pushing himself too hard. Do you intend to inspect the entire hull yourself? You need both food and rest."

Maclean wasn't the first person to tell Connor these things. Pushing himself like this was his default setting. There was work that needed to be done.

Connor sighed. "How long have we been out here, again?"

"Thirteen hours."

He'd heard Mac say it before, but somehow it hadn't registered in his brain. Now that he thought about it, he began to feel the fatigue in his muscles and perhaps even in his bones.

"Alright, you've made your point. Thanks," Connor said.

The older man nodded, looking a little relieved at Connor's response. "One other suggestion, sir."

Connor tilted his head to the side. "Now you're trying to smother me with good advice."

Mac chuckled. "I think people would benefit if you spoke to them."

"Are they getting restless already?"

Mac shrugged. "There has been some rustling in the leaves, if you take my meaning."

Connor couldn't remember when he'd slept last. It had been an early day, even before the event that had brought them here. He frowned in thought. Had it really been over a day ago?

"Okay, tell the others that we're on our way back inside," Connor replied.

"Absolutely, will do, sir," Mac replied.

Connor sent a message to the other team. Sergeant Seger and Naya were on the other side of the ship near the engine pods. Seger acknowledged the message.

Kincaid walked over to them. "I was just about to suggest that it was time for a break, sir."

"It was past time for a break, Captain," Connor replied. Major Burkhardt would've said something much earlier. Connor chided himself inwardly for that thought. It wasn't fair to Kincaid. "Captain, from now on I need to you speak up about things like this. I have certain tendencies that take over."

Kincaid frowned, looking uncomfortable at the thought of doing anything like questioning his superior. "I don't understand, sir."

"I push too hard sometimes, and it could cost us in the long run. Sometimes I need to be reminded of that. Can I count on you?"

Kincaid hesitated for a second and said, "Yes, sir."

Connor stared at him for a moment.

"You can count on me, General," Kincaid said with more confidence.

A short while later, they stepped out of their EVA suits and replaced them on the charging stations. It felt good to have them off.

Connor saw Kincaid sniff the air. "A shower would be nice,

but until we know how much water we have, it might not be an option."

Kincaid nodded. "I'm sure that news will be greeted with enthusiasm and joy, sir."

Connor chuckled. He was more than a little ripe.

"According to the ship's systems, there is plenty of water. They must've kept the tanks in use while the ship was docked," Kincaid said.

"I stand corrected," Connor said, heading for the showers.

A quick hot shower loosened tight muscles and helped him feel more refreshed overall. Now he was hungry.

Connor and Kincaid headed down the main deck to the mess hall. They entered, and the conversations hushed.

Glen Rhodes looked at Connor from where was sitting with his daughter and Jorath. A young man who had red hair was with them.

Rhodes stood. "General Gates, we need to talk."

Mac came out of the kitchen carrying two trays of food. He looked at Connor and tipped his head to a table away from the others.

"Hot meals for the both of you," Mac said.

Connor looked at Rhodes. "Come join us."

Rhodes considered it for a moment, looking a little impatient, then changed his mind. "I'll give you a few minutes to get settled."

Mac removed the cloche, revealing the juiciest, most perfectly cooked steak, and Connor's mouth immediately began to water. The steak was accompanied by mashed potatoes and a seasoned medley of vegetables.

Connor looked up at Mac. "This is quite the meal you've prepared."

Mac preened at the compliment. "It was supposed to be for yesterday in the middle of the inspection tour."

Kincaid nodded. "I remember that. It was on the schedule."

Connor cut off a piece of steak and sank his teeth into it. A savory taste explosion occurred in his mouth, and he closed his eyes, letting out an appreciative moan. "That's good. I'm glad it didn't go to waste."

"Thank you, sir," Mac replied. "The food never made it out of the storage containers. Perfectly preserved. Go ahead and tuck in."

They ate, and all the food was soon gone from their plates. Connor felt as if he could've eaten another plate of food.

Noah entered the mess hall, carrying a tablet computer. He looked at Connor and then walked over to him.

"Good, you finally came back inside," Noah said as he sat down.

Connor arched an eyebrow at his friend. "So, *you* put Mac up to contacting me."

"I might've suggested it, along with how to put it in a way that would convince you that it was the smartest thing to do," Noah said.

His tone was light, but there were lines of worry around his eyes. Connor wondered when Noah had last slept.

Rhodes walked over to their table. "I think it's time we discuss some things."

Connor leaned back in his chair. "Agreed," he said and raised his voice to the others. "Would the rest of you care to join us? I'm sure there are questions. In fact, let's get everyone here."

It took a few minutes for the others to arrive. Kincaid stood and offered his seat to Glen Rhodes, who took it without muttering a word of thanks.

Eleven people gathered around. Some were sitting at nearby

tables while others had chosen to stand. Connor remained seated, exhaustion coming at him full tilt now that he had a belly full of food.

Mac and the young man named Tim Hopper brought in a couple of carafes of coffee, which perked the rest of them up.

Connor looked at the others. "Who's in med bay?"

Mac gave him the names of the people who weren't able to make it.

"That brings our number up to fourteen," Connor said.

"Yes," Rhodes grumbled. "We're well aware of the number of us stranded on this ship. What are you going to do to get us home?"

Fear was something that could spread like wildfire in the woods during a very dry season. Connor looked at Noah, who was staring at his tablet. Rhodes cleared his throat.

"We haven't been able to contact anyone through the ship's comms," Connor began.

Rhodes narrowed his gaze. "I thought communications had been restored hours ago. Does this mean help isn't coming?"

Connor frowned. Rhodes had no idea of their current status. Hadn't Noah told them? Why would he keep them in the dark?

"I thought you knew. We restored the comms array and were unable to detect any subspace communications. We checked the entire system, and we know it's working."

"So no help is coming?" Rhodes asked.

Connor shook his head. "We haven't been able to contact COMCENT to let them know where we are."

Rhodes swung his gaze toward Noah. "What's the status of the ship's systems?"

Noah didn't reply.

"Noah," Connor said and repeated the question.

Noah looked up from the tablet, blinking. "The computer

system is coming back online. There are still failures being reported, but critical systems, such as life support, are working."

"Can we go back home? Retrace our steps?" Rhodes asked.

Noah shook his head. "The nav system can't reconcile our location."

Rhodes's mouth hung open. Similar reactions happened among many of the others.

"We don't know where we are," Connor said. "That makes going back home something of a challenge."

An uneasy silence settled on everyone in the mess hall.

"I know these aren't the answers you were hoping for," Connor said.

A young man with unruly red hair raised his hand. "General Gates, won't someone come looking for us?" he asked. "Sorry, I'm Tripp Krin, sir."

"Yes, I can tell you with absolute authority that they are already searching for us. What we need to focus on is repairing the ship," Connor replied.

"We're not qualified to repair the ship," Rhodes said. Connor's patience was beginning to slip. "And we still need to talk about what happened."

"I already told you," Noah said.

Rhodes gave him a scathing look. "Yes, your explanation is lacking. The Infinity Drive somehow engaged, bending space and throwing us away from the planet. If that's true, then you're responsible for one of the deadliest catastrophes in the history of the colony."

Connor stood. "That's enough!"

Rhodes wasn't cowed in the slightest. "I'm just getting started. He's not denying it," he said, pointing at Noah.

Connor inhaled a harsh breath, readying a reply to put Rhodes in his place once and for all.

"You're right!" Noah said. "There, you've got what you wanted. I'm responsible for hundreds of deaths."

Connor looked at him. "No, you're not."

Noah shook his head. "I was here. It's my project."

"Our project," Connor interjected.

"I'm responsible for the systems upgrade that took place. The event occurred during that, so it stands to reason that something I did went terribly wrong." He paused for a moment, looking at the other people. "I'm sorry."

Connor shook his head. "No. This is unacceptable, and it doesn't help. None of this gets us back home."

Noah lifted his gaze to Connor in resignation. "It's true."

"No, it's not. We don't know what happened; therefore, responsibility for said event cannot be assigned." He glared at Rhodes. "I don't care how much you insist on laying blame and how determined you are to drive the point home so everyone knows your voice was the loudest. It doesn't help, and it distracts everyone from what we need to be focusing on."

Rhodes sneered. "That brings me to the next item for discussion. Who put you in charge? You have no authority over anyone outside of the CDF."

Connor smiled wolfishly. "Who's going to get us home? You?" He turned to the others, stabbing them with a challenging stare. "Anyone else want to compare records on how to survive far from home with minimal resources?"

"You're out of line," Rhodes snarled.

Jorath came to his side, glaring at Connor menacingly.

Both Kincaid and Seger stepped in front of Connor. "Back off," Kincaid warned.

"You have no authority to compel me to do anything," Jorath replied, lifting his head with a stubborn glint to his gaze.

Cassidy Rhodes swooped to her father's side and speared a scathing look at Kincaid. "What are you doing to do? Shoot us?"

Connor needed to diffuse the situation before things really got out of control. "Alright, that's enough. Everyone needs to take a moment and calm down," he said.

There were a few moments of silence, and then Noah cleared his throat. "Look, if you want to blame me, it's fine. I don't care. Like Connor already said, it changes nothing. What would you rather do: argue about what he can't change, or focus on what we're going to do to survive? Those are the stakes, and no amount of bickering is going to change those things."

Rhodes placed a hand on Jorath's shoulder and the Ovarrow relaxed, backing away.

"Noah's right," Connor said. "We need to focus our attention on how we're going to survive." He'd almost said until help arrives, but he didn't want to give them false hope. He knew that by now the CDF would be searching for them. That much was true, but whether they'd find them was anyone's guess, and it wasn't looking too good for that option.

"Excuse me," Mac said. "Might I make a suggestion?" he asked, pausing for a moment. Connor gave him an encouraging nod. "I suggest that we all get some sleep. The ship is stable enough that we can afford to rest. Crew quarters are upstairs. You'll at least have a bed to sleep on. No covers, I'm afraid."

Connor looked at Rhodes. "What do you say? Want to come at this fresh in the morning?"

Cassidy leaned toward her father, speaking softly. "You need to rest."

Rhodes nodded. "Okay, we'll take this up in the morning." His shoulders slumped. "I don't even know what time it is."

A tired chuckle bubbled from Connor's chest, and soon the

others joined in. The tension drained from the mess hall, and he was thankful for it.

"It's four o'clock in the morning," Jorath said.

"Okay, we'll meet up in the afternoon then," Connor said and shared a look with Noah.

He didn't look well at all. He was blaming himself. "I need to go check on the computing core."

The others began leaving.

Connor looked at Noah with raised eyebrows.

"I'll get some rest, I promise," Noah said.

"Want me to come with you?"

Noah shook his head. "No, you go on. It won't take long."

Connor considered assigning shifts and having someone stand watch.

Sergeant Seger looked at him. "General, do you mind if I make another sweep of the ship? Not to find anyone. I'm a little restless and could use a walk."

"Go ahead," Connor replied.

They went to the upper deck, and Connor chose the nearest cabin in what was known as officer country. The cabins were more spacious. On a ship that could house just under two hundred people, they had their pick of whatever cabin they wanted.

Kincaid stood in the doorway. "General, I have a concern."

Connor turned toward him. "What is it?"

"This situation could easily become untenable, sir. Use of force might become necessary."

"Let's hope it doesn't come to that."

"It's not my first choice, sir."

"Understood. We keep the peace. We can't afford to have everyone at each other's throats, not if we're going to survive."

"Understood, sir. I'll be right across the hall."

When Kincaid left, Connor collapsed onto the bed. The smart fabric adjusted to his weight, giving him ample support. Now that he had a moment to himself, he started to think about home and family. No doubt Lenora had been informed of their disappearance. His thoughts began to wander until he was barely able to string together a coherent thought, and he was asleep in moments.

CHAPTER 9

Connor woke from a deep sleep, a little disoriented. The dimly lit officer's quarters could've been on any number of ships he'd slept on during his long military career. Sometimes they seemed to run together. He'd been dreaming but couldn't recall what it had been about. He'd been reaching across the bed, hoping to feel Lenora next to him, but unexpectedly, his hand hit the wall.

He swung his feet off the bed as he sat up. Blinking, he rubbed the sleep from his eyes and blew out a long breath. He washed his face and rinsed his mouth before rubbing his teeth with his fingers. It would have to do until he could find a toothbrush.

He felt more alert, but the muscles of his back were a little stiff from the previous day's exertions. He performed a few stretches to help loosen things up and then left his cabin. Never being one to eat breakfast as soon as he woke, he headed to the bridge.

He glanced across the corridor at Kincaid's cabin for a

second, considering waking the CDF captain, but decided not to. These were extreme circumstances, and his protective detail couldn't be at his side at every moment. They'd have to accept that. Most of the soldiers who sought out those duties had a particular stubborn streak that Connor thought was some kind of unofficial personality trait the recruiters searched for among the candidates.

With so few people aboard the ship, it felt empty as he walked the corridors, heading to the bridge. Environmental recordings played softly through the ship's speakers, which attempted to set people at ease, but it felt false in the face of their current situation. In some areas, the air smelled stale. Some of the filters had to be beyond their maintenance cycle. Swapping filters was a dirty job, especially if scrubbers were clogged.

Connor set a pace that was tantamount to a jog and had soon reached his destination. He'd expected to find Noah on the bridge, but he wasn't there. Instead, the room was empty, which was good because he needed time to consider their situation. He went over some of the conversations from yesterday. They were lost and possibly a lot farther from home than they'd initially thought. A small part of his mind searched for alternative explanations. None of it made any sense, and after giving those thoughts some attention, he pushed them to the side. He'd found himself in enough impossible situations to know that just because he couldn't figure out how an event had occurred didn't mean it was truly impossible. But that also didn't mean he wanted to waste time chasing bad ideas.

Connor had a highly suspicious mind. What other people ignored as happenstance, he didn't. It had saved his life and the entire colony on more than one occasion.

He went to a workstation and brought up a holoscreen, checking the communications array. According to the ship's computer, it was working flawlessly. They couldn't contact home or any of the deep space communications hubs they'd established over the years. In the absence of evidence to the contrary, he had to believe that the ship's communications systems were working. That meant they were outside of communication range. There simply wasn't any other explanation that fit. They needed to focus on how that had come to be. But before all that, they needed a prioritized list of action items to ensure they survived long enough to be rescued. They had to figure out where they were and ensure that they had the basics required for survival. The ship was in need of repair, and they lacked qualified people to effect those repairs, himself included. With those things in mind, he set about refining the list he'd worked on the previous day.

There was something freeing about putting things in order. Currently, their world was this ship, so it didn't take him long to refine a task list, and he even assigned responsibilities where he thought it appropriate.

The door to the bridge opened and Naya Corman entered. She was tall, with piercing emerald eyes. Her hair was a wild tapestry of auburn and gold, a similar shade to his wife's hair color.

"Good morning, sir," she said and frowned with a slight shake of her head, then shrugged. "Afternoon."

"Hello to you. We might be stuck here for a while, so please call me Connor."

She smiled. "No problem," she replied, her eyes scanning the task list. "Good, you've included the sensor array. I was going to head back out with a repair drone to replace the damaged components."

Connor nodded. "Who are you going to take with you?"

"If you don't mind, I'd like Sergeant Seger out with me

again." Connor arched an eyebrow, and she shrugged one shoulder. Then she made a show of stiffening her arms and pushing out her chest. "I know he's the pinnacle gung-ho CDF soldier type, but he's got a knack for spotting problems that other people miss. He'd make a good engineer if he was interested in changing careers one day."

Connor liked Naya's infectious enthusiasm. "You should tell him."

"Oh, I already did."

"What did he say?"

She lifted her eyebrows. "He grunted. I guess it takes time."

Connor chuckled, but then his expression became serious. "Naya, don't feel like you need to do everything on your own. I know we're not all engineers, but not every task requires that level of expertise."

She nodded. "I'll try to remember that." She pressed her lips together for a moment. "Sir, I think you need to check on Noah."

Connor frowned. "Why?"

"I don't think he's slept. He hasn't taken a break since…well, since everything happened. He pushes himself too hard. I've heard his wife admonish him about that from time to time," Naya said.

"Okay, I'll take care of it," Connor said and shook his head. "I mean, I'll check on him."

She smiled a little. "It isn't just you, sir. A lot of us are still feeling out of it. The rest helped, but it's not enough. I'll get the sensor array up and running. At least then we can pinpoint our location better."

"I'll send Seger a message that he's to assist you."

"Thank you," she replied and left the bridge.

After Connor sent a quick message to Sergeant Seger, he

tried to locate Noah but couldn't find him. Either Noah was off the ship, or he was hiding his location.

Connor stood and left the bridge. Kincaid met him in the corridor.

"Sorry, General Gates, I missed you leaving."

"It's alright, Captain. We're going to have to address some of the standing protection protocols in light of our current situation."

"Understood, sir."

Connor brought up his wrist computer and made a passing motion to Kincaid. "This is the task list in prioritized order. The highlighted section is for you."

Kincaid quickly scanned the list and hid a grimace.

"You know the saying about idle hands. People need to pitch in and help with these things. And since some of them will no doubt want to talk, tell them we'll meetup for dinner and go over our current status," Connor said.

Kincaid gave him a salute. "Yes, General. I'll get right on it."

Connor quickly narrowed down Noah's location, which wasn't any of the expected places. The *Pathfinder* wasn't a large ship, and with so few people aboard, it was easy to hide.

He walked into the control room near the robotics lab and found Noah standing, surrounded by holoscreens. He turned in surprise and then heaved a sigh.

"Should've known you'd come looking for me sooner or later," Noah said.

Connor walked over to his friend. Noah stood with an exhausted stoop, as if he was almost asleep on his feet, but he had an overtired energy that suggested he'd keep working until his body demanded that he rest.

"Why are you hiding in here?" Connor asked.

Noah's hands paused as they navigated the holoscreens. "I needed to get some work done."

Connor waited with raised eyebrows, and Noah gave him a guilty look. "All night? Have you slept?"

"I slept a little," Noah said defensively. His gaze darted to a nearby chair.

"In a bed?"

Noah looked away, shaking his head. "Too much to do." He turned his attention back to the center-most holoscreen.

They'd been through hell together, and Connor could only remember a handful of times where Noah had been this frazzled.

"Naya is heading out to repair the sensor array. She said there were some damaged components that needed to be replaced," Connor said, hoping to get Noah to engage with something other than the barrage of data windows on the holoscreens.

Noah tipped his head to the side. "I'm surprised we had spares aboard the ship."

"I didn't ask where she'd gotten the parts from."

Noah made a noncommittal noise.

"What is this?" Connor asked firmly.

"Do I really need to tell you?"

"Yeah, you do."

Noah swiped through the different sub-windows on the holoscreen and scowled. "We are so far in it. This wasn't supposed to happen."

Connor frowned in confusion. "Take a breath, Noah," but Noah ignored him. "Stop," he said, stepping toward him.

"No!" Noah moved away from Connor, and the holoscreens moved with him. "I can't stop. I have to figure this out."

"We will. We always do."

Noah closed his eyes for a long moment, his head making subtle movements in response to some inner monologue.

Connor had seen Noah upset before, but this was different—something beyond exhaustion.

"What do you know, Noah?"

Noah stiffened, and then his hands came to rest at his side. He swallowed hard and exhaled forcefully. "I was supposed to be at Jacob's school today to watch him present his science experiment."

Connor blinked at the mention of Noah's eldest son.

Noah's shoulders slumped. "I promised him I would be there. He worked so hard and wanted me to be there. He always works hard. He is so quiet sometimes but so determined. And now...I don't want to disappoint my son."

Connor was quiet for a few seconds. "I understand."

Noah nodded a little, still not facing him. "I know you do." He reached toward the holoscreen a couple of times and shook his head. "I keep thinking that the fix should be easy to unravel, that something's blocking our comms and we're still within range of New Earth. I went over the events in the logs that led up to yesterday, hoping to spot a reason, something, anything that could give me a clue as to what happened. I can't find it."

"You're exhausted. You probably couldn't find your way across the ship, and you haven't eaten since yesterday."

Noah turned toward him. "How could you possibly know that?"

"I can smell your breath from here. No food or water, and you locked yourself in this room. You probably told yourself something about not coming out until you figured out what happened." Connor stared at him, and Noah blinked. "Am I right?"

Noah rolled his eyes a little and didn't reply.

"Sometimes you can do everything right and things still go terribly wrong," Connor said.

Noah frowned and looked at him.

"Don't you remember how many times this happened during our war with the Krake?"

Noah considered that for a few moments and then nodded. "This has to be different."

"Oh yeah? Why?"

"It does. We're not at war with anyone."

"No, we're not, but," Connor said, raising his index finger, "we were working on tech hinted at by the Phantoms."

Noah heaved a long sigh. "We took every precaution that we possibly could."

"Might not have been enough."

"Could just be a coincidence."

"Yeah, right," Connor replied dryly.

Noah leaned against the wall and crossed his arms in front of his chest. "I figured with the project being on the planet that we'd be left alone."

"Maybe we were closer to a breakthrough than we thought."

"How can we prove that? I can't think of anything that would've caused this."

"I don't know, and if we start bringing up the possibility of Phantom involvement in all this, it'll be a distraction."

Noah stared at him for a moment. "You want to keep it from the others?"

"No, I just don't want to tell them yet. We don't know if they were involved, so why bring it up?"

"You know, lying by omission is still lying," Noah said.

"It's one of a few possibilities we're considering. Other than the fact that the Phantoms *might* be involved in this, we don't have any compelling evidence."

Noah bobbed his head once. "How come you're so calm?"

"Why do people keep asking me that?"

Noah arched an eyebrow.

"I have the same concerns and fears you do. I took this project because it kept me on New Earth. It was supposed to be safer than doing things on the fringe. That stuff is for Ethan, and one day, Jacob."

"Ethan," Noah said. "Only home for a few months before going right back out as part of the exploration initiative."

It had been months since Connor had last spoken with his son. The subspace transceiver network was still being brought up.

"Jacob is only eight years old, and you've already got him leaving me behind," Noah said.

"It goes by quickly. Maybe he won't." Connor regarded his friend for a moment. "So, are you going to get some real sleep?"

"What if I refuse?"

The edges of Connor's lips lifted. "I think Glen Rhodes is looking for you. He mentioned that he was particularly interested in understanding exactly what happened yesterday, and he wouldn't leave you alone until you explained it to him."

Noah's gaze narrowed. "I can't tell if you're joking or not."

Connor gave him a deadpanned expression for a few moments. "You need rest, Noah. You're no good to anyone like this. It's better for everyone if you just go along with it."

"I doubt I'll sleep."

Connor stared at him.

"Alright. Alright," Noah said, shutting off the holoscreens. "I'll try to get some sleep."

Connor smiled and gestured to the door.

"What? Are you going to walk me to my quarters?" Noah asked.

"That's exactly what I'm going to do."

Noah blew out a breath and walked toward the door. "You

know, I remember one time I tried to tell you that you were pushing yourself too hard. Do you remember what you did?"

Connor tried to remember but couldn't. "No, what did I do?"

"You had Sean and a couple of soldiers escort me from the command center. That was after—"

"Oh yeah, I remember now," Connor said and grinned.

Noah joined him, some of the tension releasing, but Connor knew it wasn't going to last.

CHAPTER 10

Near the end of the third day, the survivors had more or less adopted the same sleep schedule, which made work rotations easier. Rather than forcing the other survivors to adhere to New Earth Standard Time, Connor suggested they move the clock forward to accommodate their current schedule. Surprisingly, the others agreed to it with little argument.

Connor was sitting in the command center of the bridge, and Noah plopped into the chair next to him. Sergeant Seger sat farther away at one of the workstations. Glen Rhodes and Jorath entered the bridge and walked over to them.

Connor had set up these daily status meetings so their meals could be had in relative peace. The longer they were trapped out here, the harder it was to be at ease.

Rhodes sat, looking tired. His aged brown hair was ruffled, as if he'd been wearing a hat all day and had only rubbed his fingers through his hair after taking it off. He looked at Connor. "The purification filters are all set. I'd forgotten how much buildup could accumulate on the older Dalmore filtration system."

"You'd know more about that than I would. Thanks for getting that done," Connor replied.

Rhodes shrugged. "It's been over thirty years since I've done anything like that." He touched the side of his head. "But once I cleared away the cobwebs in here, it went smoothly."

Connor had been surprised to learn that Rhodes used to work with environmental systems before moving on to run the Colonial Requisitions Department. He'd never served in the CDF but had been involved in many other efforts that required the use of life support systems throughout the colony, both on the planet and off.

"We'll all be breathing easier because of it," Connor replied.

It had taken a few days, but some of the tension between them had eased. They had to work together to survive, so it was in their best interest to set aside their differences.

"Access to the vehicle bay and equipment has been restored," Connor said. "We were lucky that we didn't lose equipment there. It was used as a staging area for the retrofit effort. However, we don't have enough resources to repair the entire ship."

Noah nodded. "The computing core is operating at reduced capacity and cycles still need to prioritize. With the sensor array back online, I've been devoting additional cycles to it during off hours."

A wave of tension seemed to raise the temperature in the room a little. The sensor array had been fixed two days ago, and they still hadn't been able to pinpoint their location. The nav system categorized their current location as "unknown."

"Is the power core stable?" Rhodes asked.

"Yes, the core is recycling itself, but without more fuel we'll never be at full capacity in terms of power output," Noah replied.

Rhodes nodded. "Understood. Once again, I propose we

should focus our efforts on boosting the range of our communications capabilities to make contact with New Earth."

"We've already tried that twice. Doing it a third time isn't going to change the outcome," Connor replied.

A flicker of annoyance flashed across Rhodes's gaze. "But what if the signal is weakened? Please hear me out," he said, raising his hand a little. "What if the signal is weakened and easily overlooked? If we kept at it, perhaps it would be detected by a monitoring AI that would put the anomaly in front of someone to review."

Jorath cleared his throat. "This suggestion does seem prudent."

"It does," Connor replied. "We don't know which direction New Earth is in. We're just guessing, and if we try to focus subspace comms in all directions and overload our comms array, we risk losing it altogether. We have automated distress messages being broadcast at the standard subspace range."

Rhodes sighed. "Why haven't they contacted us? They should've begun searching for us by now."

Connor regarded him calmly. "There isn't a doubt in my mind that the search for us has already started. It has, don't doubt it. We need to endure long enough for them to find us."

"There are issues with this approach," Jorath said. "The ship lacks the supplies and resources to perform necessary repairs. It stands to reason that if we can't contact New Earth or any of the deep-space monitoring stations, they can't contact us either. Therefore, it becomes necessary to increase the range of our communications; otherwise, we might never be rescued."

Connor shared a look with Noah.

"He makes a good point," Rhodes said. "To be out of communication range, we'd have to be forty to fifty lightyears away from New Earth or the nearest monitoring station."

"It's more complicated than that," Connor said.

Rhodes waited for him to continue.

Connor stood and brought up a holoscreen. "This is home. New Earth. The research station is here, well away from any of our cities and only accessible through secure transportation. Noah has estimated the specific location of the planet's orbit and rotation near the time of the event. It's important to remember that this is an estimate, since logs of the event were spotty because of issues with the ship's computer systems." He paused for a moment.

"I understand," Rhodes said.

"Good. That gives us a swath of the sky that doesn't seem like much, but the farther we move away from the planet, the greater our margin of error increases."

Rhodes nodded. "That's because of the increased range."

"Right," Noah said and stood. He gestured for control of the holoscreen. "We can be anywhere in this range," he said, expanding the model of the star map until New Earth's star system was just like any other distant star. Noah made a pointing motion at the screen and a hexagon icon appeared. "This is the *Pathfinder*, and this represents our current communications effective range." A semitranslucent circle appeared around the icon. "This puts our range to about ten lightyears. Now if we focus the array, it doubles that range, but it also requires us to be precise about where we send the signal." Noah gave them a moment to absorb the information on the holoscreen. "Since the nav system can't pinpoint our location, it leaves us blind."

"Thanks for showing us this. It helps us understand," Rhodes said. "Given all this information, why can't the nav system figure out where we are?"

"Some of the data repositories in the computing core were damaged, and I've been restoring them. They were among the first things to be restored after I made sure critical systems were functioning properly."

Rhodes nodded. "So, are you saying the nav system will eventually be able to figure out our location?"

"Yes, but I haven't been able to lock in how long it will take, and we have some other decisions to make," Noah said and looked at Connor.

"We have to look for a place to resupply," Connor said. Rhodes's eyes widened and he glanced at Noah for a second. "I haven't told the others yet. Maclean informed me that our food fabricators lack bio-matter for the processing units. We basically have enough to feed us for a month. If we begin rationing, we could increase that time, but it wouldn't be significant."

"We're going to run out of food?"

Connor nodded.

"I thought we had plenty. I heard Maclean say as much," Rhodes said.

"It's not his fault. The data he was using was taken into consideration by the aft storage module dedicated for his use. It took significant damage, and entire containers were lost. To be fair, the ship wasn't stocked for a long voyage. It was stocked to make at least one meal available to the people working on the ship. That, along with snacks, so there wasn't significant bio-matter to begin with."

Rhodes sagged and rubbed his face with both his hands. Then he looked at Connor. "So we really don't have a choice."

Connor shook his head. "There is always a choice. We can stay here for a little while longer. Perhaps we'll be able to contact the CDF, but we should also evaluate nearby star systems. Maybe there will be some that have planets we can resupply from."

Rhodes looked at the holoscreen for a few seconds. "When are you going to tell the others?"

Connor chuckled inwardly. Everyone wanted to be in charge until it came time to tell people something they didn't want to hear. He'd made a career of it. "I thought we'd both do it after we're done here."

Rhodes nodded. "Yes. Okay. That will be fine." He stared at Connor for a long moment with an unasked question in his gaze.

"One step at a time. That's what'll get us through this."

Rhodes only appeared halfway convinced of it, but Connor would take what he could get.

He wished he had better news for them. Noah had been bearing the burden, mistakenly believing he could keep it from Connor. It was just a knee-jerk reaction that had been corrected.

Connor glanced at the holoscreen. They'd started scanning nearby star systems. Rhodes hadn't asked, but Connor was sure someone else would ask what they would do if none of the star systems in range had a habitable planet.

CHAPTER 11

Tyler walked toward the control room in the ship's main engineering area. The door was open and he could hear people speaking inside. As he closed in on the room, he recognized Cass's voice. She had a friendly lilt that she used to set the person she was speaking with at ease. Cass was a beautiful woman, and when he heard Tripp Krin excitedly respond to her, he knew she was laying on the charm, but he didn't know what she was after.

Tyler walked inside the control room and found Cass sitting across from Tripp Krin and another young man named Reed Davis. Cass sat slightly off the center of the chair with one of her arms over the back. She wore a light-blue ship suit that was open near the top, showing some of her perfectly tanned skin.

"Captain," Tripp said quickly, looking almost guilty. He was a civilian technical contractor for the CDF.

Reed stiffened in surprise. He couldn't have been more than eighteen years old, a common age for interns. Tyler hadn't spoken to him much.

"Am I interrupting something?" Tyler asked, looking at Cass.

She blanched a little, and he smiled.

"No," Cass said, sweetly. "I was just checking on Tripp to see how he was feeling."

Tyler looked at Tripp.

"I'm fine. I got the brace off this morning," Tripp replied.

"That's good," Tyler said.

Tripp smiled and then looked at Cass. "About the nav system. I don't know why it's taking so long to figure out where we are. Naya would be the one to ask about that."

Tyler chuckled inwardly. "What a coincidence. I was just on my way to see her. Would you like to join me, Cass?"

She turned her chair toward him, her gaze narrowing a little. Then she stood. "I suppose, since that's where you're going anyway."

Tyler smiled, then looked at Tripp and Reed. "What are you guys working on?"

"We're debugging some of the subroutines that aren't working right," Tripp replied.

Tyler looked at Reed. "What about you?" he asked.

Reed shrugged, looking uncomfortable. "I'm just helping Tripp debug the system."

"It's important work."

Reed raised his gaze to Tyler. "Is it true we're stuck out here?"

The others looked at Tyler, all of them anticipating his response.

"We're not stuck," Tyler said. "The last status report indicated that the I-Drive was almost finished going through a full diagnostic of its system."

Tripp blinked several times. "Are we going to bring it back online?"

"Not until we're sure it's safe."

Reed crossed his arms and looked away. They were scared. That much was obvious.

Tyler regarded them as he heaved a sigh. "Talk about being in the wrong place at the wrong time. I bet neither one of you was supposed to be here that long."

Both young men looked at him as if he'd guessed their thoughts.

"We were to assist with the computing core upgrade. We've never been on the ship. Our normal work location is at the central control center at the research facility," Tripp said.

Tyler looked at Reed. "And they allowed interns to participate?"

"Reed isn't just another intern," Tripp said. "He was recommended by several department heads from the Colonial Research Institute advanced studies division."

"Really? That's impressive," Tyler said to Reed.

He looked uncomfortable.

"Never been in space before?" Tyler asked.

Reed shook his head. "No. I was supposed to go on a six-week rotation at the lunar colony."

Tyler bobbed his head once. "It can be overwhelming the first few times. Up 'til now, it's been all theory and no field experiences. Am I right?"

Reed nodded.

"No worries, kid. I'll go over a few things with you and Tripp."

Tripp's eyes widened in surprise.

Reed frowned. "What things?"

"Basic knowledge about being on a ship. Safety things. Train you up on emergency procedures. That way you'll be able to take care of yourself in the event we find ourselves in need of those skills."

The edges of Reed's lips lifted, and for the first time Tyler could recall, he didn't look quite so unnerved. "I'd appreciate that very much, Captain Kincaid."

Tyler grinned. "You can call me Tyler if you want. I'm not that much older than you are." He looked at Cass. "In fact, we'll probably do some basic training for everyone. Brush up on some of those skills that might've become rusty."

Cass gave him a challenging look with a playful glint in her eyes.

Tyler looked at the others. "After we get through the basics, we'll get to the fun stuff, like space walks and the life pod systems."

"I think that would be a good idea," Reed said.

"Good, we'll talk about a schedule after dinner tonight," Tyler said. He looked at Cass. "Come on, Cass, let's go see what we can learn from Naya."

He gave the others a wave, which they eagerly returned.

Cass followed him out and they walked down the corridor for a minute.

Tyler arched an eyebrow toward her. "Chatting up the kids for information, huh?"

She rolled her eyes. "I was just talking to them."

Tyler stared at her knowingly. "Really."

"Yes, really."

Tyler arched his back, while lifting one of his shoulders, doing a good impression of her. "Am I getting the pose right? I can't make my voice go all high and enthusiastic like yours, but is this right?"

She shook her head and quickened her pace.

Grinning, he caught up to her.

"I was just trying to set them at ease by being friendly," Cass said irritably.

"Cass, come on. This is me you're talking to."

She looked up at him with those bright blue eyes of hers, and they seemed to spear him in place for a moment. "You're implying that I was flirting with them to get information?"

He smiled. "Yeah, that about sums it up."

"You're unbelievable."

"Look at it from their perspective. Someone like you walks in there and talks to them. It's enough to make them fall all over themselves to tell you anything you want to know."

She pursed her lips as she regarded him. "Kinda like you used to do?"

He chuckled. She wasn't wrong. "So, you admit to flirting just a teensy bit?"

She looked away for a few seconds. "Alright, fine. Maybe I did a little. I just wanted to see if they knew something that the rest of us were being kept in the dark about."

Tyler frowned. "We're not keeping anything from you."

"I don't believe you."

"How can I change your mind?"

She blinked in surprise. She probably expected him to keep denying her accusation.

"I'm serious. I'll answer any question you ask."

He watched as she considered it for a few moments. "Okay, there's a rumor that there was some kind of sabotage that caused this to happen. Is it true? Did someone do this to us?"

"Where did you hear that from?"

She waggled a finger in front of him. "Oh no. I asked the question. Is it true?"

Tyler sighed. "Nothing is off the table as to what caused the event. That includes someone sabotaging the ship and its systems."

Again, she looked surprised to get a straight answer from him. Then her gaze narrowed a little. "Who?"

"We don't know."

"You must have some idea."

"Does it really matter?"

"Yes, it does."

Tyler hesitated, and she stepped closer to him, chin lifted. "See, you *are* keeping things from the rest of us."

He shook his head. "It's not that simple."

"Why not?"

"Because I don't know what your clearance level is."

Cass frowned and somehow made that even look attractive. "I was cleared to be part of the inspection team."

"That's not good enough," he replied, and she started to speak. "Just hold on a second. I'm telling you the truth. There are things I'm not cleared to discuss. That's it. They're my orders."

He almost expected her to be irritated, but instead, she seemed pensive.

"Well, I suppose that's fair."

He smiled a little. "It's the truth."

"It doesn't mean I have to like it," she said and continued down the corridor.

He quickened his pace to catch up to her. "There isn't much I can do about it."

"Of course not. Your lord and master forbids it."

"Oh, come on, you can't still be mad about that."

She wouldn't look at him. "You know what? I'll talk to Naya on my own."

When she quickened her pace, he didn't chase her.

"Cass, it doesn't have to be like this."

It was the same argument they'd had over eight years ago before he'd joined the CDF.

She stopped and looked at him over her shoulder. "What? This is nothing."

Then she stormed off and Tyler decided that giving her some space was for the best. If he chased her down, they'd likely start shouting.

He sighed and gritted his teeth a little. It had been over eight years, and being around her still affected him. It affected them both. They'd been much younger the last time they'd spoken. He'd been different and so had she, but some things hadn't changed. Being around her again was a reminder of what he'd given up to join the CDF. She wanted him to be something he wasn't. At least that's what he'd told himself all those years ago. He didn't regret joining the CDF or working so hard to serve under General Gates, but maybe there was a way things could've ended between him and Cass that would've made things easier now. They couldn't ignore each other.

He increased his pace, determined to keep things professional between them. The idea felt feeble where it counted. He'd just have to settle for doing the best he could and leave it at that.

Naya Corman was working at the computing core. Cass was already there, speaking to her when Tyler joined them. They both looked at him as he entered and, for some reason, the way they regarded him made him think they'd been speaking about him.

Naya looked at Cass. "You were right, he does like to follow you around."

Cass shrugged.

"Yes, that's me, your friendly neighborhood stalker," Tyler said and joined them.

Naya grinned. "Just a little fun, Captain Kincaid."

"I'm all for having fun. I could tell you some stories here about Ms. Rhodes that would straighten even your hair, Naya," he said, noting how quickly he'd abandoned the pretext of keeping things professional. As the saying goes: When fired upon, return fire.

Naya had a tapestry of auburn and gold hair. It was tied back into a ponytail, but it had thick waves to it that had to be the envy of other women. At least that's what his sisters had always said.

Cass looked at him with only hints of her anger from earlier. "I'd have to return the favor in kind. Shall I go first?"

Naya grinned and shook her head. "Maybe someday when we're back home we can have a few drinks and you both can regale me with funny stories from ages long ago, but I do have things I need to get done."

There was something about being lost that made the thoughts of home so much sweeter.

"I'll take you up on that, unless Cass wants to back out," Tyler said.

He knew she was never one to walk away from a challenge.

She regarded him impassively. "We'll see. Maybe."

Tyler looked at Naya. "I came to check on the progress with the nav system."

"It's mapping the area but still can't identify our location."

"How could that be?" Cass asked.

"The nav system has been brought online blind. It's like being blindfolded, led out into the middle of nowhere, and then being expected to find your way home," Tyler replied.

Naya smiled and regarded him with renewed appreciation. "That's an excellent way of explaining it."

Tyler tipped his head to the side. "What can I say? I'm full of surprises."

"Indeed," Naya said. "There has been a shift in priorities for the computing core to build a reconnaissance mapping of nearby star systems."

Cass frowned. "Why?"

"Because we need resources to help with the repairs and food."

Cass glanced at Naya.

"I knew about the repairs, but we're running low on food, too?" Naya asked.

"We'll be discussing it with the evening meal. Just learned about it earlier."

"Why would this be kept from us?" Cass asked accusingly.

"It wasn't kept from you. We just learned about it today. Mac asked me to confirm what was in the storage containers designated for the mess hall. That part of the ship was damaged, and whatever was in the storage containers was gone."

"How much food do we have?" Cass asked.

"At least a month's worth. It's something we need to keep an eye on, but we're not going to starve tomorrow."

"Just a month from now," Cass replied.

Naya gave her a sympathetic look. "Focus on one day at a time and we'll get through this."

Cass's gaze softened, and she nodded appreciatively.

A month wasn't a lot of time, but Tyler also knew Mac had a few ideas on how to make their food stretch.

Tyler cleared his throat. "Have you had time to evaluate the drones?"

"Some, why?"

"Because I was hoping to use the repair drones to extract materials from asteroids or moons that have some metallicity to them."

Naya considered it for a moment and sighed. "They're not mining drones."

Tyler frowned. "They should be able to handle the double duty."

"Maybe, but Rabsaris is the expert, and he's still in sickbay."

"Are you able to get the drones working?"

"I don't know. I could end up breaking the ones that *are* working."

"Alright, I'll check on Rabsaris then."

"He got badly banged up. The autodoc has been monitoring him."

Tyler didn't know that and said so.

"Mac said the autodoc is fine for basic injuries, but for more complex things he thought it best to monitor Rabsaris's condition," Naya said.

"Who is Rabsaris?" Cass asked.

"He's a mechanic," Tyler said.

"More than that," Naya said. "He's been working on ships for over thirty years. He's better able to work on the drones. My expertise is the computing and power core. In fact, I think he might be able to improve on the repairs I had to make on the sensor array."

"We'll see about that," Tyler said.

Cass cleared her throat. "How do we pick a star system?"

"It'll have to be one that has the best chance of having the resources we need."

"What are the chances that there'll be anything we could eat?" Cass asked.

"The fabricators can use bio-matter and adapt it to something we can consume," Tyler replied.

Cass grimaced. "Sounds tasty."

Tyler chuckled. "You'd be surprised what you'd eat to survive."

"I'll take your word for it."

He left Naya to her work. A little way down the corridor, he waited for Cass. When she finally came, she looked surprised to see him.

Tyler lifted his palms. "Peace offering or a truce?"

She walked toward him slowly, full lips pursed as she considered it. "What are you doing, Tyler?"

"Things got a little heated before, and I'd rather it not happen again. I don't want there to be…" He'd been about to say, "problems between us," but he didn't think it was the best wording he could choose.

She looked away and swallowed. "You're right. We need to put our differences aside."

He nodded. "That's all I want."

Her gaze locked with his. "Is it?"

He frowned, uncertain. "Is what?"

She shook her head. "Never mind."

"This is what I mean. You can't hold me responsible when I don't understand what you're asking me."

"Subtext was never your strong suit. I'd forgotten how staggering it could be running into your blind spot."

He didn't think she was trying to insult him. "Maybe if you just said what was on your mind, I wouldn't have to guess."

She shook her head. "Don't worry about it. Everything is fine. I'll see you later, Tyler."

Everything wasn't fine. He'd tried to smooth things over between them and it kept blowing up in his face. Maybe he should stop trying. Perhaps it was better to let sleeping dogs lie.

He heaved a sigh and watched her walk away from him, which was reminiscent of what had happened between them before, except at that point *he* had been doing the walking. He couldn't change the past, and he didn't want to. Cass would need to make her peace with it.

CHAPTER 12

THE NEXT DAY, Connor and Noah were looking at the scan data for several nearby star systems. The scans left a lot to be desired. Connor tried not to let it bother him, but it did. Not having the tools they needed to make informed decisions was beginning to wear on him.

"We can't go to all of these star systems, so whatever we end up choosing had better tick most of the boxes we need," Noah said.

Connor nodded. "Any one of these four systems could work." Noah was quiet. "Go ahead and say it."

"I already said it before."

"I know, but maybe this time it'll be different."

"I don't trust the I-Drive."

"Neither do I, but we have very little choice."

Noah sighed. "What if it does what it did before?"

"Both you and Naya have checked it, and both of you said you can't find anything wrong with it."

"I know, but we could've missed something."

Connor shook his head. "That's enough. You've got to stop doing this to yourself."

"Easy for you to say."

"It is, because you're being unrealistic. You did everything right, Noah. You couldn't have prevented what happened. We don't have a choice. If we stay here, we're going to die a slow, painful death."

"I know," Noah replied irritably, and banged his fists on the workstation table. "I know. I just wish our options were better."

The doors to the bridge opened and Glen Rhodes entered, with Tyler following him.

"Gentleman, thanks for coming," Connor said.

Noah looked at him in surprise.

Rhodes came to stand next to him. "Are those the star systems?"

Connor nodded.

"Only two have an NEC-type planet," Tyler said as he scanned the holoscreen.

Rhodes frowned. "NEC?"

"New Earth Candidate planet. They are planets similar enough to New Earth that they could support life," Tyler replied.

Rhodes glanced at Connor, and he gave him a nod.

"What makes one more viable than the other?" Rhodes asked.

"That's what we're trying to figure out," Connor replied.

Rhodes glanced at the others. "How do you do that?"

"Ideally, we'd send a couple of recon drones to those systems. Their scan data would be more accurate than the long-range scans on this ship," Connor said. "However, we don't have any recon drones, so we have to pick."

"My vote is for the nearest system with the NEC," Noah replied.

Rhodes peered at the star system data on the holoscreen. "It does have the resources we need in terms of mineral ores, and there is a planet where we might be able to get some bio-matter. I don't see a downside."

"It does seem like our best option, but it's going to take us nine days to get there, so it could be our only option," Connor said.

"Nine days?" Rhodes nearly gasped. "Why will it take that long to get there?"

Connor shared a look with Noah for a second and then said. "We're taking a cautious approach to using the I-Drive. Every diagnostic and visual inspection of the drive shows that it's working."

Rhodes considered it for a moment. "I know this is a courtesy, explaining things to me, and I appreciate it. However, shouldn't we get there as quickly as possible?"

"Our resources in terms of power core capacity limit how much we can send to the I-Drive."

"I understand that, but nine days?"

"We'll push up the timetable to our destination if the I-Drive doesn't have any issues operating," Connor replied.

"Assuming everything goes well, how long could you push up the timetable?"

Connor looked at Noah, who cleared his throat.

"Four days," Noah said.

"And while we're in transit, we will need to devote computing core cycles to the nav system to help us reach our destination," Connor said.

"That means we still won't know where we are."

"Correct. Once we reach the star system, we'll be able to continue with that task."

"General," Kincaid said, "is there any evidence of an advanced alien civilization in that star system?"

Rhodes's eyes darted toward Kincaid.

"We won't know that until we reach the star system. We'll follow standard exploration protocols," Connor said and looked at Rhodes. "It means we'll reach the outer system and scan it. Then we'll decide whether we go farther in. It could be that the outer planets will have everything we need."

"What about our food shortage?"

"There are sometimes organisms that thrive on certain moons, particularly those with ice. Some of them have vast oceans. The food processors can use this material and convert it to something edible."

Rhodes nodded. "Ah, yes, I do remember reading something about that."

Connor didn't doubt it. "Okay, then we're agreed that this is our best option?"

Rhodes regarded Connor for a few moments, then looked at the others. "You clearly don't need my consent."

"But I want your input. Maybe you'll see something the rest of us have missed."

Rhodes looked at the holoscreen and rubbed his chin. "I don't see any other option. The things I'd like to see all require figuring out where we are and contacting home, both of which aren't an option. We're lost. It's time I faced that fact."

Connor bobbed his head once. "Noah, plot a course," he said and looked at the others. "Gentleman, grab a seat and strap yourselves in."

Connor sat next to Noah and opened a ship-wide broadcast. "Crew of the *Pathfinder*. Like it or not, this ship is all we've got. Qualifications aside, we are the crew of this ship, and I will address you as such. We're going to engage the I-Drive and begin making our way to the nearest star system that has a habitable planet. Report to your designated areas while we transition from n-space."

"Captain Kincaid, I want to know the moment everyone has checked in," Connor said.

"Yes, General Gates."

Rhodes looked over at Connor, considering. He looked as if he couldn't decide whether to trust Connor or not. Connor understood Rhodes better than he thought he did.

Connor reviewed the data on his holoscreen.

"I-Drive is ready," Noah said.

"General, all crew have checked in," Captain Kincaid said.

Connor looked at Noah and nodded. "Make it so."

"Engaging I-Drive," Noah said.

Connor watched as the sensor feeds flatlined and the ship transitioned into hyperspace.

"Transition complete," Noah said. "Flight time is twelve hours. Then we'll evaluate performance."

Connor looked at Kincaid. "Give the crew the all-clear."

Rhodes unstrapped himself from the chair, looking a little uncertain.

Connor smiled. "No one notices when things run smoothly."

Rhodes shrugged guiltily. "I keep waiting for something to happen."

"Hopefully, it won't," Connor said and stood.

"I have the first watch," Noah said.

"I'll take the next one," Connor said.

Rhodes looked at Connor. "Are you going to insist on maintaining a watch rotation for the entire day?"

"It's required. Someone has to be here to monitor the ship."

"Then the workload should be spread among all of us," Rhodes said.

Kincaid cleared his throat. “Excuse me, General. I can adapt one of the light-duty protocols to be used for those standing watch. They’ll have instructions to alert the ones with expertise.”

“I want to be involved in that, Captain Kincaid,” Noah said. Connor looked at him. “It shouldn’t take long.”

“Alright, I’ll leave you to it,” Connor said.

He left the bridge and Rhodes walked next to him. “Where are you going now?”

“To the vehicle bay,” Connor replied.

Rhodes pressed his lips together. “To do what?”

“I’m trying to get one of the rovers working in case we need it.”

“I had no idea you did that sort of thing.”

“I tinker,” Connor replied and tipped his head to the side, “with all kinds of things. Want to join me?”

“I appreciate the offer, but it’s my turn to help with lunch prep. I’m better in the kitchen than on a workbench.”

“A word of caution. Cooks are territorial about their kitchens,” Connor said.

Rhodes snorted. “Maclean already asserted as much.”

They parted ways, each man staying busy as best they could. Connor thought that if he became still, his mind would wander to the things outside his control. He thought about Lenora and the rest of his family. He wouldn’t allow himself to consider that they wouldn’t make it home. He just wasn’t sure what it was going to take in order to actually make that happen.

CHAPTER 13

Connor woke in the middle of the night, his mind racing, as if doing many things at once. He checked the time, and it was almost four in the morning. Echoes of dreams and thoughts permeated his mind. Now that he was awake, it felt as if he was stumbling to catch up to what his mind had been doing while he was sleeping. Waking up like this was familiar, even if it had been a while since it had happened. There were just some things that required time to marinate, and sleeping was when there were enough cycles available for his mind to work on the problems. It reminded him of the limitations they had with the ship's computing core, but perhaps in his case it was an age issue.

He'd awakened feeling restless, and he doubted he'd get back to sleep, so he went to the sink and splashed water on his face, then put on a faded-blue ship suit. Mac always had a carafe of coffee available in the mess hall, so Connor decided on a middle-of-the-night foray.

He left his quarters. The corridors were suffused by a reddish, amber-colored lighting that wouldn't stimulate wakefulness. The lighting wouldn't change in the corridors until closer to six in the morning, which was the time for an unofficial sunrise.

He entered the quiet mess hall, and the bio sensors gradually increased the lighting. He walked over to the coffee and poured a cup. After adding a generous portion of cream, he also poured some sugar into his cup.

He'd just sat down when the door to the kitchen opened and Maclean walked out. He rubbed his bald head and spotted Connor.

"Want some company, General?"

"Always," Connor replied and sipped his coffee. He let out a contented sigh. "I don't know how you do it, but this brew is really good."

Mac poured himself a cup and sat with Connor. "I try to make sure we're stocked with the best I can get. Hard-working people deserve it."

"Yes, they do."

Mac was quiet for a moment. "The secret is the proper cleaning of the entire coffeemaker. It's the only way to get that marvelous percolating goodness. Same goes for the food fabricators."

Connor nodded. "Well, I appreciate it, and so does everyone else."

Mac smiled and bobbed his head, leaning back in his chair. "Not the worst group of people to be stranded with."

Connor nearly choked on his coffee. It wasn't the first time Mac had made an offhand comment like this.

Mac grinned knowingly. "What's got you up in the middle of the night?" he asked and then rolled his eyes. "I mean, aside from the obvious."

"Just woke up. Didn't want to stay in bed anymore."

Mac nodded. "Same here. My mind tends to wander if I'm still for too long."

They lapsed into a companionable silence for a minute.

"Are you the same way?" Mac asked.

"Mostly. It comes and goes."

"Something got you up in the middle of the night. I always thought it was our brain trying to tell us something."

Connor considered it for a few moments. "Yeah, just not sure what," he replied. "What about you?"

Mac regarded him for a moment. "I'm just trying to do my part so the others can do theirs. I'm not going to figure out how to get us home, but I can make sure everyone is fed so the geniuses aboard this ship can figure it out." He eyed Connor for a moment. "I include you in that, General."

Connor chuckled and shook his head. "I'm not a genius."

"Genius takes many forms. Sure, you might not be the inventor of the I-Drive, but you've got a knack for people and seeing right to the core of a problem."

"Thanks for the vote of confidence," Connor said and drained his cup.

"If there's anyone who's going to see us through this, it's you, General. I know that comes with a lot of pressure."

Connor tilted his head to the side. "You had a thirty-year career in the CDF. Where did you serve?"

Mac smiled. "I've been around. I've served on ships, bases, and off-world bases. I didn't rise high enough in the ranks to cross paths with you, but let's just say this isn't the first time I've been way out in the deep end."

Connor stood. "Thanks for the talk."

As he was walking away, Mac called out to him.

"I once heard you say to a group of soldiers that we should play to our strengths. Yours is that you see people. Maybe what's got you up in the middle of the night has something to do with that. Just a little advice from an old cook."

"I'll keep that in mind," Connor said.

He went for a walk to clear his head. The ship wasn't very big, and he walked most of it over the next thirty minutes. What Mac said kept bouncing around in his mind. It had been a few days since they started traveling to the star system, but something kept gnawing at this thought. It was like a minor itch at the center of his back that he was only aware of in the moments before he slept. He thought it was just the anticipation of reaching the star system, but after his talk with Mac, maybe it was something else. It had to be.

Connor tried to recall what he'd been dreaming about just before he woke. It was bits and pieces of conversations, situations that he couldn't control. He began to think about the people on the ship. There weren't many of them, and all repairs requiring EVAs stopped while they were in transit. Some people spent more time together than others. His thoughts spiked. While others sought comfort in the company of others, Noah still preferred to be alone. It wasn't all the time, but it seemed to be more over the last day or so. Connor knew that he felt responsible for what had happened and was determined to figure out what triggered the event.

He considered tracking Noah down but dismissed the idea. It wasn't that he was worried about confronting his friend; he just wasn't sure the best way to go about it. Maybe Noah had learned something, and he was afraid of sharing it with him until he'd worked it all out. Connor was guilty of bearing burdens alone, and maybe his influence had imparted those practices to Noah.

Connor turned his thoughts to what Noah could be hiding. He didn't want to blindly accuse Noah of anything. He'd gotten enough of that from Rhodes.

He looked at corridor markers that labeled what was in the area, and his gaze settled on Stellar Cartography. The ship being in service for twenty years meant it had likely been part of a task force during the Krake Wars, so the ship had a holo-theater used for mapping the stars.

Connor opened the door to the holo-theater and used his credentials to open a session with the ship's computer. He considered his options for a few moments, deciding what he was going to do.

"Let's work from the top down," Connor said.

He brought up the computing core system logs and created a search that showed him Noah's activity. A long list of access log entries filled his view—too many for him to look at individually, so he created a filter to isolate the frequency of use. A new list of log entries appeared that contained automated tasks Noah had run, but recently a majority of his time had been devoted to the navigation system. The second-most entries he saw were performance reports for the I-Drive.

Connor brought up the most recent performance report and read it. The analysis showed I-Drive degradation, and it was followed by a percentage. He knew the I-Drive had been impacted, but he wasn't sure whether the degradation being recorded affected the overall performance in any significant way.

The access logs showed him that Noah had spent a significant amount of time in the nav system. No doubt he was trying to figure out their current location. Connor tried to bring up the reports attached to the access logs, but they were empty. Noah hadn't saved the reports.

He pressed his lips together and opened a session to the nav system. The status still showed their location as unknown. He brought up a model he'd been working on that contained simulations of the event. They all showed the ship leaving the planet but couldn't reconcile their location within probable ranges.

Connor stared at the holoscreen for a few moments. He removed the limiters that restricted the nav system so that it only considered probable ranges. A warning appeared about computing-core cycles. It was forcing him to limit it in some capacity. Infinity wasn't an option.

He rubbed his chin as he considered this. He'd spent time running different probability models that hadn't led anywhere. This was like beating his head against a wall and expecting a different result. It wasn't going to happen.

Connor stared at the blue, semitranslucent representation of New Earth with its planetary rings. It was slowly rotating. He reached out and stopped the planet from moving, and then he spun it until he was looking directly at the location of the research base. The assumptions being used weren't helping; it was time to consider things that weren't so obvious.

He changed the predictive focal point. Instead of the ship transiting straight up and away from the planet, he decided to have the trajectory follow a path toward the top of the planet. He gave it a range of one hundred lightyears and waited for the computer to complete its analysis.

Inconclusive. Unknown location.

Scowling, he stopped the analysis from running. Then, he highlighted half the planet and had the computer divide it into sections to run his model against. A data window appeared and began listing the iterations.

He frowned and shook his head. He'd picked the wrong side of the planet. He tried to stop the analysis from completing, but the session wouldn't respond.

He heaved a sigh and looked away, scratching his forehead. He knew the ins and outs of a nav system. He must still be tired because he knew better than to do what he'd done. This was a waste of time.

A chime sounded, drawing his attention to the holoscreen.

Connor's eyes widened. In the middle of a long list of data was a successful return, and it had a probability rating of less than one percent. He frowned and glanced at the planet. He highlighted the trajectory with the successful return, and it showed the ship going through the planet in a straight line.

"This can't be right," he said and ran the model again.

The trajectory would've destroyed the ship, but the results were the same, down to the probability rate.

Connor isolated the crazy trajectory that should've killed them and increased the distance to a thousand lightyears. As he initiated the model to run, he expected a quick return, indicating a significant error. The analysis took a few minutes to run, and a few times he thought the session was either frozen or had timed out. It did neither. The probability rate had increased to seventeen percent. He blinked in surprise and felt his heart rate increase. This didn't make a bit of sense. He knew both Noah and Naya had checked the nav system and were adamant that it was working properly.

Connor pursed his lips in thought. Then he updated the data model again, this time entering a distance of eight thousand lightyears. The computer threw up an alert, which he ignored, forcing the model to run.

Given the extreme distances and the fact that the nav system had to reconcile two distinct star mappings, it was going to take a while to run.

He walked over to one of the padded chairs and sat, extending his feet and stretching them out as he tried to block out the small voice in his head telling him how crazy this was. Lenora would've encouraged him to consider the impossible, especially when everything else he'd tried hadn't worked. It was all her years as an archeologist and piecing together the hidden history of lost civilizations speaking to him. He looked up at the artificial stars on display. Physics didn't work the same as hunting for lost civilizations, and yet here he was, out of options and way beyond all that he knew was possible.

The data model finished, and the results staggered him. He repeated the model three more times and then expanded it to include other trajectories. The error ratio increased the farther away from the original trajectory he'd begun with, which was the most accurate. Each iteration spiked his temper as he acknowledged the foolish betrayal on the part of one of his closest friends.

Connor saved the reports to his wrist computer and stormed out of the holo-theater. Gritting his teeth, he pulled up Noah's location and saw that he was on the bridge. Apparently, he wasn't the only one who couldn't sleep.

A wide range of thoughts came to his mind as he made his way there, but the most prominent one was that of betrayal. A horde of accusations came to mind, battling with his better judgement until he dismissed them all. Noah could answer for himself.

The door to the bridge opened, startling Noah. "Connor, I didn't expect to see you this early," he said and became silent. "What's wrong?"

Connor strode over until he stood across from his friend. "How long have you known?"

Noah frowned in confusion. "What do you mean? Known about what?"

"Don't play games with me," Connor said and projected the results of his analysis onto the main holoscreen. "Five thousand lightyears away from New Earth. We are five thousand lightyears away from home, and I want to know how long you've known about it."

Noah lowered his gaze, looking ashamed, and Connor clenched his teeth.

"I don't believe this. Answer the question, Noah."

"I only found out shortly after we started heading to the star system."

"That was three days ago. Why didn't you tell me?"

Noah stared at the floor. "I didn't want to believe it. I spent more than a day trying to disprove the analysis, but I couldn't. All the models I came up with show that this ship has somehow travelled through the planet and taken us thousands of lightyears from home."

Connor waited for him to continue.

Noah looked up at him guiltily and swallowed hard. "I didn't want to believe it, but here we are. Even with the differing snapshots of the star maps, they line up. Your model is accurate. Between the colossal distance and the drive core degradation issue..." He shook his head, looking like a man who had given it his all and had come up short. "Connor, I don't know if I can get us home."

Connor's gaze softened. Fear could bring out the worst in people sometimes, clouding their judgement. He sighed. "I can't believe I'm the one saying this to *you*, but you've got to have faith. It's the thing that sustains us when all else fails. I don't know how we're going to get home, but I'm not going to lose hope. We got here, which means we can get back home. It's as simple as that."

Noah's eyes became misty, and he shook his head, quickly wiping them. "I've been trying, and I can't figure it out."

"What can't you figure out?"

"All of it. How we somehow went through a planet and how

we traveled thousands of lightyears with only three I-Drive engagements." He paused for a moment, looking at the main holoscreen. "Who knows how far we would've gone if we hadn't been able to stop it?"

"I'm going to state the obvious, just so it gets out of my brain. It shouldn't have worked. The energy required to travel even a fraction of that distance wasn't available in the power core."

Noah blew out a shaky breath. "I know." He pressed his mouth shut for a second. "We stumbled onto this technology, and we thought all the probes we used developing the Infinity Drive had been destroyed somehow. It never occurred to us that they might've gone way beyond subspace communications range."

Connor remembered the project. Noah and a team of the colony's finest minds had worked on FTL for years. "Those distances would've thrown the limited nav system on those probes out of whack, which prevented them from returning home," Connor said.

"We never even considered that they were moving through solid objects. Why would anyone think of that? Our impulse was to navigate around them." He looked at the main holoscreen again. "But we did." He bit his lip, forehead wrinkling. "What if we punched a hole through the entire planet? What if I just killed everyone back home!" He snapped his fingers with a haggard expression. "And we're all that's left?" he asked. Looking away, he exhaled a breath mixed with an anguished cry. "I might've killed everyone back home."

Connor raised his hands in a placating gesture. "No," he said firmly, then came around the workstation and grabbed Noah's shoulders. "Look at me. You didn't kill anyone. You've got to calm down. We didn't kill everyone back home."

"But—"

"But nothing. There is no way for us to know until we get back home. I'm not going to let you take on all this massive guilt for what in all likelihood is not true."

"You don't know that."

Connor's gaze hardened, and it had a menacing certainty that came with the knowledge of one who had, in fact, all but destroyed an entire planet that had been home to their cruelest enemy. It had been the right decision, but the cost was weighed down by a whole lot of unanswerable questions. He wasn't going to allow Noah to take on that kind of guilt.

Connor's expression softened. "The Phantoms asked us why we only moved in space instead of through it. They must've meant literally *through* space, including planets and everything else."

"It can't be that simple."

"Why not? They must've analyzed our technology. They could've easily figured out its potential, then raised the very question that put us on this path."

Noah frowned in thought for a few seconds, and Connor waited him out.

"Sean used to joke about me trying to figure out how to teleport. That's not what this is. We're out of normal space, but..." Noah shook his head. "I can't get it straight in my head. It's dumb luck that we didn't transition back into n-space inside a planet, or worse."

"I don't think so."

"Why not?"

"Because space is vast. We'd probably have to go out of our way just to hit something. We were lucky, I'll grant you that, but it stands to reason that since we *did* move through a planet, it also stands to reason that no one was harmed in doing so."

Noah crossed his arms and sagged into the chair. He looked overwhelmed and utterly exhausted.

"Have you considered that maybe the Phantoms were aware of how close you were to making this work and caused all this?" Connor asked.

"It's all I've been thinking about. I just haven't been able to prove it."

Connor speared a look at him. "You should've come to me as soon as you'd figured this out. After the shock subsided, you should've come to me. That would've been better than spinning around in circles going crazy by yourself."

"I wasn't spinning—"

Connor's gaze hardened.

Noah sighed. "You're right. I should've come to you. Now we can both spin around in circles because I don't know how we're going to get back home."

"Well, we're going to have company doing it."

Noah looked up at him and frowned. "What do you mean?"

"Trust has been violated. This is going to cost us, and there isn't anything we can do to soften the blow. However, we can't keep this from the others. They have a right to know."

"Everything will come apart when they learn this, especially Rhodes. He's had it out for me and this project since day one."

"People are more resilient than that. I can guarantee that it's only a matter of time before Naya figures this out. Probably Kincaid, as well. Heck, I wouldn't put it past those two interns figuring it out. I managed to do it in an hour and a half, and most of that time was proving that the data model I was using was correct."

"How *did* you figure it out?"

Connor eyed him for a moment. "I checked your log activity in the computing core and noted what systems you were accessing. Then I decided to create my own data models for the nav system to analyze."

Noah gave him an appraising look. "You used access logs to figure this out?"

Connor smiled with half his mouth. "What do you think I do all day—sit back and give people orders?"

Noah snorted a little, then heaved a long sigh. He uncrossed his arms and stood. "I don't know what to say to them."

Connor had rarely seen Noah this frazzled. "Stick to the truth. It doesn't have to be pretty; it just has to be the truth. We don't soften the blow. We present the data as it is and let them decide whether it's right or not."

Noah frowned. "We?"

"I'm angry and disappointed, but I'm still going to stand by your side. Always," Connor said.

Noah regarded him. "Thanks, Connor."

"Think you're the first person to get scared and try to carry the weight of the world on your shoulders? Think again. Come on."

Noah glanced at the time. "You're going to get them out of bed for this?"

Connor shook his head. "No, but I'd like to eat a good breakfast before all the yelling starts. We need to keep up our strength."

CHAPTER 14

EATING breakfast had been the right decision. Connor watched Noah devour two helpings of eggs, bacon, fried potatoes with peppers and onions, and a large piece of banana bread. Mac had previously told Connor that Noah had skipped more than a few meals. With a full stomach, Noah looked as if he could fall asleep right there.

Before the food coma could really set in, Connor said, "You better get another cup of coffee because sleep is a long way off."

Noah nodded and went to pour himself another cup.

Connor sent a message out to the survivors, summoning them to the mess hall. Over the next half hour, people streamed in.

"I'm going to put a presentation together," Noah said.

Connor shook his head. "We need to do this quickly, and we already have the reports to show them. Once they finish eating, we'll get started."

Glen Rhodes and Jorath paused from their meal to watch them from across the mess hall. They were getting impatient.

Kincaid sat with Seger and Naya, while Tripp, Grace, and Reed sat at a table by themselves. Cassidy Rhodes was the last to arrive, and Connor watched as she went to sit with Tripp and the others.

Connor walked toward the kitchen where Maclean and his assistant, Tim Hopper, worked.

"Excuse me, gentlemen," Connor said. "Would you mind joining us out here, please?"

"At once, General Gates," Mac said and gestured for Tim to stop what he was doing.

There was only one person missing—Rabsaris Husker, who was still recovering from his injuries in sickbay.

Connor walked in front of a wide holoscreen that was across from the tables. Noah stood and joined him. The others became quiet, and there was an inaudible anticipation in the air.

Connor noticed that some of them glanced at the others, perhaps looking for some reassurance.

He cleared his throat. "We've made some discoveries that you need to know about."

"I'd like to tell them," Noah said, and Connor gestured for him to continue.

Noah faced the others. He seemed calmer than he'd been before, which Connor had expected. There was no longer any reason to hide, and it was freeing.

"This is going to be difficult for you to hear, and for that, I'm sorry," Noah said. "Shortly after we transitioned into hyperspace, I continued working on trying to figure out our current location in relation to New Earth." He paused, and the others were quiet. "I'm not going to beat around the bush on this. We're over five thousand lightyears from home."

Connor watched as each of them took in Noah's words. Kincaid and Seger looked at Connor for confirmation.

"That's impossible," Jorath said.

Noah held up his hand, imploring patience. "I will share all the data and the reports in a moment, but I assure you that the data is accurate. We *are* over five thousand lightyears from home."

Over the next twenty minutes, Noah presented his data models to support his assertion of their current location. By the end of it, most of the survivors looked as if they'd been kicked in the stomach, and Connor couldn't blame them. Others looked on with disbelief and an anger akin to that of a hunted animal.

"General Gates," Rhodes said, "do you concur with these findings?"

"Yes, I do," Connor replied. "We don't completely understand the hows and whys, but it's the best explanation we've got."

"And," Noah added, "it's one that the nav computer can reconcile."

Rhodes narrowed his gaze. "As long as the nav system is okay with it, then we should just follow blindly along? Is that your position?"

"Do you have a better explanation?" Connor asked, unable to keep the irritation from his voice.

He was getting tired of the way Rhodes's attitude shifted from reasonable to abhorrent within the span of a conversation. Several of the others watched Rhodes as if they were reserving judgement on how they felt about the news until he voiced his opinion. Such was the way of people who were overwhelmed and searching for direction.

Connor stared at Rhodes. "I asked you a question."

Rhodes looked at Noah. "You made this discovery days ago, and only now you tell the rest of us? What were you waiting for?"

Noah regarded Rhodes for a long moment. "Yes. At first I

didn't want to believe it, so I tried everything I could think of to disprove it."

Rhodes narrowed his gaze. "Then you hid the knowledge from the rest of us," he said, and his gaze swooped toward Connor. "And you, General Gates. This is hardly in keeping with the spirit of cooperation you espouse." He glanced at Noah for a second and then back at Connor, arriving at a conclusion. "You figured it out. That's it, isn't it? You figured this out and then confronted Mr. Barker about it."

Connor wasn't going to hide anything from them. "And then we came here to tell the rest of you. Now you know everything."

"That is completely unacceptable. Both of you have been operating completely unchecked for this entire voyage. We're expected to follow along because you say you know best. That's what you told us. You've faced tough situations before and that we should defer to you," Rhodes said and looked at the others. "This isn't the first time secrets have been kept from the rest of us, and now we're suffering from their recklessness. This must stop. We can't allow this to continue."

Captain Kincaid turned toward him in his chair. "You're out of line, Director Rhodes."

"No, he's not!" Cassidy shouted, cold fury in her gaze as she speared a look at Kincaid. "He's right. We've done everything that's been asked of us, but the lies and deceit keep being uncovered."

"That's absurd. We've worked around the clock for everyone's survival. It's about time all of you realize you're way out of your depth," Kincaid said.

Then the shouting started in earnest. Days of fear and frustration had built on themselves inside each of them. Connor should've known this was coming sooner or later, and he reminded himself that their reaction to the news was visceral.

They needed time to digest it. They were stuck with each other, whether they liked it or not.

Groups of people were shouting at the others, and Connor watched them. The sight of it was sickening, but if he didn't let them blow off some steam, it would be worse later. But he could only allow this to go on for so long, and it was time to intervene.

Sergeant Seger was standing like a well-muscled human wall between Connor and the others.

Seger looked at him, and Connor gave him a small nod.

Seger's voice boomed across the room, startling even Connor. The others were stunned into silence. "We will keep order here!"

Tripp Krin stormed toward him, face as red as his unruly red hair. "I'm tired of being told what to do."

Tripp began to shove, and Seger and the CDF sergeant pinned him to the deck with his arms behind his back. It had taken place so quickly that Tripp looked as if he had no idea how he'd suddenly ended up on his stomach.

"Don't make this worse, kid. I don't want to hurt you," Seger said.

Jorath started to intervene, and Kincaid blocked his path.

"Let him up, Sergeant," Connor said.

Seger let Tripp go and stood. The young man pushed himself up and hastened back. He was uninjured except for his pride.

Connor looked at Rhodes. But before either of them could speak, Noah cleared his throat.

"There is more for you to hear," Noah said, "or you can keep shouting. By all means, get it out of your system, but the facts aren't going to change. Shall I continue?"

Noah's words were like a splash of cold water on the survivors. They sat down with minimal grumbling, but Connor knew tensions were still high.

"If you can accept the fact that we're so far from home, some of you might anticipate what's next. I've been working on how to get us back there," Noah said, his voice impressively calm. "With the current I-Drive performance and without degradation, it will take us thirty-three years to travel all the way home. There's more," he said, holding up his hand before a barrage of questions came at him. "Thirty-three years is a long time, even if we had the supplies and a ship that could survive the journey. However, the I-Drive *does* suffer from degradation due to the lack of purity of the drive core. It's not meant for that kind of sustained usage. So, when I plug in the percentage decrease resulting from drive core degradation, which will grow over time, the estimate for us returning home is over two-hundred and thirty-five years."

Sometimes silence could be much louder than all the shouting in the world. This was the moment that would make or break their resolve to survive, and it was likely to go on for days.

Noah gave everyone a solemn look. He then made a passing motion with his hand, and there were audible chimes from the tablets and wrist computers the others carried. "I've made available all of my calculations and data models. Go through it as you will. The data is accurate. This is why I didn't come to you with the knowledge as soon as I learned of it. I needed time to absorb this, and then I hid from it. I was wrong. Connor confronted me as soon as he figured it out. I thought I was protecting you. I thought that since I'm one of the senior project leaders who knows the most about the technology used here, as well as what we were developing, I'm the most qualified to find a solution that will take us home." He looked at Rhodes. "You may not like what I've done, but I did it in service of all of you, as well as the fact that I have a loving wife and family I want to see again." Noah paused for a long moment. "Now you know everything, and I don't remember the last time I've actually slept, so I'm going to take my leave of you now."

Connor watched as Noah left. He'd said what needed to be said, and now the rest of them would need to come to terms with the reality of their situation.

The others were completely stunned. Rhodes looked as if he was going to call out to Noah, but Connor shook his head.

"We all need time to absorb this information," Connor said. He looked at all of them. "Take some time with this, but don't do anything rash. The only way we're going to get through this is if we work together."

"Don't do anything rash?" Rhodes scowled and shook his head. "He just told us there isn't any hope of getting home and then tells us not to do anything rash." He stared at Connor, nostrils flaring. "This is too much," he said and headed for the door. He looked at his daughter. "Cass, come with me. Jorath, you too. Anyone else who wants to join us is welcome."

The others began filing out, one by one. More than a few shared a troubled look as they left. Tripp hastened out, but Grace Mendel stayed, as did Naya Corman.

Maclean looked at Tim Hopper. "We've got prep work to do, unless you'd like to join the others?" he asked and lifted his chin toward the door.

Tim shook his head. "I'm fine right here, Mac."

Mac smiled and gave Connor a nod as they headed back into the kitchen.

Kincaid and Seger turned toward Connor.

"I think we should keep an eye on Rhodes and the others," Kincaid said.

Connor shook his head. "No, leave them alone."

"But sir, they could be planning something."

"They need time, Captain, and I intend to give it to them. They'll come around."

He hoped they would.

Kincaid considered this for a few moments. "I wish I was as confident as you are, sir."

"Maybe you need to take some time with this, too."

Kincaid shook his head. "Negative, General. I'll remain at your side."

Connor looked at the others. "This goes for everyone. Noah has been blaming himself for this whole thing since it happened. Maybe some of you agree with him, but this isn't his fault. There are some things you've not been cleared to know," he said, and then told them about the Phantoms. "All we have is a suspicion that they are somehow involved. Just so we're clear, I intend to tell this to the others as soon as they calm down. We got here. Despite everything, we travelled over five thousand lightyears faster than anyone could've imagined. And we did it in this ship. That means that this ship can make it back home. We just need some time to gather the things we need and finish making repairs."

A tall, willowy, olive-skinned man hovered in the door to the mess hall, looking confused. He had curly black hair and a cleft chin.

"Sorry, I couldn't help but overhear, and I'm not sure I heard correctly, but did you just say we're five thousand lightyears from home?"

"Rabsaris!" Naya shouted.

Connor smiled and beckoned the man over. "Rabsaris Husker?"

He nodded. "General Gates, I'm sorry. The autodoc woke me up. Said I was cleared to walk around," he said and frowned. "Are we in space?"

Connor's mouth hung open for a moment, and the others also displayed various expressions of surprise. Rabsaris was a lead mechanic, very knowledgeable about this ship and had specialized knowledge of the drones and vehicles on the ship.

"Why don't you have a seat? We'll get Mac to set you up with some food and then we'll take it from the beginning."

Rabsaris bobbed his head once. "That sounds good, General. It might take a while. My head still feels like I've taken a few too many hits."

Connor chuckled and the others joined in. Rabsaris looked confused.

"You could say that most of us feel exactly the same way."

CHAPTER 15

Connor left the robotics lab. Naya was going over the work she'd done with Rabsaris as she brought him up to speed. While the lead mechanic had been shocked to learn all that had happened to them, he didn't waste any time getting back to work. If they were to have any hope of using the repair drones for mining operations, they needed Rabsaris's expertise.

Sergeant Seger followed Connor down the corridor. The ship was quiet, and he wasn't sure where Rhodes and the others had gone. He could've tracked them via the ship's computer but decided not to.

He looked at Seger. "I'm going to take a walk, Sergeant."

"Understood, sir. I'll follow a short distance behind if you'd like some space."

While the ship had many corridors that navigated around it, its shape was more or less square, with several appendages required for flight operations. He went to the upper decks, which were largely unused. There were several cargo areas that looked intact, making him wonder if there was anything they could salvage.

He walked to the forward section and heard someone in one of the lounges. They weren't far from the command-and-control observation room.

Connor looked inside the lounge. There were several workstations along the wall, and Cassidy Rhodes sat at the one farthest from the door with her back to him. Her buttery blonde hair was tied into a short ponytail. She had several active holoscreens and was reviewing protocols to detect anomalies.

Connor considered passing the lounge, leaving Ms. Rhodes to her search, but he knew that building bridges with people necessitated reaching out to them.

He cleared his throat as he entered, and she nearly jumped out of the chair.

"I'm sorry," Connor said. "I didn't mean to sneak up on you."

Cassidy blinked several times and exhaled a long breath. "It's fine," she said and turned toward her holoscreens to begin closing them.

Connor crossed the lounge. "You don't have to stop what you're doing."

Her hand stopped in mid-motion and then settled into her lap.

Having raised a daughter of his own, he knew the value of patience and waited her out.

"I don't know if I have the clearance to look at that data," she replied.

Connor shrugged. "Given the situation, I think more than a little latitude is understandable."

She frowned in surprise and gave him an appraising look.

Connor smiled a little. "I bet you didn't expect to hear that."

She still had her guard up, but the edges of her lips did lift a little. "No, I didn't."

Connor gestured at the chair next to the workstation. "Mind if we talk for a few minutes?"

Her eyes darted toward the chair, and she looked uncertain. Then she looked up at him. "You don't like my father much, do you?"

Connor regarded her as he considered his response. "I don't hate your father. We're both doing our best to figure out a way to get home. As a father, I understand his concerns. You're here," he said, gesturing to her. "I know you're a grown woman. I have a daughter, too, who's also very accomplished, but being a father isn't something that can be turned off. So, believe me when I tell you that I understand your father's behavior."

Cassidy's expression softened. "It would be better for us all if you both put your differences aside because it's tearing the rest of us apart. I don't think we'll make it if you don't."

She wasn't wrong about that. Connor gestured toward the open chair.

Her eyes widened. "Yes, please. I'm sorry."

Connor sat. "We're all a little bit out of sorts today."

She looked away from him. "Yeah," she said quietly. Then she looked at him. "Do you mind if I ask you—actually, never mind."

Connor was quiet for a few seconds. "Why are you reviewing anomaly detection protocols?"

She frowned, and Connor gestured toward the holoscreen.

"Oh, that," she said and shifted in her seat. "I overheard part of a conversation in the mess hall about the Phantoms."

It wasn't the first time there had been mention of the Phantoms. "You must've heard of them before that."

She tilted her head to the side a little. "I'm aware that this research project was the result of an alien encounter with a species referred to as the Phantoms. The goal of the project was to reexamine FTL technology."

"That's correct."

"You said that they might be responsible for what happened with the ship. I was reviewing the protocols to see if anything had been detected."

She looked as if she'd been caught doing something she shouldn't have been doing.

"First, there's nothing wrong with what you're doing. I've found that a fresh set of eyes might notice something the rest of us miss."

Cassidy stared at him, looking slightly surprised.

Connor chuckled. "Not what you were expecting?"

"I guess not. I'm not sure what I was expecting, to be honest. I just didn't expect you to be so open about it."

"I meant what I said earlier about wanting the lines of communication open," he said, and she nodded. "Did you find anything?"

She glanced at the holoscreen, pressing her lips together. "The protocols seem to be centered around detecting gravitational anomalies. With the sensor array offline, there really isn't anything to detect."

"That's what we found as well."

"How do you expect to prove your theory about the Phantoms?"

Connor pursed his lips in thought for a second. "Think of it this way. It's similar to the way the requisitions office tries to ensure that resources aren't being wasted. When determining approval for funding a project, the review committee must understand the intent behind the project, along with its goals."

Cassidy nodded. "Yes, clear start and end goals are essential.

Otherwise, it would give rise to open-ended projects that never delivered results."

Connor tipped his head to the side approvingly. "I do hate those. To prove my theory about the Phantoms and whether or not they had something to do with the event is going to be much harder because of all the issues we've had." He regarded her thoughtfully. "You know, you might be able to help with that."

"Me? How?"

"I have a good idea how the Colonial Requisitions Office conducts its investigations and project reviews. It requires you to be well rounded, and attention to detail can definitely help."

She scratched her shoulder and then shrugged. "I still don't understand how that applies to this," she said, gesturing toward the holoscreen.

"The Phantoms can manipulate ship systems. Evidence of their involvement has been detected by small gravitational anomalies. They also claim to be able to access any data library they want, so it stands to reason…"

"That if they can access those systems to read them, they could also insert data into those vulnerable systems."

Connor smiled. "Now you're on your way to becoming a secure systems expert."

She gave him a warm smile, probably the first one he'd seen from her. Then she gave a pensive look at the holoscreens. "Where would I even begin? It's like finding the proverbial needle in a haystack."

"There lies the rub," Connor replied. "I think Phantom involvement might have been reactionary in nature. Something that didn't take a lot of prep time."

"Why do you think that?"

"Because they've shown a lot of finesse in what they've done before, and what happened to us feels more like something cobbled together at the very last instant. It's just a gut feeling I've got."

"Interesting, but it still doesn't give me a direction."

"Okay, try this on for size then. If you're investigating an accident, what are among the first things you look for?"

She frowned in thought. "If this was a technical project involving computer systems, I'd search the changelog for system management. I'd look at a list of the most recent changes and see if they were properly done. The event occurred in the middle of a major system overhaul..."

"That's right, and the others haven't been able to find anything, assuming they've had time to look for it. Would you consider looking into this?"

"What would I use as search criteria?" she asked and then said, "I'll review the proposed changes and go from there."

"Let me know what you find out."

She nodded and then gave him an appraising look. "General Gates, do you mind if I ask you a question?"

"Very well, Ms. Rhodes. What would you like to ask me?"

"You have a reputation both in the CDF and outside of it that draws certain types of people to want to serve with you. I've heard rumors about recruitment issues because of it."

Connor frowned. "Does this have to do with Captain Kincaid?" Her expression became guarded. "Actually, that's none of my business," Connor added hastily. "I've had a long career, and yes, some of the most impactful events do seem to occur around me. What would you like me to say about that?"

"Before this, I thought you encouraged that kind of behavior, but I think I've been wrong about you. I'm sorry about that."

Connor was surprised by her apology. "Much of what you learned about colonial history I've had to live through. I'm well aware of the costs involved in all those things. It's like a double-bladed knife. While I was lucky enough to have survived when others didn't, it also inspires others to try to do the same. Tyler Kincaid decided he wanted to do his part to defend the colony. I know the burden on family and loved ones can be high—never think that I don't—but if I could offer you some unsolicited advice, Tyler didn't join the CDF by choosing it over something or someone he viewed as less important. He chose it because he wanted to protect the people who matter the most. Making that kind of sacrifice has its own price for the person doing it."

Cassidy considered Connor's words for a few moments. "Thank you for the advice, General Gates. I knew Tyler before he joined the CDF. I don't know if his decision to join was as noble as you make it sound, but I will give it some thought."

Connor didn't want to get in the middle of a lover's quarrel, but he was well aware of the strains that being in the CDF had on a person and those around them.

"Cass, I thought I'd find you—" Glen Rhodes stopped speaking and stared at Connor, then glanced at this daughter for a second. "General Gates, I didn't expect to see you here."

"We were talking," Cassidy said before Connor could answer. "Actually, he was helping me understand some things about the event."

"Oh, I see," Rhodes replied.

"Dad, no. The mistrust has to stop here. Divisions won't help anyone."

Connor hadn't expected her to say that, and the surprise must've been evident on his face because Rhodes peered at him suspiciously for a moment but then relented. His expression softened as he looked at his daughter.

"You're right," Rhodes said.

Connor stood. "We're all doing the best we can."

He noticed Cassidy give her father a nod of encouragement.

Rhodes regarded Connor for a few moments. "In light of everything, it's unfair of me to be so bullheaded about this. For that, I apologize to you, General Gates. I'll try not to let it happen again, but I can't promise not to ask any questions."

"I'm not worried about questions," Connor said and extended his hand.

Rhodes shook it.

It was a peace offering, at least for the moment. Connor hoped it would carry them through whatever was coming next.

CHAPTER 16

Connor woke about ten minutes before his alarm was set to go off. The lighting in his cabin brightened, and he sighed. Sitting up, he swung his feet to the floor and rolled his shoulders, stretching them. He looked around the sparse cabin. It wasn't that he didn't appreciate the bed; it wasn't that bad, but the problem was that it wasn't his. Spending over eighteen months in his own bed had made sleeping elsewhere more difficult than it had ever been before. He scowled at the empty place next to him. He missed Lenora, the sound of her voice and all the nuances they shared. He was almost constantly reminded of her absence. The lack of that familiarity was draining him, and more recently, it was distracting him. He kept busy as much as he could, but it persisted either in the back of his mind or during a brief pause between tasks. They hadn't been apart like this in a very long time. When he'd been younger, it hadn't bothered him as much, but after being married for so long, it was unnerving how off balance he felt.

"You're getting soft," Connor said to himself with a long, drawn-out sigh. Then he shook his head. He wasn't getting soft. If anything, he was much more than he had been. He knew the incalculable value of a good marriage, and yet he suspected that his estimations fell well short of its true value.

He changed his clothes, putting on a generic, faded-blue ship suit. He felt weighed down, and it was dragging at his thoughts. They were flying a ship through interstellar space with fourteen survivors who were doing the job of flying a ship designed for five times that number of experienced crewmembers. Even with the retrofitted upgrades that allowed for a smaller crew, there were few who had actual experience serving on a ship. It reminded him of the early days of the colony when the CDF was just getting off the ground. At least then they'd had training libraries to draw upon for the purpose of educating people, but they didn't have a training library of any sort. Both he and Noah were the foremost experts, while the others were less so, with some having to draw upon experience gained a long time ago. It was a wonder no one had been seriously hurt.

Connor left his cabin and headed to the bridge. Cassidy Rhodes was already there with Grace Mendel. They'd had the early morning shift, which surprisingly hadn't bothered Cassidy at all. She said she sometimes preferred those hours rather than staying up late.

"Good morning, ladies," Connor said as he entered.

His greeting was returned in kind.

"Scans are still running," Cassidy said.

"Yes, the watch passed by uneventfully," Grace said.

"That's a good thing," Connor replied.

Grace smiled. "Oh, I know. Tripp made sure to mention it about six times during the hand-off last night."

"How's he coping?" Connor asked.

Tripp had been very upset, and it had gotten the better of him.

"He said he's doing better. That's Reed's doing, I think. But I'm hoping that some sleep will help," Grace replied.

"Me too," Connor replied.

"General Gates, do you have time for a few questions?" Cassidy asked.

"Sure, fire away."

"Why did we enter n-space so far out of the star system? Wouldn't it make more sense and take less time to go to the system's interior planets?"

"Standard exploration protocols that were adopted from the CDF. We don't know whose neighborhood we're entering, so we take a nice long look before proceeding any further."

"That makes sense, but if we need biomaterial for the fabricators to create food for us, don't we have to go to the habitable planet in the system anyway?"

"Not necessarily," Connor replied. "One of the things we learned as part of the exploration initiative was how to scavenge resources from outer planets. There's a good chance there's biomaterial we could extract from some of the ice planets orbiting the Jovian planets."

Cassidy considered this for a few moments. "Do you think there will be a hostile alien species here?"

"I don't know," Connor said and brought up the scan data. "No evidence of a technologically advanced species has been detected. If there is an intelligent species living on the habitable world, they haven't explored their own star system. I'd rather avoid contact if we can."

Grace frowned and looked at the holoscreen. "It would be nice if they helped us. I know our history of first contact doesn't reflect this, but I hope that not all the alien species we encounter are hostile."

Cassidy looked at Grace. "Don't you know who you're sitting with? General Gates was there for all the first contact with the alien species."

Grace's eyes widened, and she looked at Connor.

He wished he could offer them some encouragement, but he knew the truth. They'd only read about it in colonial history.

"It's true that I was there, and so were a lot of other people."

Grace looked away. "I feel so foolish. Uh, wow." She laughed nervously.

"Don't," Connor said. "Why don't we go over some of the ship's systems until the others arrive?"

Grace frowned and looked at Cassidy. "General, we're not qualified on any of the ship's systems."

"I know. That's gotta change."

"Are you sure about this?" Cassidy asked.

Connor chuckled. "You're not the first people I've trained. You could say that a majority of my career has been spent teaching other people."

Cassidy considered for a second. "I never thought of it like that."

"Let's get started. The others will catch up when they arrive."

Connor began going over the ship's systems. Neither woman was a stranger to the concepts, but they hadn't navigated the interface for those systems. He should've started doing this days ago. He hadn't believed they'd need it, but so many things changed by the day.

Others came to the bridge, and once they'd realized what was happening, they'd decided to stay and learn. Of all the time they'd had together on the ship, it was one of the few that Connor felt a bond with the other survivors. Often, he sought to protect others. It was in him, part of who he was, and it was a burden shared with few. But when Noah began instructing the others, that solidified what he needed to do. It established trust, and it informed the others. It was team building at its best, especially because they'd lacked it for so long, and it gave the survivors greater appreciation for what Connor and Noah were trying to do to help them return home. All the meetings in the world couldn't replace practical application that came from actually doing the things people had only read about.

The bridge was almost full, with the exception of a few of them.

"The star in this system," Noah said, "is a common G-class main sequence star, with over 1.3 solar masses. This places it on the edge of an F-class star. It blazes at a higher luminosity and has a surface temperature of about 6200 degrees Kelvin, hotter than the star of New Earth."

The star system was highly populated, with over thirteen planets orbiting it. The outer system hosted six Jovian-type planets, each with dozens of moons, with quite a few being planet-sized themselves. Sensors indicated that as many as ten of the moons were rich in metals. Connor expected that the inner rocky planets were also rich in resources. Two of the inner systems of planets were within the habitable zone, and both of them were near Earth-sized. However, only one of the planets supported life. The other was desolate, without so much as a limited atmosphere.

There were three asteroid belts in the star system. The Jovians had prevented several large planetary masses from forming, but they hadn't been pulled into orbit around them. All three of the asteroid fields were likely the victim of a celestial tug-of-war between the nearest Jovian planet that prevented the rocky planets from forming.

All the planets were in a stable orbit around the star, which indicated a certain level of system maturity.

"Do we know more about that habitable planet itself?" Rhodes asked.

Noah brought up a blurred image of it on the main holoscreen. "It's got liquid water, and there are indicators of a thriving ecosystem. It's about 0.9 the gravity of New Earth, and the surface temperature might be a bit on the warmer side. See these bands of turquoise and indigo? Those are clouds, and there's a lot of cloud cover on the planet."

Noah zoomed the image out. "And there are several rings surrounding the planet, but they're farther away than the rings of New Earth. With that kind of cloud cover, I doubt they could be seen during the day like we can see them back home."

"We haven't noted any indicators of advanced technology," Connor said.

Rhodes frowned as he stared at the holoscreen. "Just so I have this straight in my mind, we're heading to the outer Jovian that has a system of moons that have indicators of high metallicity to them. Is that right?"

"Yes. We need the ores to repair the hull and other systems. There's a long list of them," Noah replied.

"How soon before the modified drones are sent out?" Rhodes asked.

"It'll take about seven hours to reach the planet. We'll do another assessment and then deploy the drones," Connor said. He looked at the others. "Any other questions?"

None came.

"Okay, Rabsaris has updated the list of repairs to prioritize the things he needs help with between now and when we arrive at the planet. Check the roster for your assignments," Connor said.

It was nearly lunchtime by the time they'd finished, and Connor had skipped breakfast. They left the bridge, and Noah walked with Connor.

"That went better than I expected," Noah said.

Not wishing to take the life out of the general mood, Connor didn't reply.

Noah arched an eyebrow at him. "Do I want to know?"

Connor shrugged.

They were alone in the corridor, and Noah gave him an expectant look.

"After all the bad news, we're all looking for something to cling to that we hope will make a difference. Me included."

Noah frowned. "I'll take this over shouting and plotting against each other any day."

"Agreed."

Noah eyed him again. "I feel like you're about to say 'but.'"

Connor smiled. "You know me so well."

"I'd like to think I do, but there have been times when I can't figure out what you're thinking."

"We've had a nice reprieve, but it's only a matter of time before the questions come about how we get back home. Can we reverse what brought us here?"

"Theoretically? Yes."

Connor rolled his eyes. "I really hate that word."

Noah nodded. "I know you do, but it's the best one for this situation."

Connor stared at Noah for a second. "Good sleep really did wonders for you."

Noah scratched his neck, looking a little sheepish.

"Don't worry about it, Noah. It happens to the best of us. Now we just move on."

Noah pressed his lips together for a second. "I know…I

know you're leading because it's who you are. I get it. You're trying to be the glue that holds us together."

Connor snorted. "That's your job. I just lead."

"Well, you are whether you want to admit it or not. I just wanted to let you know that I'll do my part to ease the burden for you." He paused for a moment and looked away. "I just miss them," he said, his voice sounding strained.

Connor felt his throat thicken a little. "Me too."

Rabsaris came out of the airlock and retracted his helmet. His expression was grim, and Connor waited for him to finish stowing his EVA suit.

"That bad?" Connor asked.

Sergeant Seger and Naya exited the airlock.

Rabsaris nodded. "I'm sorry, General. We lost another set of drones. They're not suited for mining materials in this kind of environment. The terrain is too unpredictable, with sudden fissures and gas pockets."

Connor frowned. "I knew there would be some attrition with the drones, but it seems like we've lost a lot of them."

Rabsaris sat down and took the canister of water Connor handed him. He gulped some down and then nodded. "I'm basically putting this together from spare parts using the repair drones meant for the ship. Most of the equipment on the ship had human operators nearby. They're not meant for autonomous mining."

Connor glanced at Seger and Naya. They both looked tired. They'd been on their EVA for nine hours.

"You mentioned the environment," Connor said. "What if we went to another part of the moon?"

"I thought of that. It's a risk, sir, no way around that, but I don't think it's going to help. If the drones don't fail, then it's the cutters themselves. This equipment has been out of service for a while, and the other equipment we have isn't meant for use in space." Rabsaris paused to swallow some more water. "Sorry, I'm really thirsty. I think our best bet is to head to that habitable world. Much of the equipment here was designed for work on a planet with an atmosphere. Even if the planet doesn't have the same atmosphere as New Earth, it's going to be a lot less harsh than space. Plus, I noticed some instability with the main engine pods."

Connor's eyes widened. "How bad is it?"

Rabsaris sighed. "We're not dead. They still have a lot of life in them. We shouldn't have any issues making it to the planet, but we'll need to land the ship in order to really effect repairs."

Connor glanced at Naya and Seger. Neither of them looked surprised. They must've already discussed it.

Connor's first thought went to the possibility of being stranded on the planet. What if they couldn't leave? It would be a death sentence for all of them. While they could survive for a time, they didn't have the equipment to support them in the long term. No amount of ingenuity would change the facts.

"I'm sorry, General. I wish I had better news."

"Is this really our best option? Because going to the planet exposes us to a lot of other risks," Connor said.

Rabsaris nodded. "I can effect better repairs on the planet than I can in space. There's no space dock or repair facility here. All we've got is what we brought with us. Also, there are some sections that we should consider closing off to conserve energy and life support. I need to address the emergency patches that were put in place."

Connor knew some of the upper decks had been in a state of

disrepair when the event occurred. "Alright then. To the planet we'll go. I need you to assess the landing gear before we even make the attempt."

Rabsaris nodded. "Will do, General. The landing gear should be fine since it was in use on New Earth, but I'll do a thorough inspection and report back to you."

CHAPTER 17

Connor and Tyler walked toward the briefing room outside the bridge. Rhodes and Jorath were heading there from an adjacent corridor.

Connor lifted his chin in greeting.

"We got a message from Noah to come to the briefing room," Rhodes said.

"So did I," Connor replied.

Rhodes nodded. "Any idea what this is about? I didn't think we were landing on the planet yet."

Over the past few days, Rhodes's attitude had become much less harsh as he'd come to accept the realities of their situation. Connor doubted that many of his opinions regarding the event had changed. He still blamed both Connor and Noah for the trouble they were in, believing it was a result of some kind of negligence on their part. However, he hadn't voiced those opinions in favor of being helpful. Rhodes had accepted that the most important objective they should focus on was returning home.

Thorough investigations and finger-pointing could be done later.

While Connor thought the chances that the event that caused all this had nothing to do with negligence on the part of the project, he couldn't rule it out either. Some research pushed the boundaries of known science, and there were risks involved in any of those endeavors. Safety was always a top priority, but there was no way to reduce the risk entirely. He wasn't afraid of what an investigation would reveal. It was how they learned and improved. Many of the things he'd accomplished in his career had been put under the microscope for others to pick apart. If those investigations had really bothered him, he would've chosen a different career path.

The door to the briefing room opened, and Cassidy Rhodes leaned out, checking the corridor. She smiled. "Oh good, you're all here. Please come inside."

Her expression faltered a little when she noticed Tyler, but it was gone in an instant as she gestured for them to follow her.

"They're here," Cassidy said to Noah.

Noah stood with his back to them, facing a large holoscreen. There were many smaller sub-windows active, but Noah swiped them all away and turned toward them.

"Good morning," Noah said, and his expression faltered at Connor's expression. "It's afternoon, isn't it?"

Connor smiled. "Only by a few hours."

Noah glanced at Cassidy for a second.

"I did tell you," she replied.

He chuckled. "I know. We were making so much progress," he said and gestured for the others to sit at the long conference table.

Rhodes looked at his daughter. "What's this about, Cass?"

"About a week ago, General Gates asked me to review the data we have surrounding the event—the ship's logs and the upgrades being performed."

Connor regarded her in thought for a moment. She looked excited. "You found something."

She smiled, and it lit up her whole face. She was quite beautiful, and Connor could understand why Tyler was attracted to her.

"We both did," Cassidy replied, gesturing toward Noah.

"She asks very good questions," Noah said and then shrugged. "We're so thoroughly enmeshed with the work we do that we sometimes underestimate the value of a fresh perspective coming from someone who's outside our processes."

Connor noticed Rhodes sit a little straighter with fatherly pride as he gave his daughter an approving nod.

"Alright," Connor said, "I think you both have our attention. What did you find out?"

"I need to go over some familiar territory, so bear with me," Noah said. "This ship was being retrofitted for experimentation with the Infinity Drive. This included reducing the crew required to fly the ship, with the goal of someday making it almost completely automated. Part of that effort included significant upgrades to the computing core. Among the data components were protocols and libraries specific for I-Drive configuration and management. These were experimental protocols that were used during the development of the I-Drive itself, and when used, they linked to the nav computer. My team had reviewed the protocols and brought a proposed list to me. I've reviewed Connor's interaction with the Phantoms many times, going over the entire exchange, breaking it down by each thought that was conveyed. The Phantoms appeared assertive at some points in the conversation and actually confused at others."

Rhodes frowned and looked at Connor. "I thought they viewed themselves as our superiors, both technologically and overall."

Connor nodded. "They do. However, some of their questions had an implied context of 'why are you doing it this way?'" They were perplexed."

"That's right," Noah said. "They asked more than once why we move *in* space instead of *through* it—a question that is confusing on its own."

Rhodes heaved a long sigh. "Respectfully, and maybe with a little frustration on your behalf," he said, looking at Connor and Noah, "the question seems nonsensical. I'm not an engineer or a physicist, but don't we move in space and through it at the same time?"

"It's high concept," Connor replied. "They abducted me from among an entire platoon and brought me somewhere off-planet. I didn't realize it at the time, but they were demonstrating the concept for us."

"We think the Phantoms treat the concepts as two distinct modes of travel," Noah said. "One we're familiar with and the other is foreign when we consider the Phantoms' context."

"But with no actual basis, other than they somehow abducted you from among a CDF platoon," Rhodes said.

"Actually, there *is* a basis for it," Connor said and paused while he considered how to convey his thoughts. "This isn't absolute, so keep that in mind. During our encounter with the Phantoms, we detected a gravitational anomaly the size of a cruiser heading toward the planet, but we lost track of it. We thought they'd used the planet as cover for their escape by using the planet's gravity to slingshot around it. Now, in light of the event, I think they just travelled right through the planet. And they did it without affecting it at all."

Rhodes pressed his lips together in thought. "I was unaware of this. It was probably determined to be irrelevant for materials acquisition and review. I understand that." He blinked as several thoughts battled for prominence in his brain. "So, there is a chance that the event wasn't as disastrous as we feared?"

"I hope so," Noah said earnestly.

"We won't know until we make it home," Connor added.

Rhodes nodded once, looking relieved. "Please continue."

Noah gestured toward Cassidy. "Cass, tell them what you found."

"I created several queries that essentially highlighted the differences of any data post upgrade. As part of the process, there is an automated diagnostic of the affected subsystem that determines whether the upgrade was successful. I noticed that there were large groups of data that were altered during the upgrade. I couldn't tell what the data had to do with and brought it to Noah's attention."

"You don't give yourself enough credit," Noah said. "This isn't an all-or-nothing-type query. She managed to find partial alterations to data that almost seem chaotic on their own because they affected different things, but remember, we're looking at a snapshot of a cascade of events that also affects the systems tracking the actual changes. The affected data appears almost as if the action was reactionary in nature."

Connor's eyes widened at the implication. "Reactionary, meaning they were monitoring this. Are you saying that the Phantoms caused this?"

Noah shook his head. "We don't have a smoking gun, per se."

"What was it about the I-Drive protocols that drew their attention?" Connor asked.

Rhodes glanced at him in surprise.

Noah gave Connor a knowing look. "They were determined to be unsafe because of the loss of the probes used. We thought the probes were malfunctioning, but in light of all this, I think they may have travelled a lot farther than we'd anticipated."

If Noah was correct, there could be a few thousand experimental probes thousands of lightyears from New Earth.

"This is all very interesting," Rhodes said, "but how did a few altered protocols trigger the event that brought us here?"

"It didn't on its own," Noah replied. "Like I said, the timing of the alterations seems reactionary in nature. This is where the water gets murky because I don't have concrete answers. There were errors during the upgrade that triggered the I-Drive."

Connor frowned. "What are you saying?"

"I'm saying that what if the I-Drive was triggered as part of a host of faulty systems-check processes, and then experimental protocols that were disabled were altered just in time to prevent the catastrophe we all feared? Too many of these things happened for it not to have had someone influencing events."

Noah meant the destruction of New Earth because the I-Drive punched a hole through the planet's crust. It would've been an extinction-level event.

"Then the Phantoms were acting in our best interest?" Rhodes asked.

"We don't know," Connor said. Noah began to protest. "No, we don't know for sure. All you've confirmed is that there were outside forces that were part of the event, but we don't know how the event was triggered. We have theories. What if they caused the event and realized the impact, then sought to correct the mistake?"

Rhodes regarded Connor for a long moment. "You're suspicious of them?"

He nodded. "Always. I encountered a single being using

some kind of proxy to communicate with me. What if there are other groups that want us to fail? They could've instigated the event."

"Or," Noah said, "they could be watching out for us because they understood how close we were to succeeding."

Rhodes pressed his lips together for a moment. "How close *were* you to succeeding?"

"Closer than I thought we were. For the past eighteen months, I've revisited the old research data from the development of the Infinity Drive, prioritizing protocols that'd had the greatest chance to succeed but didn't, reexamining them with the intention of expanding our test bed for them," Noah replied.

Rhodes looked at Connor.

"We're expanding our footprint into space," Connor said, "increasing the range of subspace communications beyond what was available when the I-Drive was developed. The intent for this ship was to use it to test the limits of the I-Drive."

Rhodes stared at Connor for a moment and then exchanged a look with Jorath. "So, the intent was to one day have a crew on this ship to test the I-Drive."

"Eventually, and I do stress the use of that word. There were many milestones that had to be reached before that," Connor replied, and then looked at Noah. "So now that you know the I-Drive protocols that were affected, does that mean you have a better chance of figuring out how to get us home?"

Noah smiled. "More than I did yesterday."

"This is wonderful news!" Rhodes exclaimed and beamed at his daughter for a moment.

"We still need to map the stars and much more," Noah said.

Connor pursed his lips inquisitively and then frowned. "You said the alterations appeared chaotic."

Noah nodded, some of the excitement abating. "I have no

way to prove this, but the only way it makes sense to me is if the Phantoms were under a serious time constraint, as if they only had moments to create the changes they thought necessary, and the disarray in all the data that was affected reinforces that in my mind. It lacked the finesse of what they did before."

Rhodes made a huh sound. "What's that supposed to mean?"

"A couple of things. Maybe more. I'm not sure. What if they were far away and lacked the time to take the action they thought they needed?" Noah said.

"It does imply a limit to their capabilities," Connor said. "And they might not have been aware of the R&D facility at Whitehall in the first place."

Rhodes rubbed his chin thoughtfully. "So, they might not have been monitoring us as closely as we thought."

"Or we could've made more progress than they anticipated," Noah said.

They were all quiet for a few moments.

"This is really good work, both of you," Connor said. "You've helped shed some much-needed light on this entire ordeal." Both Noah and Cassidy bobbed their heads in acknowledgement.

"So where does that leave us?" Rhodes asked.

Connor looked away for a moment, thinking, his brain going in circle after circle of possibilities where the Phantoms were concerned. "The problems we're facing haven't changed. We still need to land the ship on the planet, which means we need to take a good long look at it to determine the best place to gather the resources we need."

"About that," Noah said. "I think we should leave the emergency shuttle in high orbit around the planet. I want to use its sensors to continue mapping the stars."

The ship had only one working shuttle.

"It'll limit our mobility on the planet," Connor replied.

Noah nodded. "I know, but there is a rover available, as well as smaller motorcycles. Scrambler models. They're pretty reliable and can handle rough terrain."

Rhodes sighed. "I don't like the idea of landing the ship on the planet," he said and shrugged. "I know we don't have a choice. I keep thinking..." he shook his head, leaving the thought unfinished.

"The risks of landing the ship on the planet far outweigh the risks of not doing it. It's as simple as that," Connor said.

"A chance to set foot on another planet isn't the worst way to spend our time," Tyler said and tipped his head to the side. It was the first time he'd spoken during the meeting, and it took some of the others by surprise. Tyler regarded them and shrugged. "There's something to be said for embracing what's next. Some people run away from problems while others run toward them."

"You'll get your chance, Captain Kincaid."

"I look forward to it, General Gates."

They spent the remainder of the time collecting data on the planet they were going to. It had extensive cloud cover, which increased its luminosity. Connor thought it was one of the brightest planets he'd ever seen.

They were still hours from putting the ship into orbit around the planet.

Rhodes sat next to Connor on the bridge. "I would've thought that this much cloud cover would've prevented life from thriving on a planet."

"It all depends on how much light penetrates the cloud cover and the type of atmosphere surrounding the planet. Even with that much cover, there could be a very lush environment. Water can insulate a planet from harmful radiation, so it is possible," Connor replied.

"Interesting," Rhodes replied. "Have you lost track of how many planets you've been to?"

"It's getting there," Connor replied, tipping his head to the side.

Noah glanced at them. "The amount of insulation that cloud cover gives the planet means that things might be bigger than we're used to. Probably lives longer, as well."

"Why is that?" Rhodes asked.

"Solar radiation triggers aging, among other things. When humans began exploring space, one of the unintended side effects was extended lifetimes. There was better shielding on the ships and stations than on Old Earth. If you've ever looked at the origins of prolonging treatments, there's quite a bit of literature that theorizes about the changing lifetimes of people throughout history."

The others became quiet, pensive, and Connor looked at Noah. "Why don't you go get some food."

Noah frowned. "Don't you want me to stick around for orbital insertion?"

"Send Naya up here. She can watch over my shoulder," Connor said and looked at Tyler. "Captain, track down Rabsaris regarding the status of the forward landing gear."

"Yes, General," Tyler replied and left the bridge.

The others left, and Connor was alone on the bridge. He cleared the main holoscreen and engaged the navigation output. Then, he enabled a sub-window with a video feed of the planet. He plotted the course that would put the ship in high orbit around the planet. They were too far for surface scanners to be effective at this range, which was why he decided to make a few passes around the planet before deciding on a place to land.

He brought up the scans of the region and noted the lack of technological development. The planet had several broken rings surrounding it, and the analysis of them indicated that there were once a few small moons that had been destroyed. The analysis of what could be an ancient debris field indicated that what caused the destruction of the moons was most likely unknown. Collision with the other moons was estimated at thirteen percent, which was virtually zero percent as far as he was concerned. Something had caused that destruction, but the only observable evidence didn't indicate what the cause had been.

There wasn't enough material in the broken rings for them to scavenge the resources they needed to repair the ship. Connor spent the next couple of hours reviewing the plans they'd put together to gather resources. He'd been to planets where both the flora and fauna were behemoth-sized, which would be a challenge. They had limited weapons capabilities. It was best if they avoided highly populated areas. They needed to gather the resources they needed, make the necessary repairs, and get off the planet.

Connor had Naya check the coordinates.

"They're flawless, sir. You didn't really need me to check them."

"Yes, I did. On a ship, work is also double checked. Usually, I'm the one doing the checking, though," Connor replied.

By the evening meal, the ship was inserted into a high orbit over the planet, and the scanner configuration was altered for surface scanning. This would take most of the night, and by morning they'd have a much better idea of where to land the ship.

The process was taking a lot longer because of the age of their equipment. Rabsaris told Connor that the scanner array had been scheduled to be replaced a month after the computing core upgrade. It would've made surface scanning occur much quicker, like it had been on the ships used for the exploration initiative. It was better that they took their time here than land the ship in the wrong place.

The next morning, Connor and Noah entered the bridge.

Noah stared at the video feed of the planet on the main holoscreen. Large bands of clouds in shades of lavender and indigo, along with white, surrounded the planet. He frowned at the sight and brought up a data window.

"Very little storm activity," Noah said.

Connor frowned. "So no rainfall?"

"At least not a lot. There are large mountain ranges, which probably feed the rivers that bring the water to different continents. It's different from other habitable worlds on record."

Connor snorted. "So, we find some out-of-the way, idyllic countryside to set the ship down."

Noah grinned and shook his head. "No."

"I know. I was only joking. Bring up the list that meets the criteria we set for the computer," Connor said.

Noah did, and they scanned the data. "Volcanic activity isn't above normal, which is good. There is stability."

The door to the bridge opened and Cassidy walked in, followed by her father.

"What's stable?" Rhodes asked.

Connor gestured toward a sub-window on the main holoscreen. "We're scouting for landing zones that meet our needs."

"Were there any signs of civilization?" Cassidy asked.

"It's hard to tell," Noah replied. "Scans show a rich topography of flora, which can cover things up."

Rhodes peered at the data and glanced at Connor. "I remember the exploration efforts for New Earth."

Connor nodded. "Remnants of those Ovarrow cities were part of the landscape. While we can't see any cities here, the standard scanning protocols don't show indicators of significant power generation anywhere on the planet."

Rhodes looked at his daughter. "It's unlikely we'll encounter any intelligent alien species. What about the other kind?"

"Just what was observed while the surface scans were taking place—a variety of creatures both land and air based. Different sizes. About what you'd expect on a habitable world," Connor said.

"Except that we wouldn't survive for very long without our EVA suits or emergency breathers at the very least," Noah said, highlighting the chemical composition of the atmosphere for them to see. Then he gestured toward a stretched-out map of the planet. "These waypoints indicate high probability rates of having the resources we need."

Rhodes peered at the holoscreen. "All mountainous regions."

Connor nodded. "We're targeting areas with relatively recent volcanic activity. The reason for that is that those areas usually produce deposits of minerals and ores we can convert into the materials we need for the ship."

Rhodes bobbed his head once. "Impressive. I didn't know the surface scanners could deduce that kind of data."

"It has specific search parameters that the analysis AI uses to estimate the likelihood of finding the things we need. No matter how you look at it, it's an educated guess," Connor replied.

Rhodes regarded him for a moment. "I get the sense that something is bothering you."

Connor sighed. "It's the lack of resources. If we had some exploration drones to send in, we could get a much more accurate view of the planet. They could penetrate the atmosphere and give us more detail on which to base our decision." He paused for a moment and then shook his hand. Speaking about the things they didn't have available wouldn't help them. The others needed hope and the ability to believe in what they were doing.

"It's not ideal," Noah said, "but it's not impossible."

They narrowed down potential landing areas, reviewing the options until a decision had to be made. General deference was given to Connor, and as they narrowed the potential landing zones, they ended up with about six areas. The planet was home to about nine continents. Some were connected while others had oceans between them.

Waiting another day to make a decision wouldn't give them better data than they already had. The state of the ship was such that further delay would cost them. Connor picked what they'd termed a volcanic valley. There was a grouping of valleys among lower-lying mountains. It must've had significant activity recently because the forests were a lot younger and more spread out than some of the other places that were more densely covered.

Noah glanced at him and spoke quietly. "Ever land a Falcon Class frigate on a planet before?"

Connor shook his head. "You?"

Noah blinked. "You're joking, right?"

"I thought it would lighten the mood," Connor said, sending an alert to the teams they had put together throughout the ship.

They'd decided to spread themselves into different parts of the ship to provide as much security as possible. It was a preventative measure in case the landing was suboptimal.

"No, I've never landed a frigate before, but I brought in a team to do it. Experienced pilots and engineers," Connor said.

Noah didn't reply right away and then laughter bubbled out

of his chest. It was contagious because Connor began laughing as well. It was just the two of them on the bridge now.

"If you only knew how many times I've been far out on the deep end, doing things either I've never done before or only heard about being done," Connor said.

Noah smiled with half his mouth. "I know. I was there for a lot of it. Let's hope this goes better than some of those other times."

Connor sent out an alert to the others, and they checked in.

"Looks like they're strapped in and ready to go," Noah said.

Connor engaged the helmet of his EVA suit and Noah did the same.

"Let's begin our descent. Set approach angle negative sixteen degrees," Connor said.

Noah repeated his instructions, and the ship angled toward the planet.

"Slow and easy does it," Connor said.

"Flight assist engaged, diverting power to the engines," Noah said.

The main holoscreen showed the nav system HUD, which duplicated what they were seeing at their workstations.

The *Pathfinder* pierced the planet's atmosphere, and eventually they were surrounded by thick clouds. The nav HUD switched to a different spectrum comprised of various scanning capabilities.

Connor checked their angle of approach, flight speed, and whether they were on track for their destination.

"Don't look so surprised, Connor. I told you I fixed the nav system."

The angle dipped to twenty degrees and then eased back to negative sixteen degrees. Maneuvering thrusters fired, keeping them from gaining too much speed. If the angle of their approach became too steep, the ship would tumble and they'd crash.

"Go to negative fifteen degrees," Connor said.

They penetrated deeper into the atmosphere but were still surrounded by significant cloud cover. Scans didn't show anything in their path. The temperatures, even at this altitude, were well above freezing and were increasing the lower their altitude became.

"Glide mode engaged," Noah said.

"Set angle of descent, negative ten degrees."

While the *Pathfinder* was considered on the small side for a former CDF warship, it still had a significant mass. There would be no masking their entry into the atmosphere.

Connor noticed Noah peering at a video feed on his holoscreen. "Did you see something?"

Noah shook his head. "No, just reminds me of Zeta-Alpha-5 where the second colony was established. It was around this altitude that we encountered flying whales."

Connor frowned in thought. "The ones that slammed into each other to fight off the other predators?"

Noah nodded. "Those are the ones. We were flying a pair of Eagle Combat shuttles right in the middle of them. Was one of the craziest things I've ever seen."

Connor remembered seeing the flight recordings of it and had to agree.

The clouds began to thin, and they were able to catch their first closeup look of the landscape.

"High amounts of oxygen, and CO2 is over four percent. Humidity is steady. Looks clear," Noah said.

The skies were exceptionally clear, giving them a lot of visibility. There were very few flat areas. The continents seemed to be made up of mountains, both extremely high and low-lying, with large valleys between them. Connor spotted rivers coming down the mountain, confirming Noah's earlier theory.

"Check it out," Connor said.

Noah looked and smiled. "This is a gorgeous world, even with a deadly atmosphere."

Connor glanced above them and angled one of the cameras. The cloud cover glowed as if it were a pale, shimmering, vast pool of light in the sky. Large areas appeared to glisten while others were dull.

"I've never seen so much refraction in an atmosphere before," Noah said appreciatively.

They watched the landscape while keeping an eye on the distant waypoint.

"We're coming on up the landing zone," Noah said.

The wide valley was just over five hundred kilometers across, and they flew toward the far end. The vegetation was less dense here, but they'd still need to create a space large enough to accommodate the ship.

"It's going to be a tight fit," Connor said.

"Firing all maneuvering thrusters for the final burn," Noah said.

They targeted the flattest part of the valley, but the topography indicated a slope.

"Deploy the landing gear," Connor said.

They waited as large panels opened, allowing the landing gear to deploy. Their control systems fed right into the flight control so they could adjust to the uneven terrain.

"Bring her down," Connor said.

The *Pathfinder* began its final descent, and all indicators remained in the green.

There was an audible clunk as the landing gear made contact

with the ground. A burst from the maneuvering thrusters eased the final touchdown, and then the engines disengaged.

Connor blew out the breath he'd been holding. "Clear across the board," he said and opened a broadcast channel to the rest of the ship. "We're clear. Begin prep for the excursion teams."

"System checks are all green," Noah said.

Connor closed the broadcast and looked at Noah. "This is when the fun begins."

CHAPTER 18

The ship had just landed, and Tyler disabled the straps that secured him in place. The others in the mess hall did the same.

"What was that loud clanging noise?" Tripp asked.

"It's just the landing gear touching down on the planet," Tyler replied.

Tripp frowned. "It didn't sound good."

Cassidy watched him, waiting for his response. She hadn't been as prickly as she had been before, and he had no idea why.

"Trust me, it's fine. It's just the landing gear absorbing the impact of the landing. If anything had broken, you'd know it," Tyler said. Tripp looked as if he was going to ask another question, but Tyler spoke over him. "Don't worry about it. Naya needs you in engineering, right?"

Tripp nodded and then left the mess hall.

Tyler walked down the corridor, and Seger opened a comlink to him. Seger's dark-skinned face appeared on Tyler's personal holoscreen. "Remember that problem we discussed earlier?"

Tyler nodded. "The lack of armament."

Seger smiled knowingly.

"What did you find? I thought we searched everywhere," Tyler said.

"Not me. Rabsaris found them. Looks like there are some hidden storage compartments near the repair shops in subsection two."

Tyler frowned in thought. They'd searched the entire ship from top to bottom, scavenging for anything useful. They'd only had a couple of sidearms between them, and he wasn't crazy about the idea of exploring an alien world with just those.

"Don't get twisted up in knots, Captain. Looks like someone made a storage compartment during deployment. Rabsaris says he's found them on other ships that were in service during the Krake War."

Tyler nodded. "They were worried about repelling boarders. What did you find?"

"Some AR-74s, grenades, ammunition blocks, and some more lightweight SMGs. Charging stations were intact and had backup power supply. They check out, sir," Seger said.

"That's good news. Did they happen to fit a few combat suits in there?"

Seger shook his head. "That would be too easy. Hidden compartments aren't that big."

"Good news. I'll let General Gates know."

"Aren't you going to help me carry all this stuff?" Seger asked.

Tyler grinned. "No, but I know just the person."

Seger stared at him. "Don't say it."

"Tripp is very sorry and wants to make amends."

"He already apologized, and now he wants to follow me around like a puppy."

"Be nice," Tyler said and closed the comlink.

He sent a message to Tripp and grinned.

"So, you've got some good news?" Cass asked, startling him.

He arched an eyebrow at her.

"I didn't sneak up on you," she said, sounding amused, and the edges of her full lips lifted. "I can't help it if I'm quiet."

Tyler resumed his pace. "Some people would call it stalking."

Cass rolled her eyes. "Oh, please."

They walked in silence for a few moments, and Tyler frowned. "Where are you going?"

"To the vehicle bay."

He blinked a few times. "That's not your assignment."

She looked up at him with those bright blue eyes and smiled sweetly. "I had it changed."

He probably stared for a second too long and then shook his head. "No, you're not coming."

He quickened his pace, and she hastened to keep up with him. He expected her to argue with him, but she didn't say anything.

Tyler stopped. "Cass, I'm serious. Stick to your real assignment—helping out with the repairs."

"I don't need your permission to go."

"Fine," he said and brought up his wrist computer. "Let me just let get Director Rhodes on the comlink here."

Just as he was about to initiate the call, Cass reached over and cancelled it. In fact, she'd backed him out of the comms system. It happened so quickly that he'd been caught completely by surprise.

"Cute," he said.

She grinned.

"You're still not coming."

Her grin faded and her expression became serious. "Why not? This isn't like those earlier EVAs on the ship."

"You don't have the training for this."

She held up one of her fingers. "Being a resident on New Earth should be training enough, or did you forget all the excursions we took well beyond the city? New Earth deep country isn't exactly the safest place to be either."

She had a point, but if he admitted it, she'd never relent.

"It's not the same. We have no idea what's out there."

"That's right. It's about time to admit you're out of your depth, just like the rest of us."

Tyler shook his head and looked at the ceiling.

"It's okay," she said softly, and it rang in his ears like a giant gong.

He exhaled forcefully and then clenched his teeth for a second. "I don't want you to get hurt."

She moved in front of him, staring up at him. "I don't want you to get hurt either, Tyler. That's why I'm going with you."

He started to move past her, but she blocked his path. "What is it? Just say it."

Tyler felt heat rush to his face, and he felt exposed and vulnerable. Somehow, she'd moved past all the walls he'd built.

He swallowed hard and looked at her. "I don't know how this is going to turn out. I really don't. I know I put on a brave face, and most of the time I really believe it, but then other times..." She stared at him. He thought she'd scowl at him or revile him, but she waited patiently, with concern. "This ship is barely holding together. Even if we get everything we need, getting home is still a long shot."

She caressed his face with her soft hands. They were warm and felt good. "I know. General Gates has been completely honest with us. I've spent some time with him. He tries to hide all the worrying, but it's there."

"He's the one man who deserves to be with his family, more

than anyone else on this ship. The same for Noah Barker. Cass, they're both living legends, and they're both scared."

"It's okay to be scared, Tyler."

"Yeah, I know."

"Do you? Doesn't seem like it."

"Fear isn't going to stop me from doing what has to be done."

"What do you think has to be done? I know what they mean to you and what you're trying to do."

"I'm trying to lighten their burden. So yeah, I'll risk my life as often as I can to take that burden away from them."

Cass tilted her head to the side, staring at him. "Now, how can you possibly expect me to stay behind after a speech like that? You think I don't want to do the same thing for my father?"

He grimaced. "Cass—" he began.

"And you need someone to watch your back," she said and smiled playfully. "I have to admit that I like the view."

He blinked and then chuckled. "I've missed you."

She smiled. "I've missed you, too."

Tyler reached out and took her hand in his. "I'm glad you're here." He shook his head and grinned. "I know how that sounded."

She hugged him and they held each other. All the fear seemed to drain away from both of them. He hadn't realized how much he'd missed her. All the years apart seemed to collapse forward.

He looked down at her. "Is it alright if I kiss you now?"

She gave him a small nod.

CHAPTER 19

Connor stepped off the loading ramp onto the damp and alien forest floor, glancing up at the brightly lit clouds above that cast an ethereal glow around the entire area. They bathed the planet in a semitranslucent slate-blue color that became morning fog in the distance. Thick trees at least ten meters across were covered with silver and red dome-shaped tops. Brownish vines of various thicknesses reached to the ground, disappearing among the younger trees and foliage. Around the base of the trees were fern-like plants, a dark green with bright red edges on each of the leaves. The ground was a blend of dark browns that seemed rich in nutrients.

Through the speakers in Connor's helmet, he was able to hear the chittering of alien songs from creatures he couldn't see, and their sounds seemed to be coming from the distance. A large shape flew overhead. It was a light-brown, bat-like creature with a feathery tail. Its wingspan was a good three meters across, and it wasn't alone. Several others flew in formation behind it. A shadowed head seemed to look at Connor for a moment before it wheeled away from him, flapping its large wings to carry it over the trees.

"Already making friends?" Noah asked.

He wore a gray EVA suit and had a sidearm on his waist. He also carried one of the older AR-74s that had been found earlier.

"Still quiet around here. All the sounds seem to be coming from the distance," Connor replied.

He looked over his shoulder and gestured toward Captain Kincaid in the rover.

The Abrams transport rover crawled down the loading ramp. They'd removed most of the seats to make room for the equipment they needed to extract the ores and minerals they were searching for.

Both Kincaid and Sergeant Seger waved as they drove by.

Noah frowned, gesturing toward the rover. "Who was that in there with them?"

"Cassidy," Connor replied. Noah chuckled, and Connor shrugged. "She set her father straight. He didn't like it, but he really didn't have a choice."

Noah pursed his lips for a moment. "Well, they were assigned to protect you, so he should be relieved that she'll be protected by qualified professionals."

Connor sighed. "On an alien world that we don't understand. Just wait until your kids are old enough to ignore *your* advice."

"When you put it like that…"

"We need the help. Hopefully, they'll be able to quickly gather what's needed so we can get out of here before we attract any attention," Connor said.

Noah frowned for a second and then looked out into the large valley. Several scout drones flew overhead, moving ahead of the rover. The vehicle's large wheels articulated high as it climbed over a thick set of roots. "I don't envy the ride they're going to have."

They watched as the rover slowly came down and continued onward. He'd had plenty of experience in off-road excursions across all kinds of terrain. That ride was going to be anything but smooth.

"Me either. Come on, let's get started," Connor said.

The hours went by, and they coordinated with Rabsaris and Naya as they set about addressing the many issues with the ship. Repair drones, each with a specialty, crawled along the hull, buzzing from place to place and stopping to fix things that needed attention.

Sergeant Seger came back with a rover full of supplies they'd gathered. He climbed out of the rover and came over to Connor. "They stayed behind, sir," Seger said. "There are rich mineral deposits here at the base of the mountains."

Several of the others came out of the ship, guiding grav platforms down the loading ramp, and began offloading the rover.

Seger went inside and replaced his EVA suit's power core. Connor grabbed a set of spares for him to bring back to Kincaid and Cassidy.

"How's it look out there?" Connor asked.

"Lively in the distance, sir. Nothing has come in for a closer look, which I think is a good thing. The scout drones spotted some large creatures about three kilometers away. Looked like some kind of predator by the way they moved. Didn't get a good look at what they were stalking, though."

Connor nodded. "I'm glad you found those rifles."

"Do you still want us to restrict our movements to the daytime, sir?"

This planet had a longer day and night cycle, but he needed

everyone to be alert. Being exhausted on an alien world would be an invitation for disaster, which was something he was anxious to avoid.

"For now," Connor said, "we'll have the scout drones patrol the area so we'll have an idea of whether any nighttime predators come poking around."

"Understood, General."

Connor regarded Seger for a moment. "What do you think of the area?"

It was a simple enough question on the surface, but he knew the CDF Sergeant would know better.

"The less time we spend here, the better, sir. There's something about this place that just feels off. I know it's an alien world, but I'd rather not draw too much attention, if you know what I mean."

"I do, and you're right to be cautious."

Seger nodded. "Looks like they're done unloading. I'll get back to it."

"Good luck, Sergeant."

The rover left, and Connor helped the others move the grav pallets up the loading ramp. Then he received a message from Rabsaris, asking that he meet him by the engine pods.

The area around the ship was clear. The plants had been burned away when they landed the ship, and Connor walked past blackened stumps on his way to the others. He spotted Noah and Rabsaris gesturing upward, and Connor joined them.

"What have you got?" Connor asked.

"Good news and bad, sir," Rabsaris said. "We're going to be down one engine pod. I can repair the others if I cannibalize parts from the most damaged one here."

"According to the away team, they've found rich mineral deposits nearby. Won't those materials help with the repairs?"

"They will, but there are limits to what the onboard fabricators can do, even with the high-quality materials available," Rabsaris said and went on to explain that some of the parts they needed could only be produced at a real shipyard fabrication facility.

Connor looked at Noah. "How much is this going to hurt us?"

"It'll reduce our speed while the I-Drive is disengaged. We're losing about thirteen percent of our engine capability. But by doing what Rabsaris is suggesting, we'll increase the performance of the other pods to almost as good as when the ship was in service. My advice is that we do as he suggests," Noah said, tilting his head toward Rabsaris.

Connor looked up at the engine pods. They were octagonal and showed signs of wear. While the ship had been in storage, they hadn't been maintained. The others waited for him to make a decision.

"I guess we're lucky that they're still working at all," he said and sighed. "Go ahead, Rabsaris. Gut it and give the other pods more life to get us home."

"Yes, General Gates."

Noah gave Connor a pensive look, considering. "How long has it been since you've used plasma cutters?"

Connor arched an eyebrow. "I could ask you the same thing."

"So, it's been a while, then?"

Connor shook his head. "No, it hasn't. You've seen my workshop."

Noah chuckled. "You mean your own personal engineering lab you've got at home, along with a few others scattered around New Earth?"

Connor had always tinkered with things—weapons and vehicles, portable power systems, and pretty much anything that caught his interest. He'd always enjoyed working with his hands. It kept his mind active and scratched a mental itch of his to put the world in order.

He chuckled. "You make it sound so secretive."

"Because I know for a fact that several significant upgrades to portable weapon's system began in a workshop near your house in Sanctuary."

Connor smiled. "Well, not all of us have research labs supported by the colonial government."

Noah shook his head. "Didn't you—"

"Let's just put a stop to this right here. What do you need me to do?"

Noah's mouth hung open in mid-sentence, and then he gestured toward the tools nearby. "Want to help me disassemble a partially destroyed engine pod?"

Connor frowned and glanced up at the repair drones working high above them. They didn't have enough drones for all the work that had to be done. Part of him wanted to scout the area. Seger had confirmed what he'd already been thinking. He attributed it to the alienness of the world they were on, but his instincts were nudging him to have a look around and assess the area for threats. But they had scout drones patrolling the area, and he'd have to rely on them.

"Alright. Let's get to work," Connor said.

Over the next several hours, they systematically removed the parts of the engine pod that they were trying to keep intact. The repair drones and Rabsaris saw to refitting them to the other pods. Aside from the EVA suit and the fact that they were on an alien planet, Connor enjoyed the hard work. It left him feeling satisfied and almost refreshed. Sometimes, he felt as if he was getting too comfortable with his surroundings. If he could actually breathe this planet's atmosphere, it wouldn't be a bad place to visit and explore. There was a part of him that really enjoyed exploring planets. This had begun for him on New Earth, and it hadn't left him. Lenora liked to tease him about being bitten by the bug, and she'd comment that it would one day outweigh the things that kept him in the CDF.

Evening was a long time coming, and since the planet rotated much slower than New Earth did, nighttime would last significantly longer than they were used to. It had been a long day, and the small crew was exhausted. Only the repair drones would keep working outside the ship.

Throughout the day, Connor had felt as if they were being observed. Sergeant Seger had mentioned it, along with Captain Kincaid. They kept attributing it to the fact that they were on an alien world. All kinds of creatures were probably watching them, but this was something different. He couldn't find any evidence of it beyond the animals they'd seen, but the feeling was still there. His instincts had never failed him in his life. He'd learned to trust them, but the question remained as to what he should do about it. Kincaid and Seger had also conveyed that they felt there was something hidden, not wanting to reveal itself. By the end of the day, they were happy to be spending the night back aboard the ship.

They kept to the ship's schedule and worked inside the ship. There was plenty to do now that they had gotten the fabricators working. As time passed, Connor had to accept that waiting for daylight to continue their work outside would ultimately increase their stay on this planet.

The dead of night passed, which led to a lengthy brightening sky, and even though, officially, morning was hours away, it was bright enough for them to leave. The highly reflective composition of the clouds lit the area, and the helmets of their EVA suits enabled them to see clearly.

Their single rover left the ship with the same away team as yesterday. Rhodes watched them go as he stood next to Connor.

"Cass is my youngest," Rhodes said and snorted a little. "They say the eldest child is how parents learn to be parents. I don't know about you, but I've found all of them unique in both the blessings and challenges they've given us."

Connor let out a quick chuckle. "I only have two, and both of them have been a handful at times."

Rhodes glanced up at him. "Plan on having more?"

Connor nodded. "Yes," he said. It was more imminent than he'd mentioned to anyone else, and it had been in the back of his mind.

Rhodes narrowed his gaze thoughtfully. "Oh," he said knowingly.

"Yeah," Connor replied dryly. Then he sighed with a slight shake of his head. "Kincaid and Seger will keep Cassidy safe."

Rhodes's expression sobered. "I know they'll try and do everything they can. I just hope they won't have to. You know?"

Rhodes had good days and bad days, like most people, Connor included. People tended to develop a pattern that formed the foundation of their lives. That pattern had been destroyed, and only fragments remained. Life beyond the familiar could shake a person to their very core. Connor tried to help them through it. He was firm when he needed to be firm and as honest as he could be. He'd lie to them if he had to, but there were lines he wouldn't cross.

"Let's get to work so we can get out of here," Connor said.

Over the next four hours, Connor helped Rabsaris remove the rest of the sacrificial engine pod. They'd taken as much material from it as they could, and Connor couldn't help but think of the ship as having a large black eye. Most ships acquired battle scars over time. Some, like the *Pathfinder's,* had to be self-inflicted to serve a greater purpose.

A request came from Mac about collecting more plants for the food processing units. Scout drones had found the specific plants they needed near the ship. Connor, Noah, and a few others went to collect the materials. The work wasn't hard, and it was good for them to stretch their legs.

Connor watched Noah stare at a large mushroom cluster near the base of a tree.

Noah looked at him and gestured toward it. "At least these are singular organisms."

Connor nodded.

"What does he mean by that?" Tripp asked. He'd just placed a large pile of reddish ferns on the grav pallet.

"Noah encountered a mushroom type of life form that was highly intelligent. It was part of a complex network that covered an entire continent. It maintained the ecosystem and had a peculiar form of mimicking types of communication," Connor replied.

Tripp's eyes widened and he looked at Noah. "That sounds amazing."

Noah turned around, frowning. "What?"

"I said that sounds amazing. The other mushroom intelligence that you found."

"It was an experience," Noah replied.

Connor resumed working, and Tripp walked over to Noah, asking him questions.

They gathered as much as the grav pallet could hold and then headed back to the ship. Some kind of movement snatched Connor's attention, and he turned toward it.

Several small creatures with large, dark eyes scurried around the base of a tree. They were humanoid, with dark gray and green skin. They moved like monkeys, but they were hairless. Their heads poked through the brush as they moved. They climbed a nearby tree, moving around it until he couldn't see them anymore. Something they'd carried reflected the light.

"What is it?" Noah asked, looking at him while he kept a hand on the grav pallet guide.

"I thought I saw some kind of light. Something those creatures carried," Connor replied, gesturing in the direction they'd gone. One of them climbed into view high above. "There, see them?"

Noah peered in that direction and shook his head. "Can't see anything. How far away were they?"

"About hundred and thirty meters," Connor replied.

His gaze sank toward the ground and there was a small light that seemed to be drawing in on itself. It winked out of existence before he could point it out to Noah. He searched the area nearby, using his enhanced vision, but couldn't find anything.

"Might've been a trick of the light. Sometimes the clouds thin, allowing a shaft of sunlight. There, see over there? There's one."

Several shafts of sunlight pierced the ground cover. They moved as if scanning the surface and quickly disappeared.

"Let's keep going," Connor said.

They resumed guiding the grav pallet back to the ship. Connor opened a comlink to the nearest recon drone, intending to have it investigate the area where the creatures had been, but it was too far away. The creatures would likely be long gone from the area if they weren't already.

Something about them tugged at his brain. He didn't want to make any assumptions and wouldn't allow a guess to form in his thoughts.

They reached the ship, and Tripp took the grav pallet inside.

Connor stood at the bottom of the loading ramp, scanning the area.

Noah stood quietly at his side, and after a few moments, he asked. "What is it?"

He shook his head. "Not sure. I thought I saw something."

Noah peered into the valley and frowned. "Shouldn't the others have been back by now?"

Connor looked at the time on his HUD, then nodded. He opened a comlink to the rover, but there was no response.

"They're not at the rover," Connor said, and then tried to raise Kincaid. The comlink connected and Connor heard sounds of breathing on the other end.

"Captain, what's your status?" Connor asked.

"There are more coming from over there," Kincaid said. "No, don't shoot… Because they're not hostile."

Connor heard a garbling sound from the comlink that wasn't interference.

"We're not alone, General. Repeat. We're not alone here," Kincaid said.

"They can detect the commlink, and it's agitating them," Seger said.

Connor's eyebrows pushed forward as he focused on his hearing, trying to glean as much as possible. He tried to add Kincaid's camera feed to the comlink, but it wouldn't work.

"General—" Kincaid began and was cut off.

Noah stared at him, waiting.

"The others are in trouble. They've encountered something," Connor said, marching up the loading ramp.

"What did they encounter?"

"I don't know. It sounded like there were a lot of them. They detected the comlink," Connor replied.

"How?"

"I don't know. Kincaid was trying not to antagonize whoever they are."

Noah nodded. "There are some charged power packs ahead."

They needed to replace the power core of their EVA suits. He would've liked to have a combat suit, but they didn't have any. At least they had a rifle.

"What should we tell the others?" Noah asked.

Connor considered it for a few seconds. He couldn't just leave without anyone noticing. "We have to tell the others."

Noah arched an eyebrow. "Before or after we leave?"

Connor gave him a pointed look. "When did you become such a rebel?"

"I know how you like to operate."

"If we just left, it would create more problems than it prevents. I'll tell the others," Connor said.

He opened a broadcast comlink to the others on the ship and told them what had happened. "Noah and I are going out to investigate. Rabsaris and Naya, continue organizing and making the repairs. Everyone else, help them. I'll be in contact. You can track our progress via our comlinks."

"General Gates," Rhodes said, sounding winded, "I must insist that you take Jorath with you."

Connor exchanged a look with Noah. "We'll move faster on our own."

"He can help you," Rhodes demanded. "He's going to follow you whether you allow it or not."

The airlock to the vehicle bay opened and Jorath walked out. He wore a dark EVA suit and carried one of the AR-74 assault rifles.

"General Gates," Jorath said, "I will come with you. I'm

afraid I haven't been completely honest about my presence on the ship."

"What are you saying?" Noah asked.

Connor narrowed his gaze a little. "You're Director Rhodes's bodyguard."

"Assigned protection. I also have a role in the Colonial Requisitions Department. Evaluations specializing in construction services inspections."

"Mekar?" Connor asked. The Mekar were a faction of Ovarrow who joined the colony and had helped them fight in the Krake Wars. Most Ovarrow at that time had basic military training.

"Ovarrow security services that served with the liaisons before we became colonial citizens," Jorath said.

"Why didn't you mention any of this before?" Noah asked.

"It wasn't relevant to the current situation," Jorath said.

Connor's gaze flicked to the rifle. "It's not designed for Ovarrow."

Ovarrow had oversized hands that made handling colonial weapons a challenge.

"My training includes field certification for this rifle, even the older series. I assure you that I can operate this weapon with proficiency," Jorath replied.

Connor considered it for a few seconds. They needed to leave, so he had to make a decision. "I'll allow you to come, as long as you follow my orders. Is that understood?"

"I will assist you, General Gates."

Connor shook his head. "Not good enough."

Jorath regarded. "I assure you—"

"Jorath, we're going to what could potentially be contact with a hostile alien force. There can only be one person in charge. I can't afford to have you acting on your own."

Jorath sighed. "I will follow your orders, General Gates. I will not do anything that puts the lives of the others in danger."

Noah eyed Connor. Three of them armed were better than just the two of them.

Connor gave Noah a nod. "Alright, let's go."

CHAPTER 20

THEY LEFT THE SHIP, and Connor set a quick pace. The EVA suits assisted the wearer with repeated movements, which enabled them to move quicker and for longer stretches of time. It wasn't the same as a combat suit, but it was better than no assistance at all.

Connor led, while Noah and Jorath followed. All reservations about Jorath's abilities to keep up with them were soon gone. He moved like an Ovarrow soldier, keeping a steady pace while checking their surroundings. Connor had trained more than enough soldiers to recognize when someone had the proper training.

"I tasked scout drones nine and seven with flying ahead toward the others," Noah said.

They weren't stealth recon drones, so there was a good chance they'd be detected. At least they'd know the lay of the land.

They had little in the way of equipment—just a field kit with basic survival equipment and their rifles. As they travelled,

Connor tried to listen for weapons fire but hadn't heard anything. He couldn't be sure if that was a good sign or not.

They headed for the nearest mountain, and a waypoint on their HUD marked the location of the rover. The alien forest was both alive and distant, as if the creatures that lived here were keeping away from them. Connor had experienced similar behavior only when in the presence of a dangerous predator.

As they traversed the area, he couldn't detect any sign of a threat. He checked the drone video feeds, knowing the analysis AI would highlight potential threats. The data was sent to their individual EVA suits, which were highlighted on their HUDs. They avoided both slippery and rocky terrain, and a path was marked for them to follow. The marked path was a suggestion, and sometimes Connor chose an alternative path. The EVA's suit computers adapted accordingly.

The Abrams rover was parked near the base of the mountain. It wasn't damaged. Connor peeked inside and saw that the vehicle still had plenty of power. His HUD updated with the last location of the away team's comlink signals. They'd gone offline almost an hour ago.

"Something has to be interfering with the comlink signals," Noah said.

Connor nodded and sent a quick update back to the ship. "I've let the others know that we've reached the rover."

The scout drones alerted them and a video feed came to prominence on their HUDs. The away team was below the drone, surrounded by alien creatures. Kincaid had his hands in front of his chest in a placating gesture. Then he looked up at the drone, and the video feed severed. A message on Connor's HUD indicated that the signal had been lost.

"Did you get a good look at them?" Noah asked.

"Not really. They were surrounded," Connor said. There was no recording of the video feed, so he couldn't bring it back up.

"General Gates, we must reach them quickly," Jorath said.

They left the rover, heading to the others. They were only half a kilometer away. They passed by the worksite where they'd been extracting the minerals and ores. They'd left the site for some reason, and Connor thought they might've been lured away.

Connor slowed his pace as they approached an outcropping of large boulders. He glanced up, searching for alien watchers above. It was what he would've done.

"I detect no scouts, General," Jorath said.

Connor nodded. "Okay, we go slow. I don't want to run in there blindly," he said and advised them to be quiet.

They moved quietly, avoiding anything that would give away their approach.

As they came closer, Connor heard Kincaid speaking.

"I can't understand you," Kincaid said.

There was a garbling sound like an agitated chittering. It reminded Connor of a recording of people speaking played back at high speeds.

Connor came to the large base of a tree, which had more than enough room for Noah and Jorath to join him.

Connor leaned around to look at the open area. Kincaid and Cassidy stood on top of a small boulder. He tried to spot Seger but couldn't find him.

"They're just drones," Kincaid was saying, gesturing to an area in front of him. Among the brush were the broken remains of the scout drones. "They help us to see," he said, gesturing at his eyes and then above them.

Connor leaned farther away from the tree to get a better look at who Kincaid was trying to communicate with.

There were over twenty of them. They were short, perhaps five-and-a-half feet tall, and thin, with furry brown hair. Large, tan-colored ears extended from their heads and ended in triangular points. They had hooked snouts, and their mouths moved rapidly as they spoke. Their movements were fast and energetic. They wore some kind of uniform that had metallic accents and belts. Some of them had sleeves of bright chrome. A ring of chrome glowed around the base of the boulder that Kincaid and Cassidy stood on.

Connor crossed a gap between the trees and motioned for the others to look.

The aliens didn't appear to carry any weapons, but there were thick bands on their wrists.

Connor brought up his wrist computer and engaged the translator interface. It began recording the alien language. Hopefully, it could decipher it.

Jorath stared at him. "They're unarmed."

Noah shook his head. "We don't know that."

"A show of force is required," Jorath said.

Connor shook his head while watching the analysis AI make extremely slow progress detecting the alien language.

"Just wait!" Kincaid said urgently.

Connor saw that the chrome ring hovered above the ground about halfway up the boulder.

"They're in danger," Jorath hissed.

"Get his thing off of me!" Seger shouted.

Connor peered in Seger's direction. He was a short distance behind the boulder. A thin, glowing metallic shaft extended from the ground and split, and the ends wrapped around Seger's hands and ankles. He struggled to move but couldn't.

Jorath lifted his rifle, and Connor shoved it down.

"No," Connor said.

Jorath relented and waited.

Connor tried to think of a way to get the upper hand. Firing their weapons on them at this point would've been foolish. Seger wasn't hurt, just immobilized. He heard Noah say as much to Jorath.

"I'm going to try to talk to them," Connor said.

"How?" Noah asked.

Connor raised his wrist and showed the others his personal holoscreen. The translator interface and gone through many iterations over the years, but one of the most significant increases in sophistication came from their enemies known as the Krake. They'd had to create their own translator interface as they waged their inter-dimensional war. The Krake had been driven to communicate with their victims so they would know that the Krake were superior to them. Colonial scientists had reversed engineered the technology and further adapted it based on human linguistics. The translator had been augmented as they encountered other species.

Noah nodded. "What if they don't listen?"

"Then we use force," Connor said and looked at Jorath.

"Understood, General," Jorath replied.

Connor stepped away from the trees and walked toward the group of aliens surrounding Kincaid, Cassidy, and Seger. They noticed him almost as soon as he stepped out, and the entire group turned toward them at the same time. Their movements were precise, and Connor's pulse raced. Some of them lifted their hands toward Connor, and the metallic bands around their wrists glowed.

Gripping his rifle in one hand, Connor lifted his other hand. "Hello, I don't mean you any harm. They are with me," he said, gesturing toward Kincaid and the others and then back at himself.

Several of the aliens began speaking, and Connor glanced at his holoscreen. Several new data feeds were added to the language analysis AI as it attempted to decipher their language.

Jorath moved to his side and lifted his rifle.

"Only at the armed ones," Connor said.

One of the aliens, who was closest to Kincaid, walked toward them. Jorath pointed his weapon at the aliens who had their wrist weapons pointed at them.

The alien walking toward them moved slower, as if he didn't want to startle them. He wore a long green shirt that had some kind of silvery humanoid emblem on its chest. It was mainly a head, and the body was stretched around it in concentric circles. Connor stared at it for a moment and then noticed that there were other depictions of the same emblem on the others.

Connor lowered his rifle, allowing it to hang from the straps, leaving his hands free. He lifted his wrist, showing the approaching alien on the holoscreen.

"This is trying to decipher your language," Connor said.

The alien peered at it with dark eyes. They were full of intelligence, and Connor hoped he understood that Connor didn't want this to escalate.

Connor glanced at Jorath. "Lower your weapon a little," he said evenly.

Jorath blinked in surprise and then slowly lowered his weapon.

Noah stood by Connor's other side, keeping careful watch on the aliens.

The translator chimed softly, and Connor looked. There were several sample scripts for him to play, so he selected the first one.

A quick chittering sound came from his wrist computer and the alien closest to him stared at it. The other aliens tilted their heads, as if they were hearing something for the first time.

The alien in the green shirt gestured toward the others, and they lowered their weapons. Most of them looked reluctant to do it. There was a soft glow of light on the alien's shoulder, and a spiral of shimmering metal detached from it, hovering just above. It was a three-dimensional, octagonal shape that had a faintly glowing pale light in the center. The alien stared at Connor as if waiting for him to speak.

"I'm Connor Gates. We mean you no harm."

The light pulsed, as if detecting his words. There were garbled sounds as the octagon spun faster. Then it slowed, and his words were played back to him.

The alien peered at him for a long moment. He spoke with a quick chittering sound, and a translation came from the octagon. "Phendran, Loremaster." The voice sounded like an altered tone of what Connor had used. It was lighter and even.

Connor gestured toward him. "Phendran," he said and then pointed at his chest. "Connor."

Phendran repeated the gesture and then repeated the words.

Connor motioned toward Kincaid and the others. "They are our companions," he said, then gestured toward himself and the others.

Phendran glanced behind him and then back at Connor. His attention shifted toward his wrist computer, as if considering it. He then touched the octagon, and a small beam of silvery light came toward Connor. It was so quick that Connor had no chance to react. Several tiny beams split from the end and attached to the holo-interface.

"Connor?" Noah asked.

"It's a data connection," Connor said. "Two-way connectivity detected."

Phendran calmly waited. A band of semitranslucent green

appeared in front of his face, originating from a spot on his forehead.

"They're scanning the computer."

Jorath leaned toward Connor. "This is intrusive."

"We did the same thing on ancient Ovarrow computers that survived your war with the Krake. It was how we made the first translators to communicate with your species."

Jorath huffed out a breath and became still.

The alien's holoscreens were smaller, and all were a shade of green. They appeared at the same time, and the aliens stared at them intently.

Connor looked at the data window on his holoscreen, and a list of protocols scrolled down the screen. "They're uploading data."

"Yes," Phendran said. "Quicker communication capabilities this way."

Connor blinked in surprise and looked at him.

"That is the goal," Phendran said. "The process will complete momentarily."

Noah made an impressed "huh" sound. "That will help."

Connor glanced at his friend. "Different from the other times we've established first contact with an alien species."

Noah nodded, but the aliens began speaking to each other, drawing their attention.

Jorath frowned and looked at Connor. "They're speaking in native Ovarrow."

Connor glanced at his wrist computer for a second. "They must've detected your language in the translator interface."

"That's impressive," Noah said, and Connor agreed.

The beam of light went out, and the data connection on Connor's wrist computer showed that it had severed. There were several new data libraries, along with new options available on the translator program.

Connor looked at Phendran. "Can you understand me?"

"Yes, communication options are now available," Phendran said.

Another alien stepped toward them. He had shimmering metallic sleeves and the bearing of a soldier. "Intruders, why do you plunder from here?"

"We do not know if they are intruders, Dedicated Scastars," Phendran said.

"What else could they be, Loremaster Phendran?" Scastars asked.

"They can speak for themselves," Phendran said and looked at Connor.

The exchange was quick and was through before the translation came over the speakers in his helmet.

Connor had to be careful. How he handled this exchange would determine whether the situation escalated to violence. He glanced at the alien named Scastars for a second and then looked at Phendran. "What is a Dedicated?"

"He delays his response. He has something to hide. Look at them all. Guarded expressions. Weapons. They should be brought to the Aczar Major," Scastars said.

"They are cautious," Phendran replied and looked at Connor. "And understandably so." He glanced at his holoscreen for a moment. "A Dedicated is a title afforded to protectors and enforcers of the covenant. It's how we of the Aczar remain in harmony, each with a contributing role to ensure our survival."

Connor glanced at Scastars. A Dedicated was some kind of soldier. He looked eager to act, as if he could barely contain the energy inside him. "We didn't know this was your territory. We were in need of supplies and chose this place to gather them."

Scastars swung his gaze at Phendran. "He admits his crime. They are intruders. They came here to steal from us. They'll expose us. They are the source of the disruptions of the sky."

"This is a misunderstanding," Connor said.

Scastars ignored him. "What say you, Loremaster. If you won't give me clearance to act, I will have no choice but to alert Aczar Major about these events. The council will convene."

Phendran regarded his companion for a moment. "I will not prevent you from doing your duty, Dedicated. However, I will communicate with them because that is how we acquire knowledge."

Without a reply, Scastars and the other Dedicated left them. More than half the aliens went with him.

Phendran calmly looked at Connor. "How have you come to be here?"

"Our ship was damaged, and we needed to gather supplies to fix it. Our analysis of the area showed that this area had most of what we needed," Connor replied. He looked up at Kincaid and Cassidy. They were still standing on the boulder, and Seger was restrained by the shimmering metallic frame. "Will you please free my companions?"

Phendran turned toward them and gave them an appraising look. "Kholva, release them."

One of the aliens walked to the boulder and touched the metallic ring. It retracted, becoming palm-sized, and Kholva placed it on his belt. It then disappeared, as if it had merged with the material on his belt. Then, he walked over to Seger and removed the restraining apparatus.

Connor tilted his head to the side.

Kincaid needed no further prompting and slid off the boulder. He turned and caught Cassidy as she did the same. Seger bent over and retrieved his rifle from the ground. The aliens followed his movements closely.

The three of them walked over to Connor. None of them looked any worse for wear, but they were still alarmed.

Connor looked at Phendran. "Thank you."

"What is your species called?" Phendran asked.

"We're Human, and this is an Ovarrow," Connor replied, gesturing to Jorath.

Phendran regarded Jorath for a long moment. "Much like a Dedicated."

"General," Kincaid said, "they surrounded us. Caught us completely by surprise. I think they have some kind of cloaking technology because we didn't detect them at all."

"Understood," Connor replied. He looked at Seger. "Are you alright?"

"Yes, General. They trapped me before I could get my weapon ready. It was the fastest thing I've ever seen."

Phendran looked at Connor. "You're their leader?"

"I am."

"This reference—general—is a show of respect. I understand this. My title is that of Loremaster, keeper of knowledge and mediator among the Aczar, ensuring harmony among my species."

"A pleasure to meet you," Connor said. "We didn't know there was an intelligent species living on this planet."

He wondered how large their population was and how they'd hidden themselves from the ship's scanners.

"Would you have come here if you had?" Phendran asked.

"Yes, but we would've tried to communicate with you first," Connor said.

"We detected your ship and its landing in this region."

Connor noted the distinction and believed that Phendran

meant them to be two separate instances. He hadn't disclosed when they detected the ship.

Jorath leaned toward Connor. "Our presence here has upset them. Perhaps we should leave before things become worse."

"You worry that you will be trapped here. It is not my intention to see that you are trapped," Phendran said.

He had a precise way of speaking that reminded Connor of someone who was extremely shrewd and not to be underestimated.

"My companion is worried that others of your kind will seek to keep us here against our will. Given the way our companions were treated, I share his concern," Connor said.

"I understand. With regard to your companions, they were about to attack us, so Scastars and his Dedicated prevented this from happening. It was only after this occurred that communication was attempted," Phendran said.

"You startled them. They were unaware of your presence. I would've reacted the same way," Connor replied.

"Ah, but you haven't. You assessed the situation from behind those trees. Then you decided to attempt communication before use of force," Phendran said.

How did he know we'd been hiding? Connor glanced at the others. Shock registered with both Noah and Jorath. Sometimes the direct path was the only one worth taking.

"You knew we were watching you?" Connor asked.

"Yes."

"All of you?"

Phendran stared at him for a quick moment, and he looked pleased. "No, General Gates."

He considered asking who else knew but decided to move on.

"If you were aware of us the moment we landed on your

planet, why did you wait so long before contacting us?" Connor asked.

"Caution was advised. We decided to observe and then investigate."

Connor couldn't fault that logic. "Do you have ships of your own?"

"We do not explore the stars," Phendran replied.

"Could you explore the stars if you wanted to?"

"We are not ready."

Connor considered Phendran's answer. Given the level of technology they had, he wondered why they hadn't explored their own star system.

"Neither were we when we began exploring the stars," Connor said.

Phendran frowned and glanced at his companions. Some kind of unspoken communication seemed to occur among them. Then Phendran looked at Connor.

Connor glanced at the emblem. "Who is that?"

Phendran looked down at this chest for a second. "That is our Great Mentor, who has guided us and protected us. He has kept us on the righteous path."

"That's interesting," Noah said quietly. Phendran looked at him. "What is the righteous path?"

"We seek to be like our Mentor. Avoid exploring the stars, because of the darkness that lies in wait there. It's what led us to this planet."

Connor's eyes widened and he looked at Noah.

"You've explored," Phendran continued, "therefore you must've encountered the evil darkness that resides out there."

Noah mouthed the word, "Phantoms?"

Connor lowered his chin a little. Could this species have

been in contact with a Phantom? Or maybe they had encountered some other hostile alien species.

"This isn't your home world?" Connor asked.

"Long ago we were guided to this world where we would be safe, as long as we didn't draw attention to ourselves," Phendran said.

Connor glanced at the other aliens, the Aczars. There seemed to be disapproval in their gazes as they regarded him and the others.

Kincaid cleared his throat, and Connor looked at him. "General Gates, I don't understand. Are they saying they've encountered the Phantoms?"

"That's exactly what they're saying."

CHAPTER 21

Phendran gave Connor an appraising look. "I'm not familiar with the concept of a phantom."

Connor looked away while he considered his answer. His mind raced with possibilities. The Phantoms had had a hand in the event, but could they have guided them here to this star system? Normally he wouldn't attribute capabilities to an adversary that hadn't been proven to exist, but the evidence was stacking up.

Connor covered his mouth for a moment and rubbed the stubble on his chin. He looked at Noah. "It can't be an accident that we're here."

Noah sighed, looking relieved. "I'm glad you said that because I've been thinking the same thing for the past ten minutes."

Phendran made an impatient noise. "This conversation is perplexing."

Connor pressed his lips together. The Aczars were easily

agitated and highly intelligent. Once again, being direct with them seemed like his best choice.

"We encountered a species that advised us the same thing as your mentor," Connor said.

Phendran blinked and several of the others looked as if they were about to become agitated. "Do you have evidence of this encounter?"

Connor shook his head. "Not with me, but I can describe it for you, and then you can judge for yourself."

"That would be helpful, General Gates," Phendran replied.

Connor recounted his experience with the Phantoms, how they'd first assisted New Earth's interstellar probes to reach Old Earth's star system, and then the events when they'd taken a more direct approach with the encounter he had with them over eighteen months ago.

Phendran hardly moved as Connor spoke. Rather, he listened intently, as if he was committing it all to memory.

"Does the description of our encounter align with your own experience?" Connor asked.

The Aczar name Kholva stepped toward Phendran. "The ship. We should focus on their ship. Right now, it is a lure."

Phendran considered this for a few moments and then looked at Connor. "Space travel has been banned. The presence of your ship is an abomination to the Aczar."

"Then we'll leave," Connor replied.

"That might be for the best."

"You didn't answer my question. Does our experience with the Phantoms align with your own?"

Phendran bridged his fingers in front of his chest. "How did your species react to your encounter?"

"It's still being discussed."

"Yet you still explore the stars."

"Yes, we do."

"But the warning. The Phantoms are your superiors. Why wouldn't you heed their advice?"

Connor glanced at the other Aczar and then at Phendran. "Just because a species has superior technology doesn't mean they are wise or even all-knowing. We'll decide for ourselves what is in our own best interest."

"But the warnings are true. You should've yielded to them."

"We'll have to agree to disagree on that."

"A peculiar concept—one that doesn't reach consensus."

Connor tilted his head to the side. "Does your species agree on everything?"

"No, but to maintain harmony, we follow the consensus of the majority. When this fails us, we seek out the mentor for guidance," Phendran said.

Connor's mouth hung open in shock. Phendran had said they could communicate with the Phantoms.

"How do you seek out guidance from the mentor?" Noah asked.

Phendran stared at him intently. "By initiating communication with him."

Him, not them, Connor thought and stared at Phendran. "Is there a mentor here on this planet?"

Phendran looked as if the question perplexed him. "Yes, he's been here since the beginning."

"Would it be possible for me to speak with him?" Connor asked.

"Access to Salpheth is restricted," Phendran replied.

"Salpheth? Is that his name?"

"That is what he called himself. In your encounter, didn't they tell you their personal designation?"

Connor shook his head. "It was a construct. Artificial."

"Yes, because they exist outside of this reality. We seek to ascend as they have."

"Which you plan to do by remaining ignorant of the universe, hoping they'll come back to you one day? Is that your plan?"

Phendran looked away, uncertain. It was the first time he'd looked unsure of himself throughout this entire conversation.

"Salpheth guides us. Salpheth protects us."

The other Aczar repeated Phendran's words. It sounded practiced and absolute, as if it formed the bedrock of their entire society.

"This troubles you," Phendran said.

"Yes, it does," Connor replied. "My experience with anyone in power is that if they are left unchecked, they become corrupt. Blind loyalty leads to ignorance and hardship."

"We are neither blind nor ignorant."

Connor didn't see the point in belaboring the point. No one who was blindly ignorant would admit it because their entire world would collapse around them.

Phendran peered up at him with an expression of great scrutiny. "You don't see us that way. I can see it. You believe we are willfully ignorant."

"I didn't say that. You said that."

"But those are your thoughts."

"I'm concerned..." Connor began and paused for a moment. "I'm concerned that you've been misled, and it's hobbled the development of your species. The Phantoms over-generalize probable outcomes and have adopted a broad approach to influencing intelligent species. It lacks the individualistic nature unique to us all, which is to say, to put it bluntly, that their arrogance blinds them to what is possible."

Noah looked at him in shock.

The phrase "in for a penny, in for a pound," came to Connor's mind. "Furthermore," he continued, "I don't think we arrived here by accident. I think we were sent here by the Phantoms."

"For what purpose?"

"To meet you. We explore with the hope of building alliances so we can learn from one another, increase our understanding of the universe. If we do encounter 'great evil,' we can make our stand together."

Several of the Aczars appeared confused, as if the concept of alliances were a foreign concept to them.

"Then you have done the exact opposite of what was advised. This will lead to your destruction. Why would the Aczar be a part of that?"

"Our experience teaches us that there are no guarantees at all. Our homeworld was attacked, and it had nothing to do with our efforts to explore. Our enemy sought my species over sixty lightyears to our first interstellar colony world. So, our experience is much different from yours. Evil sought us out, and we had no choice but to face it with everything we had. We were lucky enough to survive, and it made us better than we were before. I don't know your entire history. In different circumstances, what your species has done to survive might've been the best choice. I'm not here to judge you. However, I don't think our being here is an accident. The only way for me to confirm this is if I can speak with your mentor…Salpheth."

Phendran was quiet for a long moment, considering. "Please allow me to confer with the others."

He turned, and the Aczars walked a short distance away.

Connor gestured for the others to gather around. "What do you think?"

Noah blew out a breath. "Honestly, I'm still trying to keep up."

"I think we should return to the ship and get out of here as quickly as possible," Seger said. "They're dangerous and high-strung. Unpredictable."

Kincaid nodded. "I agree with him. Even with our weapons, I think they could overwhelm us."

"They can't be that superior to us," Jorath said.

Kincaid shook his head. "They wear their technology. Some of it you can barely see. Those belts hold a host of tools I've never seen before." He paused for a second. "It's like our nanorobotic ammunition blocks but with way more capability. We shouldn't underestimate them."

Seger nodded. "It's like they each had a small army of tiny robotic assistants. I have no idea how they power them all. The apparatus that held me was incredibly strong and the fastest thing I've ever seen."

Kincaid nodded. "It's like they anticipated all our actions."

"They might've done just that," Noah said.

Connor looked at him. "What do you mean?"

"See how fast they talk? Their movements are quick, too. Maybe this species simply processes thought faster than we do. Some kind of super-speed intelligence."

Connor glanced at the group of Aczars for a second. "They could just be enhanced."

"Definitely," Noah agreed. "Nobody was waving any weapons around, but I still felt like we were treading on thin ice."

Connor nodded. "They certainly seem quick to judge."

"Did you mean what you said?" Cassidy asked. "About the Phantoms. That they somehow sent us here?"

Connor nodded. "Yes, I think the odds are staggeringly against the chance that we just happened on this civilization."

She frowned for a second. "But why would they do that? Seems odd. I mean, we're so far from home."

"She has a point, sir," Kincaid said. "As far as targets go, this has got to be one of the tiniest ones out there."

"Not if they anticipated a breakthrough with the I-Drive," Connor said.

Noah nodded. "That supports the theory that the Phantoms were more aware of the I-Drive's potential than we were." He bit his lower lip for a second. "Do you think they'll let us speak with this mentor, Salpheth?"

"I don't know. I keep trying to put myself in their position, and then the answer becomes no. He's a national asset. I bet they restrict access to Salpheth even among their own species."

Phendran stopped speaking with the other Aczar. They all stopped speaking at the same time, and then began walking back to them.

"If they won't allow us to speak with Salpheth, we'll leave. Head back to the ship as quickly as possible and leave the planet," Connor said.

"I still can't reach the ship via comms," Noah said.

"Understood. Here they come," Connor replied.

CHAPTER 22

Connor watched as Phendran and the others approached with pensive expressions. Phendran walked slower than the others, but they deferred to him.

"Consensus has been reached," Phendran said. "We will not grant your request to meet with Salpheth."

Connor regarded him for a few seconds. "Aren't you curious? Don't you want to know how he'd respond to what we've shared with you?"

"An inquiry will be raised."

Connor narrowed his gaze inquisitively. "Are you allowed to contact Salpheth? Do you have authorization?"

Several of the Aczars let out a shrill cry, glaring at him, and Phendran regarded him.

"You are not familiar with us or our ways," Phendran said and looked at the others until they became quiet. Then he directed his gaze at Connor. "As Loremaster, I have authorization to contact Salpheth for guidance."

"So, it's really your decision, then. *You've* decided that we can't meet Salpheth," Connor said.

Phendran gave him a wry look, looking slightly amused. "No decision is made in a vacuum."

"I understand. Then allow us to return to our ship and we will leave your planet in peace," Connor said and paused for a second, pursing his lips thoughtfully. "You're curious about what I said, but I don't understand what's preventing you from seeking out the truth."

"I *am* curious. What would you do in our position?"

The question was simple enough, but Connor knew better. "It depends on what I was hiding."

The others became still, and silence mushroomed between the two species.

"You *do* understand," Phendran said, looking pleased. "What would you ask Salpheth?"

Connor had to be careful with his response. One wrong word might close the door on this chance to speak with a Phantom. "I'd like to hear what he has to say about our experience with his species. Maybe he'd give some guidance to us. I'd also like to know more about him. It might help us shape our opinions of the Phantoms or influence our policies regarding the advice they give."

Phendran considered this for a few moments. "That is a request I can grant."

Connor blinked in surprise. He wasn't expecting Phendran to change his mind so quickly and wondered if he'd just been testing Connor.

He decided not to press Phendran on the issue. "Thank you. When can we meet him? There are limits to how long our EVA suits can operate until they need to be recharged."

"Very well. Right now. Please step closer and we'll show you the way," Phendran said. He gestured toward the others, then looked at Connor. "Do not be alarmed. We will surround you for the transition. Follow me."

Connor looked at the others. Kincaid and Seger were waiting for his orders. Cassidy gave a worried glance at the Aczars, and Jorath took up a position behind her. He gave Connor a level look.

"We're with you, Connor," Noah said.

Connor followed Phendran toward a steep cliff face of dark rock. The emblem on Phendran's chest glowed with a pale light and part of the rock wall reacted. Bands of glowing metal appeared, then flashed, and a dark passageway opened. Connor had to duck his head to fit through it, as did some of the others.

Phendran kept walking, not checking to see if they were following. Once they were all through the hidden door, it sealed up behind them. A pale green light came from shimmering rings on the walls. They were in a metallic corridor.

Thankfully, the ceiling was higher, and Connor could stand up straight. Phendran led them to the end of the corridor. It looked as if there was only a wall. Then a long oval of light glistened, making the solid-looking wall waver until it was gone. It reminded Connor of the pools of light from his encounter with the Phantom. Those had been some kind of portal.

Phendran turned and looked up at Connor. "You are familiar with these."

He nodded. "Where does it go?"

"I'm taking you to see Salpheth. It won't be long now," Phendran replied and stepped through the light. There was a faint hissing sound as he passed through.

"Is that it? Is that what you saw?" Noah asked.

Connor nodded. "Yeah, that's it."

He considered saying something to the others to set them at ease, but it would've been a mistake. They were at Phendran's mercy and had to see this through.

Connor stepped through the door and, as he touched the light, his EVA suit registered a significant temperature drop. He stepped out into a large room. There were purple crystals along the far wall. They looked like naturally occurring growth.

Phendran stood in the center of the room. "Please join me here."

Connor walked over to him, and the others followed.

Kincaid came to his side. "I had no idea this was all inside the mountain."

Connor glanced at Phendran. "I'm not sure we're inside the mountain."

Kincaid frowned and stared at Phendran.

"How far have they taken us?" Cassidy asked.

Phendran's gaze settled on her. "I've taken you to a place of communication. It is here that you will be able to see Salpheth."

She looked at Connor. Phendran hadn't answered her question.

Connor gave her a reassuring nod and then looked at Phendran. "Please continue," Connor said.

The other Aczar stayed by the far wall, near where the door had been. Once the last of them came through, the door of light became dark. Connor searched for some kind of control panel or other means to use the door, but there wasn't anything. The Aczars appeared more at ease, making Connor think they weren't as comfortable on the planet's surface.

Something like a holographic interface appeared in front of Phendran. Connor peered at it, seeing tiny specs of metal the consistency of fine sand form the interface. Colonial holographic interfaces were composed of light and charged particles that reacted to human touch. The Aczar interface was physical and impressive.

The Aczar interface expanded to form a very large screen that expanded the entire width and height of the room. It blocked their view of the wall in an expanse of darkness. Then the screen abruptly changed, displaying a distant view of a large energy sphere that was semitranslucent. Golden waves washed over it in constant intervals, swirling in some places before they dissolved for brief moments and then reformed. A grayish humanoid figure floated inside the sphere. The figure spun toward them as if aware of their presence. The view on the screen closed in on the sphere until it was pierced, and they were able to see the figure inside. It had a similar musculature to that of a human. Its torso was bare and glistened in the light. The face was blank, without lips or a nose, but wide, large, teardrop-dark eyes regarded Connor intently. Its body seemed to give off pale light with spots of darkness. There was a motion to it that made Connor uncertain what he was seeing. Despite having masculine musculature, it had no male genitalia at all, nor nipples or a belly button. There were no indications that the being in front of him had been born so much as hatched or created some other way. Its head was elongated, and pale flaps of skin went down its back, disappearing from view.

The Phantom regarded Connor and the others intently. Cassidy drew closer to Kincaid.

Thick lips appeared on the Phantom's face, giving him a grim appearance.

Connor took in the sight of the Phantom. It was similar in appearance to the construct he'd seen before, but there were differences. The creature in front of him was a living being and not a construct made of light. He was tall, at least two and half meters in height.

Phendran studied Connor's and then the others' reactions. "This is Salpheth, the Great Mentor of the Aczar."

Salpheth's gaze drifted toward Phendran for a long moment and then went back to Connor and the others.

Connor heard Noah whisper an almost silent prayer.

"Visitors to the planet Ichlos, how have you come to be here?" Salpheth asked.

His deep voice sounded clear, and yet it was also as if certain tones dragged behind, like some kind of delay.

"We came here on our ship," Connor replied.

"They traveled from beyond the star system, Great Mentor," Phendran said.

Salpheth regarded them for a moment and then gazed intently at Connor. "Do you speak for the others?"

"Yes," Connor said. "We're from another star system far away from here."

"I know the star systems in this region. None of them had intelligent life capable of traveling the great expanse," Salpheth said and paused for a moment. "Your ship must then be capable of traversing the extremely vast distances."

Salpheth looked away from them, drifting off into his own thoughts.

"How long have you been here?" Connor asked.

He raised his gaze toward Connor. "Since the beginning. Why did you come to this planet? The Aczar have gone to great lengths to hide themselves."

"Their ship is in need of repair, and they landed on the surface to gather materials," Phendran said.

Salpheth considered this and looked at Connor. "My appearance doesn't surprise you. You've seen my species before."

"A construct of your species, yes," Connor replied.

Small golden waves shifted behind Salpheth. Connor glanced at Noah, who was accessing his wrist computer.

"I would very much like to see your ship. It must be truly remarkable to have brought you so far," Salpheth said.

"I'd be happy to show it to you if you'd answer my questions," Connor replied.

He didn't like that Salpheth was so interested in their ship and had no intention of bringing the Phantom anywhere near it. There was something off about his interest in it, as if he was more interested in their ship than the fact that they'd come to this planet.

"I will answer your questions and then you'll answer mine. Is that agreeable to you?"

"Seems fair," Connor said. "Why were you left behind?"

Salpheth's head cocked to the side, surprised, as if Connor had exposed something he'd thought to keep hidden.

"I've encountered your species before," Connor said. "They told me they travel the galaxy. Observe alien species. They don't stay in one place for very long."

Salpheth turned his head, and one of his dark eyes peered intently at Connor. "What else did they tell you?"

"They warned me about the dangers of exploring the galaxy. They warned me about the Vemus and that we should stay within the star systems we've already explored."

Salpheth waited for Connor to continue speaking, but Connor decided to wait him out. He wanted to know Salpheth's reaction.

"The fact that they took the time to address you directly should leave you in awe. It is a privilege granted to few."

Connor shook his head. "Not quite. It's more like they left me and many other people with a lot of questions. You see, they did a lot more than speak to me," he said and went on to explain what else the Phantoms had done—how they'd followed the Colonial Exploration Initiative and visited New Earth in secret, accessed all their data libraries, and more.

Salpheth was quiet, hardly seeming to move as Connor spoke to him. He noticed that Phendran watched Salpheth intently during the whole exchange.

"So, you see, they took more than a passing interest in us. Maybe some things have changed since you've last seen them," Connor said.

"All these things and you still doubt the knowledge that has been given to you?" Salpheth asked.

He hadn't denied Connor's assertion that Salpheth was a prisoner and had been left behind by his own species. It made him more suspicious of the alien than he'd been before.

"I don't doubt that the Vemus are formidable," Connor said, "but I don't see how restricting ourselves in a lame attempt to avoid notice is a solid, long-term strategy for our survival." He glanced at Phendran for a second. "Doing that would only keep us ignorant for longer, and how would that serve future generations?"

Salpheth regarded him. "I see. Blindly exploring the galaxy, trusting in your own experiences to deliver you from any and all dangers, including the Vemus. That is your decision."

"We've been better served relying on our own experiences than trusting other species' certainties regarding what direction we should to take."

Salpheth leaned forward a little. "I can't decide if it's supreme arrogance or the fact that you've somehow survived where hundreds of other species have failed that feeds this bravado."

Connor frowned. "Hundreds of other species?"

"Do you know how old we are? Do you think we've only

travelled this galaxy? My time here is but a moment by comparison."

"And yet, *you* were left behind."

Salpheth's gaze narrowed. He didn't like being reminded of that.

Connor looked at Phendran. "Why do you keep your 'Great Mentor' in prison? What would happen if he escaped? Has he escaped before?"

Phendran's eyes widened in surprise, and Connor glanced at Salpheth.

"Why do you let them keep you imprisoned?" Connor asked. He stepped closer to the screen. "If you're so intelligent and powerful, then escaping should've been easy for you. Maybe you can't escape, or maybe you are waiting for something. In which case, that leads me to believe you have other motives." Connor paused for a moment, then asked. "Why are you manipulating them?"

"I've guided the Aczar. Their development has been exceedingly rare," Salpheth said.

"And yet they're reluctant to go on the planet's surface. They're hiding here, and I can't figure out what the motivation is for doing this to them." Connor said.

He looked at Salpheth and then at Phendran. The Aczar stared at him as if he'd obtained a new understanding. Connor was beginning to wonder if both the Aczar and Salpheth were stuck in a kind of stalemate.

Connor looked at Salpheth. "You've been keenly interested in our ship and our ability to travel vast distances. Don't you already possess this knowledge?" He gestured toward Phendran. "Based on what I've seen, the Aczar have technology enough to do the same. Why have you stopped them?"

"Indeed. My species has a compulsion to catalogue species

who have the potential to grow beyond their limitations. Your ship and the fact that you've come so far is of interest to me."

Connor frowned. "How could you possibly know how far we've traveled?"

"I've visited galaxies and have a breadth of knowledge that greatly exceeds your own."

Connor knew a bluff when he saw one. "Then it shouldn't be a problem for you to tell me how far we've come to get here."

Salpheth's gaze narrowed, and Phendran watched him intently.

This wasn't the first alien he'd encountered with a colossal superiority complex. He wouldn't underestimate him, but that didn't mean he'd submit and allow the pompousness to go unchecked.

The edges of Connor's lips lifted. "Would you like me to tell you?"

Salpheth was silent.

"I would like to know," Phendran said.

Connor looked at Phendran and his gaze softened. "We've traveled over five thousand lightyears to get here."

Phendran's eyes widened and then he looked at Salpheth.

The Phantom considered this for a long moment. "This is the reason others of my kind have taken such an interest in you. You've experimented with technology that is beyond your comprehension."

"That's where you're wrong," Noah said. "It's well within our comprehension, otherwise we wouldn't be here talking to you."

Salpheth's dark eyes considered Noah. "Just because you've gained the use of a particular technology doesn't mean you've mastered its application." He looked away from them, peering at something offscreen. Then he turned back to them and looked at

Connor. "They will never allow you to leave this planet. The Aczar are committed to the covenant."

Connor frowned and looked at Phendran. "A decision hadn't been reached yet about that."

Phendran frowned. "I'm unaware of any decision that has been made."

A bitter chuckled came from Salpheth. "A Loremaster no longer has insight into those decisions."

Phendran looked away, uncertain.

"Is that true?" Connor asked. "Will you stop us from leaving?"

"No," Phendran said, glaring at Salpheth for a moment, then looked at Connor. "I wouldn't stop you from leaving."

"Stop playing games with me. Can you take me back to my ship?"

"Yes, of course."

"Interesting exchange," Salpheth chortled, "considering the fact that neither of you knows where the ship in question is currently located." He stared at Connor, looking smug. "Even now, your ship is being moved."

"Moved!" Cassidy exclaimed, eyes filled with worry. "What about the others on the ship?"

"Irrelevant," Salpheth replied.

"Stop it!" Connor shouted. "There's no way they could move the ship."

"He's right," Noah said. "Assuming they could access the ship, there's no way they could fly it."

Salpheth hovered smugly, looking as if he had some hidden knowledge. "This is why you should restrict your activities. You think you know the limits of what is possible, but be assured travelers, you have only scratched the surface."

Connor looked at Phendran. "Is he lying to us? Could you move the ship somehow?"

Phendran considered it for a second. "It is possible."

"Where? Where would they take it?" Connor asked, ignoring how his brain refused to accept that the ship had been stolen.

"I don't know," Phendran said.

Connor believed him. "We have to get out of here."

Phendran looked away from him, uncertain.

"The Aczar detest spaceships," Salpheth said. "It seems that you'll be trapped here for a very long time."

CHAPTER 23

CONNOR IGNORED Salpheth and focused on Phendran.

The other Aczars stepped away from the far wall, and both Kincaid and Seger lifted their weapons.

"Wait," Connor said and looked at Phendran. "Take us out of here. We need to get back to our ship. We've got people on there."

Phendran looked at Salpheth. The Phantom had become quiet as he watched them intently, almost challengingly.

Connor's heart pounded, and the urge to take action was beginning to override all other ideas.

Phendran remained quiet, but his eyes darted back and forth as if his mind were racing.

"Fine, you stay here, but we're leaving," Connor said and spun away from Phendran and the giant screen that showed Salpheth's prison.

He walked toward the area of the wall where the door had been, and the other Aczar moved to block his path. "Open this door. Take us back the way we've come."

They didn't move.

Over to the side, the young Aczar named Kholva frowned.

"You," Connor said, pointing at him. "I'd rather avoid violence, but you're leaving me with little choice. Will you open the door?"

Kholva's eyes widened as if he was surprised at being addressed. Then he looked past Connor at Phendran. "Loremaster, I seek guidance. These actions don't seem right."

"Because they aren't. Your people are taking what's not rightfully theirs. It's called stealing," Connor said.

Phendran began muttering softly and his eyes became distant.

"What's wrong with him?" Noah asked.

Connor looked at Kholva.

"He accesses the archive. He's deep inside it," Kholva said.

Connor brought up his wrist computer and tried to reach the ship, but the comlink wouldn't connect. Either the signal was being blocked, or they were too far away.

Kincaid and Seger had their weapons pointed at the Aczars, who stood poised with their own hands raised. A faint glow came from their metallic bands.

Shooting their way out wasn't really an option. Instead, Connor turned toward Phendran and crossed the distance to him. Salpheth hovered on the screen, watching him intently.

"Phendran, you have to listen to me. You've been manipulated. Salpheth manipulates you as a way of keeping your species under his control."

"You're wasting your time," Salpheth said. "They will never waver in their commitment to the covenant."

He'd sounded frustrated, as if he was speaking from experience. Connor knew he couldn't trust Salpheth, but his response seemed genuine.

"Phendran," Connor said. "This fanatical dedication to a limiting philosophy has kept your species stagnant. Even if you can't see it, you can't go along with what's being done. Trapping us here is a death sentence. We cannot survive here."

It was the first time he'd admitted it, and he knew the others were staring at him. Connor ignored them, hoping to see Phendran snap out of whatever he was doing. After a few long moments, Connor reached for his weapon. He turned toward the other Aczars, raising it. Then he dove to the side, and a flash of light came.

Several metallic frameworks lunged toward him, and it took him a moment to realize that they were frozen in place under a meter from reaching him. He scrambled out of the way.

"Stop, General Gates. I've heard you," Phendran said.

Connor glanced at him. Phendran closed the screen, cutting off their view of Salpheth.

Kincaid gasped. "They're frozen!"

Connor peered at other Aczar. More than half of them were frozen in place and looked unaware of what was happening.

"They are immobilized. Come. Come. I will help you," Phendran said.

He hastened to the wall, and Connor followed.

Kholva looked around, shocked, as were several Aczars.

"Peace, Kholva," Phendran said. "A temporary reset of their Saruvian Assistants. They'll soon come out of it."

"As you say, Loremaster," Kholva replied.

"What the heck just happened?" Seger asked. He had his weapon pointed at a motionless Aczar, as if expecting him to move at any second.

Phendran looked at Connor. "General Gates, your weapons are not needed now. I've neutralized the threat. I cannot allow them to be harmed."

Seger and Kincaid looked at Connor.

"Lower your weapons," Connor said and looked at Phendran. "I cannot reach our ship. Are you blocking the signal?"

Phendran's eyes flicked to the side. There was a faint bluish glow around his dark eyes, and this was the first indication that the Aczar had neural implants. "Try it now."

Connor tried to open a comlink to the ship, but it failed to connect.

"We could be out of range," Noah said, peering at his personal holoscreen intently.

"We are inside the mountain where we found you. It should be within range of your communication devices," Phendran said and frowned.

"Unless they took our ship out of range," Connor said.

He lifted his wrist computer and accessed the control interface of the scout drones. Only two were online. He sent a command for them to return to the ship.

"Two drones online. They might've been missed. They're traveling back to the LZ," Connor said and looked at Kincaid. "Monitor their progress, Captain."

"Yes, General," Kincaid replied.

Connor turned toward Phendran. "Take us out of here."

Phendran hesitated and then pressed the palms of his hands together in front of his chest. "I can take you back to your land vehicle, but I don't see how that will help," Phendran said.

"Why not? How far could the ship have gone?" Seger asked.

Phendran was about to respond when Kincaid said. "General Gates, you need to see this." He made a passing motion.

The scout drone's video feed came to prominence on Connor's wrist computer. The site where the ship had been was empty. The ship was gone. Connor blinked and watched as the drone's camera panned around, searching for the missing ship.

The surrounding area was undisturbed. The ship was simply gone.

Cassidy peered at his holoscreen and let out a half-startled cry. "Where is it? What about the rest of them?" She spun toward Phendran with a snarl. "My father is on that ship! Where have they taken him?"

Phendran blinked, taken aback by her vehemence.

"Answer her," Connor demanded, his tone sharp.

"They are likely still on the ship."

"What do you mean 'likely'?" Cassidy said.

"The Dedicated wouldn't have had time to take them off the ship. They would've moved the entire ship with everyone inside. It's the only explanation that makes sense," Phendran said. He moved toward the wall and a door of light appeared. "Please follow me."

Connor looked at Cassidy. Her shoulders were drawn up tight and her mouth was a grim line. "Cassidy, we'll find them. You have to trust me. I promise you that we'll find them."

She stared at him for a moment and then nodded. Kincaid came to her side.

Connor looked at the others. "Let's go," he said and walked through the door.

It was much like seeing a flash of light and then they were somewhere else. It was quick, and aside from a drop in temperature detected by their EVA suits, he didn't feel a thing.

They entered a short corridor carved from a pale-colored stone. It was smooth and seamless, and it led to another room.

Phendran stood at the end of the corridor. "Hurry, I need to close the door so the others won't be able to trace where we went."

Connor and the others quickly walked toward him, along with Kholva and a few of the other Aczar.

Kholva gestured toward the door, and it became dark.

"Come. Come," Phendran said and entered the room.

The room was carved in the same manner as the corridor. It was well lit with soft yellow lights. Mosaic patterns covered the floor and formed complex patterns that seemed to draw the eye on a journey.

Phendran walked to the other side room and a metallic workstation rose from the floor. A holoscreen became active and a series of symbols flashed by that Connor couldn't read.

"I'm searching for your ship," Phendran said.

"Why did they take the ship?" Connor asked.

"I can only speculate," Phendran replied as his hands darted through the holoscreen. Multiple sub windows appeared, and Connor lost track of them all.

Connor waited for him to continue, but he didn't. "Speculate away."

"The covenant decrees that all technology is concealed. Your ship was likely taken because it violates one of our most sacred laws."

Noah shook his head. "This seems a bit extreme. We could've just left."

Connor frowned in thought for a second. "That might satisfy your laws, but there has to be another reason."

Phendran nodded. "Salpheth. He must've had them take your ship."

"Why?" Noah asked.

Connor's eyes flicked toward the ceiling for a second. "Because he wants to escape."

"It's impossible," Phendran began and stopped.

Noah gave Connor a knowing look. "It's not the ship, it's the I-Drive. That has to be what he needs."

Phendran's hands dropped to his side, and he looked away.

"Phendran," Connor said, "Salpheth is a prisoner, but he's also somehow made you dependent on him."

"He's guided our innovation with his wisdom—" Phendran began and stopped. "I am a Loremaster. We know our history and ensure the adherence to our covenant. It is up to us to discern what is compliant with it, and that includes Salpheth in our development. We've followed his guidance."

"What about the ships your species used to come to this planet?" Connor asked.

"They were all destroyed. Our ancestors abandoned the old ways that… we had to renounce them." He glanced at Kholva and the other Aczar, looking determined. "Apprentices, students of the lore, I'm going to help these travelers recover their ship. This will be in violation of Aczar Major right up to Baeqex. Scastars will have expedited this. They'll repurpose the materials from their ship, but I won't allow this to happen."

Kholva glanced at the others for a second. "Why do you do this?"

"There are secret archives. They are the historical account of the three uprisings, containing the recorded history that led some of our ancestors to abandon the covenant from Salpheth."

"The uprisings, but all of them were stopped and their harmful teachers destroyed," Kholva said.

"Not all of them. This is why I help these travelers, as well as to stop Salpheth."

Connor frowned for a second. "He must've tried to escape before or instigated the uprising at the start."

"They were dark moments in our history. Many died. However, we must prevent your ship from being dismantled," Phendran said.

"How can you find it?"

"Loremasters are what you might call information specialists. I'll trace Scastars and his team, and they will lead us to your ship."

CHAPTER 24

PHENDRAN CALLED Kholva and another Aczar named Vorix to help him. Several workstations rose from the floor and Connor watched how they used them. Their movements revealed a mixture of different hand gestures, but there were also long pauses, leading him to believe they were using some kind of neural implant. Connor was no stranger to using a neural implant, but there was a general preference among people to use their hands to control a computer system.

Noah looked at him nervously. "I hate being this cut off."

"Yeah, me too," Connor said. "I'd ask you to try to infiltrate their systems, but it might do more harm than good."

Noah nodded. "It's better to just keep an eye on them." He blew out a shallow breath and shook his head.

"I know. They move so fast, it's hard to follow," Connor said.

He didn't like feeling so helpless. He had to rely on Phendran's help, but it also meant that if Phendran suddenly changed his mind, he wasn't sure what they would do. The other Aczars were much younger than Phendran, and they regarded him as an authority figure. If Phendran betrayed them… Connor let that line of thinking go. It wasn't going to help.

He looked at Kincaid and the others. "Did you see how they operated the door?"

Kincaid shook his head. "Negative, sir. I think they must transmit their authorization via their implants."

Connor nodded. "That's what I thought as well."

Seger leaned toward him. "It'll be a real crap-fest for us if they change their minds about helping us."

Kincaid nodded and waited for Connor to respond.

"You're right, it would be. But they also seem open to reason. As long as we don't give them a reason to change their minds, hopefully, we'll be fine."

Connor chided himself inwardly. He'd just made "hope" their strategy. "We should also pay attention and look for opportunities to change the status quo."

"Understood, sir," Kincaid said. "It would be best if we could reach the ship while they're transferring it. How would they even move a ship this big?"

"I have a few ideas about that," Connor said.

Noah looked at him in surprise. "You do?"

He nodded. "Yes. They could have some kind of atmospheric tug ship that simply hauls it away to another location. Phendran said they didn't infiltrate the ship, so they didn't fly it out of there. I didn't expect they could do that. The other way I thought of is pretty farfetched." He paused for a second. "What if they deployed some kind of mobile gateway?"

Noah frowned. "Instantaneous travel or, as others prefer to call it, teleportation?"

Connor nodded.

"A door that big, though?" Kincaid asked.

Connor shrugged. "What difference does it make?" He

gestured toward the wall where the door had been. "If they can make a door that size, why not a bigger door?"

Noah chuckled a little. "Don't worry about it, Captain Kincaid. He's been doing this to me since I met him." He frowned for a moment. "I don't know. It's one thing to have a facility—hidden facility—with a network of these doors used for travel, but it's quite another to just be able to put up a mobile gateway to anywhere you want."

"I hope you're right," Connor said.

"Why don't we just ask them?" Cassidy said, lifting her chin toward Phendran and the others.

"I'm aware of your comments and speculations," Phendran said without turning toward them.

"Joy, they can hear us," Kincaid said softly.

Connor walked to Phendran. "So, are we close to being right?"

"Your speculation is accurate in that we do have these capabilities, but mobile teleportation on such a scale is limited. It is likely that the Dedicated used a team of vehicles designed for moving mass quantities," Phendran said.

Kholva turned from his workstation. "I've found what you asked, Loremaster. It is as you say."

"I was afraid of that," Phendran said and gave Connor a remorseful look. "You will not be murdered as you feared you would be. They intend to give you a facility to live out the rest of your lives."

Cassidy gasped, and Kincaid muttered angrily.

Connor regarded Phendran for a moment and then shook his head. "No, they won't."

"That's what the decree states."

"I don't care what it says. We'll be exploited for our knowledge and then discarded because we'll outlive our usefulness.

Why else would they do this?" Connor asked and then gestured at the screens. "Look how hard it was for you to find this information. They intend to keep us a secret."

Phendran glanced at the workstations, looking conflicted. Then something small flashed on one of the screens, drawing his attention.

"Think it through," Connor pressed. "Why do you need to study the I-Drive if you never intend to leave the planet?"

Phendran turned to him. "That isn't the covenant. We were to conceal ourselves and increase our understanding of the universe so we could be like the Great Advisor. This includes perfecting ourselves, being in harmony with our Saruvian counterparts." He frowned for a second, then held up one of his hands and the metallic wrist bands expanded to form a spinning octagon. There was a bluish glow coming from the center. "This is our counterpart—an artificial life created to help us ascend. They speed up our development and understanding. It was a gift to us from Salpheth."

Connor looked at it.

Noah leaned toward it a little. "You've achieved a synergistic relationship with an artificial life form?"

"Indeed, they have," a voice with warm overtones came from the octagonal form. "We are the Saruvian Robotic Assistants. We serve the Aczar, defend them if necessary."

Connor's eyes narrowed a little, and then he looked at Phendran. "How do you know it's not controlling you?"

Phendran shook his head. "The same way you know that none of us are controlling you," he replied, gesturing at the others. "Trust and a relationship of equals at its core."

Connor glanced at Noah, who tipped his head to the side in agreement.

"I think we're getting sidetracked," Noah said.

Connor considered Noah's words for a few moments, remembering his experience with the Phantoms. He'd encountered a construct, which was some kind of radically advanced machine that was connected to the Phantoms. He looked at the metallic octagon.

"Our implants are extensive," Phendran said. A bluish glow came from his eyes and around his head. It even extended down his arms.

"Okay, but we can't stay here. We have to get back home," Connor said.

Noah cleared his throat. "Are you sure about that?"

Connor arched an eyebrow. "What do you mean?"

"I mean, yeah, we have to get home, but the coming here part," Noah said, giving Connor a meaningful look.

Phendran glanced at them. "No subvocal communication among you. This is a hinderance."

Connor pressed his lips together for a few seconds. "We think that the Phantoms might've intentionally sent us here to make contact with you."

"Why would they do that?"

"Maybe they wanted us to check on you? I don't know. I'll ask them the next time I speak to them," Connor said. His tone was sharp, and he was becoming frustrated. He sighed. "Maybe they think there could be an alliance between our two species."

Phendran's eyes widened. "For what purpose?"

"To help each other. To learn from one another. You said that your ancestors encountered some kind of great evil out in the deep dark. We were attacked by something the Phantoms believe is beyond our ability to deal with. Yet, here we are," Connor said.

"How would this alliance work?"

"I don't know. I'm not the person who gets to decide these things. I do know that an alliance will never happen if we're forced to stay here. You said you'd help us find our ship. Are you changing your mind about that?"

"No," Phendran replied quickly. "I've made my decision, and I am committed to following through to its completion."

He had a very matter of fact way of speaking that left Connor with little doubt that the Aczar meant what he'd said. Connor hadn't expected this. They were two completely different alien species, but maybe Noah was right and the Phantoms had sent them here for a purpose. Either way, he appreciated that Phendran and the others were willing to help them, but he wasn't sure what it would cost them in the long run.

"Where are they taking the ship? I doubt it could be far, not if they want to keep it a secret," Connor said.

"I thought they would take it to a storage facility, but I was wrong, so I'm continuing the search," Phendran said.

"Loremaster," an Aczar said. Her voice was higher than the others, and her features more delicate.

Connor hadn't noticed before, but there were a few female Aczar among them.

"Vorix, what have you found?" Phendran asked.

"Salpheth has urged Scastars to secure the ship to prevent the Humans from taking it away from them. Primary objective is to preserve a high energy output machine capable of spatial manipulation."

Connor frowned, trying to make sense of what she'd said.

"They're talking about the Infinity Drive," Noah said. "A 'high energy output machine capable of spatial manipulation.' I'd say that is an accurate description of what it does."

"Makes sense," Connor said.

Phendran brought up a new screen. "Carriers are moving your ship. I've located them."

"Are we able to see it?" Connor asked.

The video feed was strange. It wasn't an actual video but a feed built from metallic particles that modeled the camera feed. It showed a series of smaller ships with an atmospheric design. They were sleek, black, oval-shaped airships with some kind of energy field that surrounded the *Pathfinder*. Connor saw chunks of the ground that had been taken from where the landing gear made contact.

"Looks like an artificial gravity field," Noah said, sounding impressed.

"But those ships are so small. How could they produce enough power to maintain and control the gravity field?" Kincaid asked.

Noah glanced at Phendran. The Aczar had focused his attention on a different screen.

"They must have more efficient power generators than we do. I haven't detected much of a heat signature from anything we've seen so far," Noah said.

"When we pass through the door, my suit registers a drop in temperature but then returns to normal," Connor said.

"That's got to be part of it," Noah said and shook his head, "but we don't have time to chase this down now. Look how small those ships are, and yet they can move not only our ship but the ground beneath it where the landing gear touched down. That's high-precision work for a gravity field. I'd love to—Never mind."

Phendran snapped his hands away from the screens with a snarl of frustration. All three workstations sank to the floor. "I know where they're taking the ship, but my activity is being monitored."

"Will that be a problem?" Connor asked.

"Eventually. Come, I'll take you to your ship," Phendran said and hastened to another part of the room where he opened a door.

Kholva and Vorix quickly stepped through. Phendran gestured for them to go first. They all went through the door and entered a plateau high in the mountains. The bright light startled them for a moment.

"Phendran," Connor said, "what if we get separated? How can we find the ship? We can't even travel here without your help."

Phendran gestured for them to keep moving and then looked up at Connor. "I can share part of my Saruvian Assistant with you, but since you're not Aczar, it'll be a limited capacity."

"Should I be concerned?" Connor asked.

"Yes, because I'm not sure whether it will work, but I'm willing to try."

"I don't understand," Connor said.

"There is a chance you'll be rejected."

Connor blinked. "Wait a second. I just want a way to use the doors and find our ship. I can't allow your robotic assistant to breach my EVA suit. I'm just looking for a way to interface with your systems if we become separated."

Phendran didn't speak for a few moments, then stopped walking. He extended his hand toward Connor with his palm facing outward. Connor hesitated for a moment and then did the same. A sleek silvery line detached from Phendran's wristband and slithered onto Connor's hand. It moved fast and coiled onto the back of his glove. The bluish glow faded, now looking like a metallic patch on his glove. It was inert, and Connor stared at it for a moment.

"It'll remain dormant until it is needed," Phendran said.

"How's it going to know if I need it?"

"Think of it as being on standby. It still monitors and is aware of the surroundings," Phendran replied.

Kholva led them across the plateau and came to a stop near a group of boulders. The surrounding area shimmered, revealing a bullet-shaped aircar. It had a gleaming silver surface that reflected the area around them, and an oval-shaped hatch appeared, spilling light from the opening.

"We must use this vehicle to reach the facility where your ship is being taken. They won't be able to track our movements in this," Phendran said.

Kholva and Vorix hastened up the ramp. The doorway was small, and Connor's group had to squeeze through. Along the interior walls were several small seats that were appropriately sized for an Aczar.

Noah glanced at him. "This is going to be cozy."

There wasn't much room inside, and when the door rematerialized, it felt like they were on top of one another. Connor turned toward the front where Phendran sat.

"Flight controls ready," Kholva said.

"Take us out," Phendran said.

The Aczar ship lifted off the ground, and Connor didn't feel the movement at all.

Kincaid was next to him. "We're really in it now, sir," he whispered.

Connor nodded. "You've got that right."

CHAPTER 25

THE ACZAR AIRCAR flew away from the plateau, descending to an area above the alien trees.

Connor glanced at his wrist computer and the piece of Phendran's Saruvian Robotic Assistant near it. He frowned, considering.

Kincaid glanced at it. "Sir, what is that?"

"It's supposed to help us if we get separated from them," Connor said, lifting his chin toward Phendran and the others.

"It might not be safe. Want to transfer it to me?" Kincaid asked, lifting his hand.

Connor shook his head. Noah leaned to the side, peering at it thoughtfully. "We need to get a message to the others."

Kincaid nodded. "Agreed. I can't imagine what they must be thinking."

"I'm more concerned with what they're doing," Connor replied.

"Rabsaris and Naya should be able to keep them from doing anything foolish," Kincaid said.

"I can't get a comlink to the ship," Noah said.

"What about the shuttle? Does it have subspace comms?" Kincaid asked.

Connor shook his head. "No, it's been out of service for too long."

He brought up his wrist computer and was able to establish a comlink to the two scout drones.

"What are you going to do with them?" Kincaid asked.

"I'm not sure, depends on what we find with the ship. Right now, I have them tracking our location," Connor replied.

"Phendran," Noah said, "do you have a visual on the ship?"

"Stand by," Phendran replied. "Yes. I'm afraid I'm only able to show it up here."

Connor peered at the main console in the front of the aircar. It showed the *Pathfinder* suspended in the air, with eight smaller ships flying nearby. There was some kind of tether attached to the hull. It glowed a little and then spread across the entire ship. Other bullet-shaped aircars were flying nearby, but these had weapons mounted on them. They flew in escort-formation.

"Phendran," Connor said. "I need to send a message to my people on our ship. Do you know of way we can do that without alerting the escort ships?"

Phendran considered it for a few seconds. "We cannot maintain stealth and ensure a message is delivered."

Kincaid looked at Connor. "Our scout drones won't get past those escorts. Their coverage is effective."

Connor pursed his lips in thought for a moment. Then he brought up his wrist computer.

"What are you going to do?" Noah asked.

"First, I'm going to craft a message for the others. They need to prepare for boarders," Connor said. Cassidy blinked in surprise but didn't say anything. "It's only a matter of time. They need to be advised of the current situation and that we're working on a way to help them."

Noah frowned. "How are you going to get the message to them?"

Connor smiled and arched an eyebrow. "You of little faith," he said while opening a comlink to the shuttle.

"The shuttle," Noah said, thoughtfully.

"Let's see if we can give them something to chase."

Kincaid looked at him. "You're going to remote pilot the shuttle? It's not the most agile spacecraft out there."

Connor nodded. "I know. I'm just going to engineer a buzz of the tower, see if I can get them to chase it for a little bit and give the drones a chance to reach the ship."

Kincaid blinked, and then he nodded. "Clever, sir. That's really clever. Are you sure the drones can reach the ship? We'll lose our only shot at getting them a message."

"I think they can," Connor said. "Just need to get them close enough to send the message."

"He's right," Noah said. "Those are some kind of gravity tethers. They're not blocking anything. They just maintain a field, and the tugs are dragging the ship to wherever they're taking it."

"Why don't we just try to return to the ship, assuming the shuttle-bait maneuver works?" Kincaid asked.

Connor continued entering the message for the ship and said, "It might come to that, but we could also be just as trapped as the others."

"Some of the point-defense systems are functional. We could have them use them to clear a path. Give us a chance to get out of here," Kincaid said.

The others looked at Connor. The CDF captain was exploring their options.

"If one of us was on the ship, I'd consider it," Connor said.

"Maybe Rabsaris or Naya Corman could get the defense systems to work, but they don't have the training or the know-how to actually use them."

Kincaid's eyes sank for a moment, and he shook his head. "I'm sorry, sir. I'm just trying to figure out a way to help them."

"I bet Mac would know," Noah said. Connor looked at him and shrugged. "He's seen combat before. You could tell."

"Then he can help defend the others if it comes to it," Connor said.

Noah nodded. "I can make a flight maneuver ready for the shuttle. Nothing fancy, like you said. Do you want to check it?"

"Do I need to?"

Noah blinked. "Uh, no, well, maybe you should. Just in case."

Noah lifted his holoscreen toward Connor and he checked it. "That's good. Just have it exit the atmosphere. Hopefully, it'll be able to outrun them."

Noah nodded. "Shuttle is on its way."

Connor finished compiling his instructions for the ship and uploaded them to the scout drones.

They didn't have long to wait for the shuttle to make its appearance. It was on an intercept course with the ship.

"Let's hope they take the bait," Connor said.

If it didn't work, he'd have each of the drones try to reach the ship on their own.

Connor watched the shuttle fly in a direct path toward the ship. The airtugs didn't slow down, but the escort ships took the bait. All of them darted toward the shuttle, fast. The shuttle increased its velocity and rose at a sharp angle.

One of the escort ships dropped away from the pack and flew back toward the ship. There was nothing Connor could do. The scout drones were already on their way.

There was a slight delay in tracking the scout drones' location because Connor didn't want to maintain a comlink in case it could be traced. As the drones got near the ship, the tracking signal was lost.

Noah frowned and looked at Connor. "How are we going to know if they received the message?"

"I gave them a way to signal us," Connor said.

They waited about ten minutes before Connor asked, "Phendran, are you able to give us a closer look at the ship's forward section?"

A new window appeared with a video feed that was much closer to the ship.

"That can't be from here," Noah said.

"It's not," Phendran replied. "This is from one of the airtug ships. Is this sufficient?"

"It's fine. Can you pan it to the left more?" Connor asked.

They waited and the video feed shifted.

"That's good. You can cut the feed," Connor said and looked at the others. "Message received."

Kincaid and Noah exchanged looks. "How do you know?" Noah asked.

He thought he'd told them, but he must not have. "They rotated the comms array ninety degrees from center."

"How do we know it wasn't already in that position?" Kincaid asked, then held up his hand. "I'm sorry, it's just that there is a chance it could've already been like that."

Noah arched an eyebrow and looked at Connor.

"Yeah, but the transceiver was rotating as well. Trust me, they got the message," Connor replied. He looked at Noah. "What's the status of the shuttle?"

"Making its way to the upper atmosphere," Noah said and

peered at this screen in thought. "Looks like they've slowed their pursuit."

"They will not leave the planet's atmosphere," Phendran said.

"They won't or they can't?" Connor asked.

"They can't. There is a limit to how far from a power source our ships can go."

Connor considered this for a few moments.

"Sir, is he saying that their ships, including this one, are remotely powered?" Kincaid asked.

"That is correct," Phendran replied.

"That's a limiting design," Kincaid said.

"I think that's the point," Connor replied, regarding Phendran for a few seconds. "Do you know where they're taking the ship?"

"There are several places they could be taking it," Phendran began to say and then stopped speaking. Several messages appeared on his screen, and Connor couldn't quite make them out.

Connor looked at the other video feed that showed their ship. Several more escort vehicles had returned to it. "Can you slow them down?"

"Yeah," Noah said. "If those ships draw power from somewhere else, can it be disrupted?"

"Loremaster, I've determined the final destination of their ship. Making data available to you now," Kholva said. He'd been working from his own screen, hardly making a sound.

Phendran peered at the data, looking troubled. "Peculiar," he said and turned toward Connor. "The facility is near where Salpheth is located."

Connor's gaze narrowed. "That can't be a coincidence."

"No, it's not."

"It'll be even more heavily guarded than this," Connor said. "We have to slow them down. Give us a chance to reach the ship."

"What do you intend to do after that?"

Connor stared at him for a moment. "Leave. We return to our ship and then we leave."

"But the airtugs will not let you go," Phendran said.

"I think I have a solution for that," Noah said.

Connor held up his hand. "Hold that thought," he said and looked at Phendran, raising his eyebrows. "Salpheth?"

"I'm not sure," Phendran said.

"He wants the ship. Can you tell if he's being moved?"

"That's impossible," Phendran said.

"Oh yeah? Then why is our ship being taken to him right now? This isn't what you expected. There is more going on here than we were led to believe." Connor gestured toward the video feed. "This only makes sense if Salpheth is trying to escape. And he must have support, which means there will also be those willing to stop him at all costs."

Kincaid leaned forward. "He means us losing our ship." There was a dangerous edge to his voice.

Phendran blinked, his eyes darting to each of them, and then he turned back to his console.

Kincaid began to speak.

"Give him a chance to work," Connor said.

"This is spiraling out of control. We have to—"

Connor leaned toward him. "Listen to me," he said quietly. "We were never in control. The only thing we can do is influence what we can. I don't see a way for us to reach the ship without their help. Do you?"

Kincaid considered for a few moments, looking troubled. Then he shook his head in short jerks.

"I'm sorry, sir."

Connor glanced at the back of his glove where the Saruvian robot was. It glowed for a moment and then became dull. He looked at Phendran. "If Salpheth were being moved, wouldn't someone be alerted?"

"Not if he had help. The Dedicated in charge of him might not be aware of it. I'm trying to confirm his location," Phendran said.

"What about slowing down the airtugs?"

Phendran looked at Kholva. "See to it. Decrease power draw, but don't cut them off completely."

Connor approved. If they just slowed them down but still kept moving, it wouldn't arouse suspicions until it was too late.

"Salpheth is being transported," Phendran said.

Connor considered this for a moment and then nodded slowly. This whole thing was being coordinated, and they'd been one step behind this entire time. He felt like something slithered inside his stomach, and he looked at the video feed.

"The armed aircars," Connor said. "Who's in charge of them?"

Phendran frowned and didn't reply.

"If they're on the opposing side, they could just fire their weapons on the ship. If they destroy it, Salpheth can't escape."

Moments after he said it, several of the ships banked away from the *Pathfinder*.

"I have to warn them!" Phendran said.

Connor watched with gritted teeth as the alien attack ships were about to attack the *Pathfinder*.

CHAPTER 26

Phendran spoke so rapidly into his comlink that by the time the translation came through, Connor and the others were barely able to keep up. The remaining armed escort ships hadn't moved, but they must've noticed what happened.

"We have to help them. Does this ship have any weapons?" Connor asked, looking around, trying to find anything that could be considered a weapons system.

Phendran kept speaking on the comlink, but Kholva looked at him.

"This ship isn't equipped with any weapons capabilities. It's a stealth transport ship."

"How about speed? Can it keep up with those ships? Will they fire on us when we reach them?" Connor asked.

Kholva looked uncertain and glanced at Phendran.

Something must've kicked the pilots in the remaining escort ships into gear because they changed their formation, rotating around the *Pathfinder*, putting themselves into the path of the oncoming ships. Three of the ships darted toward the others, firing some kind of green energy lance. The other fighters rolled out of the way, altering course, then returned fire. The ships and the weapons were fast.

"I can barely track them," Noah said.

"I know, it's hard. They're agile," Connor replied.

"The battle steel hull of the *Pathfinder* should give them some protection against those weapons," Noah said.

Green energy lances found their mark on the escort ships, and the pilots had to maintain the angle to penetrate the hull of the other ships. Connor was able to spot where they concentrated their fire. They sought to disable rather than destroy, which gave him more insight into the Aczar. How long before the tactics changed?

Connor tried to think of a way they could reach the *Pathfinder*, sneak aboard, and escape. The escort ships needed to be neutralized. As soon as they engaged the *Pathfinder*'s engines, they would turn their weapons on them, and they didn't have a means to defend themselves from the onslaught.

"The airtugs are slowing down," Kincaid said.

Phendran had become quiet, and Connor thought he looked frustrated.

"What is it?" Connor asked.

Phendran studied the video feed of the attack with a pained expression, and Connor understood.

Kincaid leaned toward Connor. "What's going on? Why isn't he doing something?"

"He *is* doing something," Noah replied. "I just can't figure out what it is."

Connor studied the screen, and the energy lances seemed to be firing with increased intensity. Several ships had crashed.

Connor looked at Noah and the others, knowing what they were witnessing. "This is the beginning of a war."

Noah blinked. “Are you saying we’re the catalyst of a civil war among these people?”

Connor nodded and looked at Phendran. “That’s it, isn’t it? This is the beginning of it.”

Phendran lifted his gaze toward him, resigned. “We only sought to break Salpheth’s hold on us. Decrease his influence. It has been slow going, but everything has accelerated. Now it’s growing out of control.”

Phendran glanced at the other Aczar on the ship, looking regretful, and Connor understood. Phendran had the look of someone who understood the cost that such wide-sweeping change would have on this generation and the generations to come. It was something he’d had to live with, as well. Wars had a way of going far beyond the best of intentions, taking on a life of their own.

“It’s not too late,” Connor said. “We can stop Salpheth.”

“How can we do that?” Phendran asked, then shook his head. “You don’t understand what he’s capable of. What he’ll do.”

“He can’t escape if we remove the means of his escape. We need to reach the ship before him. If you can give me some time, we can get our ship out of here. Then you can deal with Salpheth however you see fit.”

Phendran considered this for a few moments. “But the Phantoms who sent you here. They had a purpose. They wanted our species to meet.”

Connor considered that for a few seconds, and the others waited. “One thing at a time.”

“There is wisdom in what you say. I just don’t see a way forward, and that is unsettling. Even now, Salpheth makes his way to your ship.”

Noah blew out a breath. "It's the Infinity Drive. That's what he wants."

"The fact that he wants your ship is obvious, but you've said that it is in need of repair. I fail to understand why Salpheth chooses to act now. If I can't figure that out, I can't hope to come up with a way to prevent him from achieving his objective," Phendran said.

"He intends to use the Infinity Drive," Connor said. "It's how we got here. He said he understood its uses better than we do."

"That's debatable," Noah said.

"Agreed, but he has something in mind for it. He's willing to risk everything to take it from us. We have to beat him to the ship," Connor said. The others looked at him, some with mild surprise. "We need to stop him."

Phendran looked up at him. "How do you intend to do that?"

"I'm not exactly sure." Conor said, and Phendran stared at him. "I don't have all the answers. I know we need to defend the ship from Salpheth and whoever is helping him."

"That would be the Khronax. They are a division of the Dedicated. Zealots for him," Phendran said.

"Zealots," Connor said. He'd seen fanatical loyalty among the Ovarrow, the Krake, and in their own history. "All the more reason for us to get back to the ship."

"But how will you stop them?" Phendran asked.

"We set a trap," Connor said. "He'll want to reach the ship intact, or his plan will fail. That gives us a window to reach the ship, too. We have defensive measures in place that will help."

Phendran's gaze narrowed. "What defensive measures?"

Connor gave him a hard look. "I thought you wanted to help us. We both want the same things. Help us return to the ship.

Kholva said that this ship has stealth capabilities. Can't you use that to get us there?"

Phendran's gaze slipped into a kind of calculation while he considered it. "Desperation motivates Salpheth to this course of action, and desperation is what drives our reaction."

The tension among them increased.

"Doing nothing is unacceptable," Connor said. He wasn't sure if Phendran's commitment to helping them was wavering. If it was, he'd have to take matters into his own hands.

Phendran gave him a knowing look, as if he'd anticipated his thoughts. "To your ship then. Without a plan."

Connor's muscles loosened a little. "We have a saying about the best laid plans. They sometimes go by the wayside."

Phendran frowned in thought for a second and then turned back to the controls.

Noah leaned toward Connor. "Good job. For a second there I thought he was going to backtrack."

Connor nodded. "Me too."

"What do you intend to do to stop Salpheth?" Noah asked.

Kincaid and Cassidy stared at him.

Seger lifted his rifle. "I say we shoot first and ask questions later."

"I agree," Kincaid said. "Especially after hearing about the Zealots. It makes me think they'll take out whoever gets in their way."

Connor nodded. He knew the others on the ship were preparing for boarders. They'd be armed, but none of them were soldiers. He looked at Kincaid and Seger for a second. The Aczars had subdued them before they'd had a chance to respond. He didn't know if their rifles would be able to stop them.

"Okay, listen up. This is what we're going to do," Connor said.

Kholva looked at them. "Excuse me, General Gates."

Connor looked at the young Aczar with raised eyebrows. "Yes?"

"We would like to help you," Kholva said, gesturing toward the others. "On your ship."

Connor wasn't sure what combat skills Kholva, or the others had, and his first instinct was to deny the request. Then he changed his mind. "Okay, you want to help, you can help, but you have to do as I tell you."

Kholva and the others considered it for a few moments. "That is acceptable. We will help in any way that we can, and perhaps bring to your attention ideas and capabilities that you might not be aware of. Please continue."

Connor glanced at Phendran, but he was busy flying the ship.

"Okay, this is what we'll do," Connor said and began laying out his plan to defend the ship.

CHAPTER 27

To the untrained eye, a battle was chaotic, but to Connor it was familiar. No matter how long it had been, it was as familiar to him as breathing, and it surprised him at how fast he adapted. He was older, and after surviving so much, he knew a few things about conflict. The untrained and inexperienced sought to bring order back into their worlds, but a battle was different. Some things could be controlled but not others. The best they could do was influence events. That was why Phendran had stumbled at the decision point of whether to continue helping them or not. Connor supposed this was the same or similar to other Aczars. They moved and thought quicker than people, but that had limitations he hoped to take advantage of when the time was right.

Phendran flew them low, almost hugging the treetops of the alien forest, which had something to do with how the Aczar tracked ships. They were racing to catch up to the *Pathfinder* and were almost there. Armed escort ships waged a battle nearby, while several armed ships maintained protective coverage of the *Pathfinder*.

"I'm unable to locate Salpheth," Phendran said. "My contacts indicate that he's switching modes of transport to evade detection. I believe he won't make a run for your ship until he's much closer."

"Understood," Connor said and looked at Noah. "What's the ETA of the shuttle?"

"Three minutes. Do you really think they'll fall for the same trick twice?"

"Maybe. They're more preoccupied now. My guess is that one side or the other will chase it. Regardless, it adds another layer to this, and the more distracted they are, the better the chance we'll have of reaching the ship," Connor said.

Sacrificing the shuttle wasn't his first choice, but he had little choice.

Phendran increased their velocity, and they rose into the air. Connor wanted a bird's-eye view of the ship before making their approach. He was playing a hunch about the way the Aczar thought. They'd gone to great lengths to inhibit their ability to travel off planet, so they tended to view threats in a linear fashion. Connor had faced enemies in just about every environment imaginable and sought to use every advantage he could to increase their chances of success.

An alarm flashed on one of the sub-windows, and Phendran quickly acknowledged it. "We've reached the limits of the direct power interface. We'll soon be out of range," he said.

"Understood," Connor said.

Once they passed out of range, the ship would go offline. Their trajectory took them in a wide arc that would put them in the vicinity of the *Pathfinder*. The Aczars' tracking capabilities were limited to power signatures. Once those were gone, they were essentially blind. With so many things happening at once, Connor thought their chances were better than average to pierce the defensive coverage of the armed escorts, and that required that they delay powering up their aircar until the last possible moment.

Connor glanced around the cabin. Everyone was tense but determined. When Connor explained his plan, Phendran and the Aczars with him had been shocked, but Noah and the others were quickly on board with it.

With the lack of power, the dampening field was offline, and they had to strap themselves to their chairs as best they could. The chairs were smaller, meant for the Aczars, and the seat restraints were meant for Aczars, too.

Kincaid and Seger made good use of their combat knives, cutting the straps so they could tie them together. It wasn't safe. If the ship crashed, they would be tossed about the cabin. Connor and Noah had multipurpose protection suits on under their EVA suits. It added some protection, but at the speeds they were going, a crash would overwhelm those protections as well. Phendran promised to avoid crashing the aircar.

Kincaid sat next to Cassidy and Seger sat on her other side. Both soldiers clung to her, forming a protective bubble.

Noah glanced at Connor. They sat on opposite sides of the cabin. He arched an eyebrow. "Want to get cozy?"

A shallow chuckle escaped Connor's lips. "Yeah, that would be a sight."

Noah glanced at Phendran for a second. "I'm glad he's at the controls. We need their reaction times if this is going to work."

Phendran assured them that he could get the power back on and perform the aerial maneuver that would take them precisely where they needed to go. They were contending with the pilots of the armed escort ships whose reaction times were similar to Phendran's.

Connor thought about his son, Ethan. He'd been an excellent Talon V pilot before choosing to command exploration ships for the Colonial Exploration Initiative. He could've handled this kind of stunt, but he'd rely on the fighter's computer systems to assist. Phendran was doing the same but relying on his Saruvian Robotic Assistant. Connor didn't completely understand what the robotic assistant was capable of, but they were something that all Aczars used. Humanity used artificial intelligence to assist with so many things, but there were always constraints in place. If the technology the Aczars used was heavily influenced by Salpheth, could it be trusted?

"I wish there was a way to stop Salpheth from even reaching the ship," Noah said.

"There isn't," Connor replied.

"I know, I just wish there was."

"Maybe if we had more time and more help, but this is too well-coordinated. He's got them all doing exactly what he wants them to."

Noah was quiet for a second and then said. "I guess that makes us the wild card in all this."

"He probably thinks he can outthink us as well, or the risk we pose is negligible. A lot of arrogance with him."

Noah looked away, then his eyes widened. "I think there's a way I can use that."

"How?"

Noah was about to reply when a sudden buildup of force pressed them into their seats. Without inertia dampeners, they were feeling the full effect as the aircar bulleted toward the ground.

Connor gritted his teeth and clenched his gut. He couldn't remember when he'd last eaten, but whatever was in his stomach sloshed around.

Noah groaned. "I'd forgotten what this is like. Oh, I might be sick."

"Tilt your head back and look up," Connor said.

Noah did and took several breaths. He shook his head. "This is the reason I stopped—" He bit back what he was going to say, glancing at Kincaid and the others. "So much for the living legends."

A chuckle bubbled up from Connor's chest and he rolled his eyes. "I'm glad I can count on you to focus on what's important."

Noah sighed with a grin, looking better.

Phendran shouted a warning, and the power came back on. The shock was so much that Connor felt it in his bones. One moment it felt as if he were bearing the weight of the world on his entire body, and then the pressure eased.

They'd purposefully overshot the *Pathfinder,* and Phendran swung the ship around. The CDF shuttle flew nearby and suddenly banked to the side.

"Stealth protocols have engaged," Phendran said.

The remaining armed escort ships flew toward the fleeing shuttle. Bright flashes came as they fired their energy lances at the ship. The shuttle managed to avoid fire for a few seconds, leading the ships farther away before it was tagged. Several lances pierced the hull and the rear engines. The shuttle quickly lost altitude and began a violent roll.

Connor lost sight of the shuttle and watched as they approached the ship. Phendran increased their velocity, and they swooped down, flying underneath the ship. He decreased the velocity as they approached a maintenance hatch. They were within the gravitational field put forth by the airtugs that still carried the ship.

"Another ship approaches on the other side of the

Pathfinder," Phendran said. "It's a stealth transport like this one, only bigger. It has to be Salpheth."

Phendran deployed some kind of locking clamps that attached to the *Pathfinder*'s hull. Connor untied his straps and helped the others.

"The atmosphere on the ship differs from on your planet," Connor said.

"It won't be a problem," Phendran replied.

Metallic pieces of their clothing began to glow, then gathered near their necks. A silver faceplate formed and glowed in a pale green along the edges, illuminating their brownish hair. "This will enable us to survive in your ship's environment," Phendran said.

Kincaid and Seger stepped out of the aircar first and checked the area, then Connor followed.

As soon as Connor was out of the aircar, several comlinks connected at the same time. They stood on the hull of the ship and Kincaid already had the maintenance hatch open.

"Comms are back," Noah said.

Phendran and the others followed them.

"General Gates," Naya Corman said, her voice coming over comms, sounding relieved.

"We're back. I'm glad you got the message because we don't have a lot of time. Hostile forces are inbound," Connor said and proceeded to fill her in.

Once they were inside the ship, Noah came over to him. "I need to get to the I-Drive."

"What are you going to do?" Connor asked.

"I think I can set a trap for Salpheth, if he makes it that far," Noah said.

Phendran looked up at him. "Salpheth can track energy

sources. He'll make his way to the single highest power draw on the ship, which I presume to be this I-Drive."

Noah nodded and looked at Connor. "Just slow him down and give me time to get things set up."

"You still haven't told me what you're going to do," Connor said, not liking how vague Noah was being.

"I think I can use the drive core to either trap him or send him away, but I can't do it from here," Noah said as he backed down the corridor.

Connor gave him a nod. "Do you need help?"

Noah smiled. "Yeah, but you need it more. I'll be fine." He turned and ran down the corridor at an all-out run.

Connor gestured for the others to come closer.

"General Gates, we can come to you," Naya said.

She was on the bridge with Glen Rhodes and the other civilians.

"Negative, stay on the bridge. You can help me from there. I have things I need you to do, so stand by," Connor said.

"One more thing, General Gates," Naya said. "We've observed the decreased velocity of the airtugs. There is chance that we could use our engines to break free of them."

"Understood," Connor replied. He'd hoped this was true and looked at Phendran.

"Without knowing the capabilities of your ship's engines, it's impossible for me to predict whether this is true."

"Okay," Connor said. He wouldn't rule it out, but he doubted the Aczars would simply watch them escape, especially if Salpheth was aboard.

Two men came down the corridor, and Connor recognized Mac and Tim Hopper. Both were armed with AR-74s.

"I'm not going to the bridge, Tyler, so stop telling me to," Cassidy said.

Jorath looked at her. "Please, you'll be safer there with the others."

Cassidy shook her head and looked at Connor. "Please, General, I can help you. There aren't enough of us to make a stand."

Connor removed his helmet and EVA suit, stowing it at the recharging base. He regarded Cassidy for a moment. There was fear and fierce determination in her gaze, and she wasn't wrong. She'd kept a level head throughout this entire ordeal, and he doubted she'd freeze up at the first sign of battle. "You can help, but you'll do exactly as I say. Captain Kincaid is my second, so if he gives any of you a command, you'll follow it without question. Understood?"

Connor's gaze swept over the others, including them in his assertion. Something unspoken passed between Kincaid and Jorath. Cassidy would be looked after whether she wanted it or not.

"Okay, we're going to split up into teams. Kincaid, you take Cass and Jorath and hold the position in corridor 3B. The objective is to slow them down. Fall back as needed and we'll meet up at the drive core," Connor said and looked at Seger. "Sergeant, you take Rabsaris and Hopper and cover corridor 7J. Mac, you're with me, along with Phendran and the others."

He intended to funnel the enemy toward him, and both Kincaid and Seger knew it.

"Understood, General," Kincaid said and gestured for the others to follow him away.

Seger was only a few steps behind, heading off in a different direction.

Mac glanced at the Aczars for a second and then at Connor. "Made some new friends?"

"And some enemies. Come on," Connor said.

He led Mac down the corridor, going across the ship.

Mac looked at Connor. "Are they even armed?"

"We can defend ourselves," Phendran said.

"If you say so," Mac said, and looked at Connor. "How do you know where they'll board from?"

"Because I opened the vehicle bay doors," Connor said.

Mac blinked. "And you think they'll just take the bait?"

Connor nodded. "They think they're superior," he said and quickly filled Mac in about Salpheth.

"General, there is some kind of interference with our sensors at the vehicle bay," Naya said.

"Understood. Close all the doors between us and them," Connor said.

Rabsaris activated his comlink. "General, I've got several mid-sized maintenance drones in that area. They might be able to slow them down."

Connor lifted his wrist computer and brought up the video feed from the corridor near the vehicle bay. A bright flash came from the vehicle bay doors and eight Aczars entered the corridor. Metallic bands on their wrists were glowing. Hovering behind them was an energy field with Salpheth in the middle. There was something else in there with him, but Connor couldn't get a good look at what it was.

The Zealots raced to the maintenance drones and attacked, splitting them into pieces. The drones hadn't even moved and just fell to the floor. Connor hadn't seen how they'd attacked.

Mac muttered a curse and looked at Connor with wide eyes.

The others on the team channel became quiet. They'd all seen what had happened. They'd need to keep their distance and engage them from afar.

The Zealots approached one of the doors and used their

Saruvian Robotic Assistant to force the door open. It barely slowed them down.

There was something about the containment field for Salpheth that interfered with the video feed, causing it to cut out.

Connor and the others reached the corridor that led to the drive core and main engineering. He hoped that whatever trap Noah was cooking up would work.

"They're coming up on your location, Captain," Connor said.

"Understood, sir," Kincaid replied. "We're in position."

They were down an adjacent corridor. Kincaid and Jorath took up a position on either side and waited for the first of the Zealots to pass by. One of them peered down the corridor and then moved on.

Kincaid waited until Salpheth came into view and fired his weapon. Super hardened alloy darts hit the energy field. Bright blotches mushroomed across the field, and it moved to the side, bouncing off the wall.

The Zealots threw themselves into view, blocking the way for a few seconds. Kincaid kept firing his weapon and a Zealot fell to the deck, wounded. Then the others raced down the corridor toward Kincaid and the others. Metallic legs spread from their backs, propelling them along the walls and ceiling faster than the Aczars could ever run. Both Kincaid and Jorath fired their weapons at full auto. Several of the metallic legs broke away, causing the Zealots to stumble, but they still came.

Kincaid yelled for the others to fall back, and they retreated down the corridor, closing the doors as they went. The chase was on.

Mac blew out a long breath. "If they catch up to them…"

Connor peered at the wounded Zealots in the corridor. They

weren't dead. He looked at Phendran. "What's happening to them?"

"They're bodies are being repaired. Emergency medical treatment is being rendered. As long as their critical systems are undamaged, they will survive, but it will take some time."

The remaining Zealots formed a tighter perimeter around Salpheth's containment field and then slowed down.

Connor pursed his lips in thought. "I've got an idea."

CHAPTER 28

"NAYA," Connor said. "I need you to be ready to increase power to the artificial gravity fields on my command."

"I can do that, sir, but I can only cover short sections at a time. Noah is charging the drive core, and we're limited by the power core's capacity. How much power do you need me to divert to it?" Naya asked.

"As much as you can. Stand by," Connor said. "Sergeant, they're making their way to you."

"Understood, General. We'll be ready," Seger replied.

By the time Salpheth and his Zealots reached the corridor Seger and his team were covering, they didn't take the bait. Instead, they hastened past and didn't engage at all.

"They won't fall for it this time, General," Seger said. "Want me to pursue them?"

"Keep a safe distance and follow, then wait for my orders," Connor replied.

He'd wondered how fast the Zealots would adapt. There were a few main corridors that went the length of the ship. Salpheth directed his Zealots into a robotics repair station. Connor couldn't be sure how they communicated. The Zealots spread out, leaving a path for Salpheth.

He watched as a bright burst of energy came from the containment field, leaving a giant hole through the wall and the equipment beyond.

"Walls can't stop these things?" Mac asked.

"Evidently not," Connor said.

Phendran peered at the video feed and looked up at Connor. "He's taking the most direct path to the drive core."

Connor considered diverting the power, wondering if Salpheth would blindly follow it.

"General, the invaders are taking out entire systems at a time. It's limited my abilities here on the bridge," Naya said.

"Understood. Pass systems control to me for this sector," Connor said.

A new menu of items appeared on his wrist computer, and Connor minimized it. He peered down the length of the corridor, waiting, then looked at the others. "When they reach the corridor, we'll attack."

Phendran eyed him for a moment. "They'll expect it."

"We only need to slow them down to give Noah the time he needs."

Phendran nodded. "We'll engage the Zealots. I might be able to take control of the containment field."

Connor frowned. "How?"

"It has to be that one of the Zealots with Salpheth is maintaining the field. It'll be difficult to get close enough."

If Phendran could take control of the containment field and disable it, that would give Connor the opportunity he needed to take out Salpheth once and for all.

A bright flash came from the end of the corridor, and the temperature in the area surged.

Connor brought up his rifle and fired a three-round burst. The first Zealot sank to the deck, not moving. Connor quickly aimed for the nearest and fired again. The Zealot he aimed for this time jerked out of the way much faster than Connor had anticipated. Other Zealots burst through the opening and raced down the corridor.

Connor took cover while Mac continued to fire his weapon. Phendran and the other Aczars waited.

"Whatever you're going to do, do it fast!" Mac shouted. "Slippery bastards."

Connor brought up the control interface for the support systems in the area and increased the artificial gravity field in the corridor. The Zealots racing toward them stumbled to the deck. Their Saruvian Robotic Assistants tried to heave them back up, but the field was too strong. The power required was immense and couldn't be maintained for long.

"Now!" Connor shouted.

He spun from cover and unleashed a barrage of heavy fire from his weapon. Mac joined him. They had to compensate for the gravity field as it exerted tremendous forces on anything in range, which included the high-density darts being shot from their weapons.

Salpheth emerged from the hole, the energy containment field blackening the surrounding walls. Connor fired his weapon and blotches of light mushroomed for mere moments, but nothing penetrated the field. The bodies of the Zealots were locked into place on the deck, and Salpheth took in the sight.

The power cut off in the corridor, and the only light came from Salpheth's containment field. The surviving Zealots stirred, but Salpheth raced past them, and the containment field shoved them out of the way. Bolts of golden energy lanced toward the walls, racing toward Connor and the others.

Phendran pulled Connor out of the way as Salpheth blurred past them. Connor stumbled as heat stole the breath from his lungs, making him gasp.

"The field is unstable!" Phendran warned.

Connor raced to the door and peered down the corridor. Mac was regaining his feet from across the way and looked no worse for wear. Connor spun toward the drive core and ran.

The energy field was almost too bright for him to look at. He tried to spot the Zealot who was maintaining the field but didn't see one. Could Phendran have been wrong about that?

Connor heard weapons firing from farther down the corridor behind them but had to ignore it. Salpheth must be stopped. If he destroyed the I-Drive, they'd be stranded here for a very long time.

The wide doors to the drive core were already open and Salpheth was inside. The power to the area returned as Connor ran toward the doors. Phendran and Kholva raced past him and beat him inside.

Connor went through the doors and saw Noah pinned against the wall by one of the Zealots. The Zealot appeared unconscious, but the robotic assistant pinned Noah in place.

Noah looked at Connor, eyes wide, and then at Salpheth.

Phendran stood outside the containment field. Salpheth and one of the Zealots were inside it. The Aczar was within its own individual field and looked to be unconscious.

Salpheth ignored them and stood gazing at the drive core, studying it.

Kholva stood next to Phendran, and they both thrust their hands, which were covered with glistening metallic gloves, into the energy field and seized the Zealot inside. Metallic legs extended from their backs and heaved. The Zealot was pulled from the containment field and Salpheth spun toward them. The Phantom pushed out with his hands and a torrent of energy expanded toward them. Phendran and Kholva were shoved back and violently hit the wall. Connor dove to the deck, narrowly avoiding the energy field.

The deck began to shake, and the shaking spread to the entire area. Salpheth looked around in surprise.

Naya must have engaged the engines in a last-ditch effort to escape the Aczar. The *Pathfinder*'s engines were straining against the gravitational fields used by the airtugs. The colossal forces could tear the ship apart.

Connor looked up and saw something move in his peripheral vision. He pushed to his feet and saw Salpheth phase through the drive core's containment field. The Infinity Drive core was a black sphere about the size of a combat shuttle. Since the charging process had begun, waves of deep purplish energy washed over. Salpheth hovered near it as a being of light and shadow. Then he extended his arms toward it.

"Connor!" Noah called out to him.

He turned toward Noah and started toward him. A loud screeching scream came from the core.

"You have to engage the drive. It's the only way," Noah said.

Connor's eyes widened.

Alerts appeared on the nearby holoscreens, warning of a huge power surge. Salpheth's containment field spread away from him, beginning to envelope the drive core.

Connor looked at Noah. "Where will it take us?"

Salpheth began bellowing in triumph.

"Not us. *Him!*"

Understanding blazed a path in Connor's mind. He raced toward the workstation and brought up the protocols for the

Infinity Drive, hesitating. All the alerts warned him against exactly what he was about to do. He looked at the drive core. The large black sphere wobbled, as if it was coming out of alignment. If he overloaded the core, he could kill Salpheth using the Phantom's energy against him, but if he engaged it… He peered at the protocols Noah had set up. There were too many of them and it was all too complex. If he did this, they might never escape, but he trusted Noah.

He gritted his teeth and engaged the Infinity Drive.

The ship shuddered violently, and Connor saw a fierce bright light within the drive core. There were two equal portions of light and darkness, both blinding in their own ways. Then, a deep basso groan that sounded like a great behemoth emanated from the entire core.

Salpheth spun toward Connor, his hand extended accusingly. Connor braced for some kind of impact, but then something latched onto Salpheth, pulling him away. The remnants of Salpheth's containment field shredded, taking the Phantom with it as it was sucked into the Infinity Drive. The core spun wildly for a long moment, then seemed to right itself as if whatever was interfering with it were suddenly gone. Then the drive powered down.

Phendran raced to Connor's side, eyes wide as he stared into the drive core. "What happened to him?"

The ship shuddered with increasing intensity. Connor wobbled on his feet as he sought to regain his balance.

Kholva went to help Noah, who had fallen to the deck. The Zealot who'd been holding Noah in place had run out of whatever powered his robotic assistant, and he was dead.

Klaxon alarms blared from overhead. Connor moved to the nearest workstation and opened a comlink to the bridge.

"General, they're attacking the ship," Naya said.

Noah came to his side and brought up a holoscreen.

Phendran looked up at Connor. "They believe Salpheth is on this ship."

Connor frowned while he considered his options. "Naya, are we able to break free of the airtugs?"

Naya blew out a frustrated breath. "Unclear, General. It could go either way," she replied, her voice sounding strained. "Sir, what do you want me to do?"

Connor clenched his jaw. The Aczars were firing their weapons on his ship, and they couldn't fire back. He gave a slight, frustrated shake of his head. "Power down the engines. Do it now," he said and looked at Phendran. "Can you get them to stop firing on our ship?"

Phendran blinked in surprise. "You're surrendering?"

Some of the others had made it to the drive core.

Captain Kincaid regarded him in disbelief. "Sir?"

Every fighting instinct in him demanded that he not surrender, at least until he'd seen the barrage of alerts on Noah's holoscreen. He might console himself later that he'd thought of it as a strategic retreat, but that would've been a lie. Even if they broke free of the airtugs and outran the armed escort ships, where would they go? They couldn't make their repairs any better now than they could before, and they were likely in worse shape than they'd been before.

Something almost broke inside him as he faced an uncertain future. The only way they survived with a real chance of getting home was to surrender to the Aczars.

Connor looked at Phendran. "Yes, we're surrendering. Tell them we will cooperate."

Phendran gave him an appraising look. "And Salpheth?"

Connor glanced at Noah, who was stone-faced. "He's gone."

"Perhaps I will delay in sharing that information. It'll give them a reason to cooperate," Phendran replied.

Connor's eyebrows raised in surprise. "Are you sure about that?"

"General Gates, I promised I would assist you. As I see it, nothing has changed about that. Please allow me access to your communication systems so that I might send them a message."

"I've got it," Noah said and gestured toward his workstation.

Kincaid stared at him for a second. "Do you have any orders for me, General?"

Connor blew out a long breath, feeling tired and frustrated. They were looking to him to lead them. He'd been in that role for so long that he'd gotten used it, but there were times when it might've been nice to let someone else lead for a while.

He pushed those thoughts away. They were the thoughts of someone who was exhausted, and he didn't have time for it.

"We need to secure the prisoners. Assuming there are prisoners?" Connor asked.

"I will come with you," Kholva said.

"There are some. Seger is covering them from a distance," Kincaid said.

Connor turned toward Phendran and waited.

The Aczar turned from the communications interface. "They won't attack as long as you allow the airtugs to bring you in."

"To destroy our ship?"

"I don't think so," Phendran said. "At least not yet. I'm afraid that's the best I can do at this moment. There has been a great upheaval, and there are many who seek answers."

Salpheth was gone, but they were still living by the moment, and their future was uncertain.

CHAPTER 29

THE ACZAR WERE adept at hollowing out space underground and inside mountains, and they moved the *Pathfinder* to another underground space. It had been five days since they'd first arrived, and Connor still wasn't sure what to expect. His meetings with the Aczar Ruling Council liaison made him feel like he was being kept in the dark as to their intentions, and those intentions seemed to change. Phendran assured him that bringing the ship to this place was for their protection. It was essentially a large warehouse for holding material and wasn't the processing plant they would use to dismantle the ship.

After the initial shock of the recent events had worn off, the crew of the *Pathfinder* got some much-needed rest, but as time passed, Connor and the other survivors became restless. The bodies of the Zealots had been retrieved, along with the prisoners. Phendran had left them, but communication protocols had been given to them to contact an Aczar liaison named Khetis.

The Aczars appeared preoccupied with the fallout that was making its way through their population at the loss of

Salpheth. Many Aczars viewed the Phantom as some kind of spiritual leader. Once Phendran had convinced them that Salpheth was no longer on the *Pathfinder*, the leader of the Dedicated began to search elsewhere for the Phantom. They believed that the Khronax faction had taken him somewhere. There was also a reformist faction that had been brought to the forefront and was negotiating with the other Aczar factions.

Connor had shared what happened with the liaison, Khetis, and given a statement about his encounter with the Phantoms. His testimony had Phendran's support. Then it seemed that the Aczar Ruling Council had shifted its attention elsewhere, which left Connor and the others in limbo.

The Dedicated had given them strict instructions to remain aboard their ship, and various plants and protein sources for the ship's food processors had been given to them so they wouldn't starve.

The door to Connor's quarters chimed, and he answered it.

"Good morning, General," Rabsaris said.

Connor waved him inside, and they sat at a small table.

"I found some more areas of the hull that have been repaired," Rabsaris said, excitedly. "Not just repaired. The workmanship is beyond the specs for when the ship was first built."

Connor frowned. "Are you sure?"

He nodded. "I looked up the specifications myself and compared them to what the drones found. We've got an unknown benefactor who's helping to repair the ship, but I can't figure out when the work is actually being done. Are you sure this wasn't arranged by Phendran or someone else?"

Connor shook his head. "I haven't spoken to Phendran in days. The only contact I've had with the Aczars is with Khetis." He had to keep the frustration from his voice. Khetis wasn't forthcoming with any information and seemed to take their requests with extreme reluctance.

"Regardless, most of the exterior damage in the battle has been repaired."

"What about the internal damage?" Connor asked.

Rabsaris snorted. "Ongoing. That tends to happen when walls are completely burned through by some kind of high-energy weapon. It's remarkable that the damage hadn't spread."

Connor stood. "I think that was his intent."

Rabsaris frowned. "I don't understand."

Connor stood and opened the door, and Rabsaris joined him in the corridor. "Salpheth wasn't trying to destroy the ship, at least not yet. He needed to use the I-Drive."

Rabsaris pursed his lips in thought. "I'm better at fixing things. I'm afraid I can't offer you much in the way of knowledge about the I-Drive. I can tell you that the power core has stabilized. We're running at about sixty percent capacity, and that won't change unless we get a new core. We've been engineering bypasses to get critical systems back online."

"The new core is back-ordered," Connor said.

"Like a lot of things. Also, we've been making use of the materials gathered before everything went…well, you know."

"That's good. How about the engines?"

"Aside from the extreme stress they were under from trying to break free of those airtugs, they're going to be fine. If there wasn't a mountain above us, I'd say we could fly out of here in a day or so."

That was good news.

"Understood. Thanks for the update," Connor said.

Rabsaris left him, and Connor headed to the bridge, meeting Naya and Noah on the way.

"Still waiting on the diagnostic to finish. Salpheth really messed things up," Noah said.

Connor knew that both Noah and Naya had been going over the Infinity Drive from top to bottom. No one knew how the I-Drive worked better than Noah, which was one of the benefits of being its inventor.

"Still no idea where Salpheth went?" Connor asked.

It hadn't come up yet, but it was only a matter of time before the Aczar pressed them for that information once they accepted that the I-Drive had sent Salpheth away.

"Not exactly," Noah said, and Connor frowned. The answer hadn't changed since the event. "I know you hate that," Noah continued with a guilty shrug. "It doesn't appear that the drive used the coordinates I specified. If it had, I would've been able to determine that from the logs."

"I know. I engaged the drive. Could he have done something to it?"

Noah frowned doubtfully. "We've talked about this before. I don't see what he could've done. You said he looked shocked, so wherever he went, it was a surprise to him."

"I'm glad he's gone," Naya said. "I say we leave well enough alone."

"Agreed," Noah said and palmed the door controls for the bridge. "I'm still seeing occasional power fluctuations from the main power core."

As they entered the bridge, Connor asked, "What do you think is causing them?"

Noah chuckled a little and his gaze rose to the ceiling for a moment. "Aside from the fact that the core was due to be replaced, degradation of the core itself, the containment area, and the lack of high-grade materials to effectively recycle it are all top of my list."

Connor arched an eyebrow. "So, it's old."

He nodded. "It's old."

Rhodes entered the bridge and joined them.

"I'm glad you're here," Connor said to him. He had a daily check-in with the Aczar, and he didn't want to be late.

Rhodes smiled a little. "I'm glad I could help."

He'd asked Rhodes to observe his meetings with Khetis. Despite their differences, Rhodes was excellent at reading the undertones of communication, whether it be written or spoken. This was probably why he'd risen so high within the Colonial Requisitions Department.

A video comlink request came in, and Naya put it on the main holoscreen.

Khetis, the Aczar liaison, peered into the camera. He had fine, light-brown hair that covered his entire face. The hair of his snout was a lighter tone, indicating his age. His dark eyes were wide set and stared intently.

Connor saw that the collar of Khetis's shirt was metallic, which was part of his Saruvian assistant.

"General Gates, I offer greetings on behalf of the ruling council of the Aczar."

"Thank you, Khetis. I, too, offer greetings both to you and the ruling council," Connor replied and introduced the others.

The meetings always began the same way, and at this point, their greetings were a bit tedious. The Aczar were sticklers for observing formal address. It made Connor wonder how much of that extended throughout the entire species—not that he was a stranger to formal proceedings, but eventually, when it was just a small group, a certain amount of informal communication was to be expected.

Khetis's opening questions inquired as to their wellbeing and the status of the people on the ship. It was more of a formality than a genuine inquiry as to their actual wellbeing.

"Honestly, we're getting tired of the view," Connor said, forgoing his normal response.

Khetis tipped his head to the side. "As you've already been informed, this location is for your protection."

"We appreciate it. We've also cooperated with you, but at some point, I would like an answer to our request to leave the planet," Connor replied.

"The data provided about your Confederation is being discussed among our leaders. However, we have other pertinent efforts that require our immediate attention."

"Okay, and not to sound unreasonable, but how long do you intend to keep us here?"

"General Gates, we requested that you remain with your ship. It's safer for us all if these conditions remain."

Connor regarded the liaison for a long moment. "Have you located Salpheth?"

"We have not," Khetis replied and paused for a moment. "I do not believe you appreciate the current struggles your presence is causing. As you are aware, space travel is forbidden to the Aczar, as is the development of technology that encourages those endeavors."

"I'm aware of your laws concerning space travel. But we were unaware of those laws when we came here. As I already told you, we hadn't detected your species at all, so how can we have caused any offense when your species goes to such lengths to conceal its presence?"

Khetis blinked, and his head twitched to the side a little.

Connor couldn't be sure what was having the biggest impact on the Aczars—the fact that Salpheth was missing or that they'd been visited by an alien species.

Khetis looked away from the camera for a moment. "General Gates, I've been asked to convey a request about your ship. We'd like to understand how it operates, particularly the device you call the Infinity Drive. We've been made aware that Salpheth was intrigued by it, therefore it warrants our attention."

Connor considered this for a few seconds. "We've shared information about our ship. The feedback you gave us was that you didn't believe the I-Drive sent Salpheth anywhere."

"That is still our assessment. Our experience with Salpheth is greater than yours. He represents an ascended species whose achievements are overwhelmingly superior to ours. This also makes him cunning and on the run."

Connor stared at him intently. "In other words, you've lost your prisoner and now have become desperate enough to consider alternative explanations." He paused for a moment, and Khetis didn't reply. "I'd like to speak to Phendran. He had a better understanding about Salpheth than you do."

"Loremaster Phendran is unavailable."

"For how long? When will be available?"

"I don't have this information."

"Can you get that information?"

Khetis gave him an oblique look. "I will convey your request."

"You've said that before, but nothing ever comes of it," Connor said.

The others on the bridge became still. This was the hardest Connor had pushed Khetis for answers.

"What about our request for more information about your ship?"

Connor leveled his gaze at him. "I'll consider it."

Khetis's gaze narrowed, then he tipped his head to the side and severed the comlink.

Connor shook his head and sighed. He turned to the others. "This isn't getting us anywhere."

Rhodes pursed his lips. "Oh, I don't know about that."

"What do you mean?"

"I think they're running out of options. Like you said, they can't locate Salpheth. That has to be putting tremendous pressure on them," Rhodes said.

Noah nodded. "They all but worshiped Salpheth, even though they kept him as a prisoner. They didn't keep it a secret either."

"I don't know about that," Connor said. "Yes, they revered Salpheth, but as to what the general public knows about it is beyond us."

"And now they're curious about the I-Drive," Noah said.

Rhodes nodded. "That is a major concern."

A comlink chimed on Connor's wrist computer.

"General," Kincaid said, "There's something you should see here near the port airlock."

"What's happening?" Connor asked.

"Part of the EVA suit you were using is glowing."

Connor frowned, and the others became quiet.

"I'm on my way."

They left the bridge, making their way to the airlock.

"Why would your EVA suit be glowing?" Rhodes asked.

Connor began to shrug, and then his eyes widened. He looked at Noah.

"I thought Phendran took it with him," Noah said.

Rhodes looked at both of them expectantly, eyebrows raised.

"I was given a piece of their technology in case we got separated so we wouldn't be trapped. I completely forgot about it. I thought Phendran had taken it back, too," Connor said.

Since they'd been restricted to the ship, they hadn't used their

EVA suits. The last time he'd seen it was when he returned it to the charging cradle.

"That can't be a coincidence," Rhodes said.

Connor considered it for a moment. "You're right."

"I don't understand," Naya said.

"Why do I feel like someone is about to squeeze the trigger, and we're caught in the crosshairs," Noah said and then looked at Naya. "Connor presses Khetis for answers and they respond by requesting more information about our ship. Then the piece of their SRA that was left behind suddenly starts glowing. It's quite a bit more than a coincidence."

Naya frowned. "SRA?"

"Saruvian Robotic Assistant. I think it was named for the inventor of the technology. I had to give it an acronym just to speed things up," Noah replied. Then he arched an eyebrow. "Maybe we should rename the Infinity Drive."

Rhodes frowned, and Connor rolled his eyes, shaking his head.

Noah smiled, pointing at him. "You didn't think I was serious, did you?"

Connor stared at him for a long moment as they walked down the corridor and then shrugged. "I wouldn't be surprised. I mean, you *do* crave constant attention."

Noah's mouth hung open, shocked. Then he snorted, and Connor grinned.

They made their way to the airlock. Kincaid and Cassidy were just outside.

"What happened?" Connor asked.

"I had everyone clear the area. It just started glowing. I didn't touch it," Kincaid said.

Connor peered inside the room. A dull greenish glow reflected off the wall behind an EVA suit.

Connor moved to step inside and Rhodes grabbed his arm.

"Are you sure about this?" he asked.

"Phendran gave it to me. I doubt he'd do that if he thought it was dangerous."

"Yeah, but what if it's not from Phendran? What it's from one of those Khronax?" Rhodes asked.

Connor stopped in mid-stride and gave Rhodes an appraising look.

Rhodes shrugged. "I'm just saying."

Kincaid blew out a breath and looked at Connor. "He's got a point, sir. I should check it."

Connor shook his head. "No," he said. Kincaid began to protest. "No! It's not them. They were nowhere near this ship. We went through all the areas the Khronax had been and didn't find anything. Furthermore, Phendran and the others investigated those areas and were satisfied that nothing had been left behind. This is a piece of his SRA."

"Understood, sir," Kincaid replied.

Connor stepped into the room and walked to the station where his EVA suit was located. The others also stepped inside but kept their distance. Kincaid had his sidearm out and ready in case it was needed.

Connor tapped the controls, and the cradle holding the EVA suit lifted. The suit slowly spun toward him, displaying a medallion-size medal on its chest. The edges slowly pulsed in a pale green light, as if it was on standby. He was reminded of early rules he'd instilled in the soldiers who explored alien ruins with advanced technology—look, but don't touch. It had saved lives, and now he was about to do the opposite. Phendran had assured him it would be safe.

Connor reached out toward the metallic disc, and it flared to life. A ripple crossed the metal, and part of it reached toward his hand. It was cold to the touch but soon warmed as it snaked around his wrist, becoming the metallic band he'd seen other Aczars wearing.

Connor peered at it, and the pulsing light quickened. Several symbols appeared on top of it and then changed to English.

They won't let you leave. Prepare yourselves.

Connor's mouth hung open a little, and the others came over. They read the message and silence grabbed hold of them.

"Don't all speak at once," Connor said, breaking the silence.

Noah pressed his lips together for a second. "He's warning us."

"Who?" Rhodes asked.

"Phendran," Connor said. "We've got to figure out a way to leave."

"Sir," Kincaid said, and Connor looked at him. "This could be a trap. Someone could've sent this message to get us to do something drastic, which gives them an excuse to justify doing whatever they want."

Connor didn't reply right away, choosing to consider what Kincaid had said. "That's true. Someone could be manipulating us, but that possibility doesn't change the fact that we need to figure out a way to escape." He glanced at the others for a moment. "It's better if we exercise our own fate, rather than allowing someone else to decide it for us."

The others were quiet for a few seconds, and then Noah said. "Amen to that."

CHAPTER 30

Later that afternoon, Connor met with the others in the conference room near the bridge. The mood on the ship had become somber in light of Phendran's warning. They'd had a breather to collect themselves, and Connor went with Noah to inspect the ship's systems.

Rhodes sat across from him. "That message is pretty vague. What does he expect us to do?"

"Figure out a way to leave," Connor replied.

Rhodes's eyebrows drew together, and he looked away. It wasn't a good sign. They were losing confidence, giving in to the enormity of their situation. In their minds, the mountain above them was crushing their hope. Connor wasn't immune to it, but he drew from a foundation of fortitude that forced him to think beyond whatever situation he happened to be in. There was a way out of this mountain. They just needed to put their heads together and figure it out.

He glanced at the Aczar tech on his wrist. It was the size of a large bracelet and fit much like the health-monitoring bands people wore. Earlier, he'd glided his fingers over it, wondering aloud about how to take it off. To his surprise, the bracelet came off his wrist and returned to a medallion shape. He then moved his wrist over it, and the medallion surrounded his wrist, becoming a thick bracelet. After trying to give it a few commands, which yielded no results, he hadn't done anything else with it.

Naya walked in and took a seat to Connor's right.

Rhodes finally lifted his gaze to Connor. "They can't decide what to do with us."

"I think competing factions are trying to control the decisions being made," Connor said. He scratched the stubble on his chin for a second. "They're going to try to take the ship away from us. It's just a matter of time."

Rhodes stared at him for a long moment. "Surrendering to them was our only option. It gave us the time we needed to repair the ship." He paused with a thoughtful frown and lifted his hand, palm up a little. "But we can't stop them."

Connor shook his head. "The ship has no ammunition for the weapons systems available, and we've only got about a dozen assault rifles. I doubt we'd slow them down if they really wanted to storm the ship."

When warships like the *Pathfinder* were decommissioned, one of the first things to go were the ammunition stores and weapons systems that could be salvaged for other ships. Connor had mainly gotten the ship for their research project because it required a major refit of its systems. It was a blank slate for them to use for experimenting with the I-Drive.

Rhodes looked as if he'd swallowed something foul. Then he heaved a sigh. "I know you're just being honest, but…"

"That's the reality of the situation. The sooner we accept it, the better off we'll be."

"You're not leaving us with a lot of options. I can't see just turning the ship over to them and hoping they have a way to keep us alive."

Connor glanced at the others around the table and tipped his head to the side. "Well, that's unacceptable, so we need to come up with other options." He leveled his gaze at Noah.

Noah bit his lip for a second. "The engines are functional. In theory, we could fly the ship out of this mountain. There's just the problem of getting past the doors, armed forces, and other defensive measures that they have stationed nearby."

"About that," Naya said. "I've been using the ship's sensors, and I've detected increased impact events in the surrounding area. There's a battle being fought nearby. I think the Aczars are fighting among themselves."

Rhodes frowned. "How can you be sure?"

Connor glanced at the data Naya shared. "Because the impact events are different from seismic events. The analysis AI can differentiate between the two."

Rhodes looked at the data on the holoscreen across from them. "But why would they bombard the area and this mountain in particular?"

"Warring factions vying for control. If they can't find Salpheth, why not go after the one thing Salpheth wanted enough to try to escape for."

Rhodes pressed his lips together and looked away while he considered it.

"General, I have an idea," Kincaid said.

"What is it, Captain?" Connor asked

"Send out a small team to open the doors so we can fly the ship out of here."

"Aren't they watching the ship?" Rhodes asked.

Kincaid nodded. "They are, but I've sent out a recon drone over the past few days and they haven't detected it."

Connor's eyebrows shot up. "What?"

Kincaid flinched. "I repaired one of the scout drones by using parts from the maintenance drones that were destroyed by the Khronax. Then, I launched it out of the small maintenance hatch near the sensor array."

Seger cleared his throat. "We got the idea of trying while disposing of wreckage from the attack. Things that couldn't be salvaged."

Connor regarded the two soldiers. "Disposing how, Sergeant?"

"It started off by clearing away a ruined sensor that fell off the ship," Kincaid said. "We thought for sure the Aczars would notice, but nothing happened. This was the day after we got here. So, we decide to do a penetration test to see if the Aczars would notice something else coming off the ship."

Rhodes frowned. "A penetration test? With what?"

The edges of Seger's lips lifted. "We had a throwing contest."

A soft chuckle escaped Connor's lips, and Rhodes looked at him.

"I fail to see the humor in this," Rhodes said.

"You'd be surprised how many things happen because of things just like this," Connor said, gesturing toward the two soldiers.

Kincaid looked relieved. "Then we decided to repair one of the drones and have it fly around the chamber. We kept it high above us. I'm not sure why the Aczars made this chamber so big. I guess they don't do things by half." He paused for a moment, considering. "Anyway, I think they have limited detection capabilities."

Rhodes shook his head. "I find that hard to believe for a species that is afraid of being detected."

"It could be that the drone was simply too small," Kincaid said.

"Or someone is helping us," Connor said.

"Agreed," Noah said. "I'd rather not assume that they can't see us because they already demonstrated that they could. They took out the recon drones we had when they took the ship. It's probably limited by an active sensor capability."

"And you don't think they're keeping an eye on us?" Rhodes asked.

"I didn't say that," Noah replied calmly.

"Someone is helping us," Connor said and looked at Kincaid. "How far were you able to send the drone?"

"We made it past the first set of doors," Kincaid replied.

"What about low-altitude testing?"

Kincaid shook his head. "Not yet."

"So, all we've got is the fact that the drones aren't detected at the higher altitude."

"But it stands to reason, sir, that if someone is blocking the detection of our drones, maybe they'll do more if we give them a reason to," Kincaid said.

Connor considered it for a second. "What do you propose?"

Kincaid glanced at Seger for a moment. "That Seger and I use the drones to take us to the first set of doors and then ensure they're open long enough for the ship to fly through."

Rhodes huffed out a breath. "You can't be serious. What happens when they detect you?"

Kincaid smiled. "We fly out of there before they can catch us." He looked at the others and then at Connor. "Look, I get it. There's a chance that we could be left behind. We don't want that to happen, but isn't that why we're here? We take the risks so others don't have to."

Rhodes shook his head and looked away for a moment. "What about Cass?"

Kincaid met his gaze. "She's the reason I'd be doing this, sir."

Connor understood exactly where Kincaid was coming from. He'd put his life on the line so many times that it eventually became somewhat commonplace. Lenora had gone to great lengths to make him understand that this shouldn't always be the case. There were times when it was appropriate, and then there were times when it wasn't. The arguments came when they didn't agree on when that should be. It was a difficult balance to maintain with those you loved.

Kincaid looked at Connor. "This is a good plan, sir. Noah has already said the ship could fly us out of here."

"That's true," Connor replied evenly. "The Aczar would likely have some kind of response for that event. And then we'd have to find a way to pick you guys up."

"I was thinking that perhaps Phendran could lend a hand with that. Maybe even assist with the operation," Kincaid said.

Rhodes looked intrigued by that, but Connor had expected nothing less from the CDF captain. This wasn't something he'd just thought of in the moment. He'd carefully considered it.

"We've got another option," Connor said, looking at the others until his gaze settled on Noah.

Noah flinched. "Oh, Connor, I don't know about that. We were lucky to survive it once."

The others frowned, and Rhodes asked. "What's he talking about? What option?"

The edges of Connor's lips lifted a little, and he gave Noah a knowing look. "The way I see it is that it's our *only* option. We use the I-Drive to get out of here." He looked at Kincaid and Seger. "All of us."

Rhodes blinked several times and then looked at Noah.

Kincaid frowned with his mouth partially agape.

"That's a better plan," Seger said slowly and shrugged, giving Kincaid a pointed look. "It is."

Rhodes recovered from shock. "Can it be done?"

"It already *has* been done," Connor said and looked at Noah.

"Yeah, but we didn't know what was happening," Noah said.

"We were going to have to try this sooner or later," Connor said. Noah shuffled his feet, looking uncertain. Connor expected that millions of ideas were flying through his head. "Hear me out. Without Salpheth, the Aczars are facing an existential crisis. They've hinged who they are on him, as if they were intertwined. Now that he's gone, they'll need to decide who they are going to become." He gestured toward the impact data Naya had shared earlier. "This isn't going to be a peaceful transition. We've seen hundreds of examples of this in our war with the Krake. How many Ovarrow civilizations faced a similar dilemma before the cycle was broken? The likelihood of us surviving that isn't good. It's time for us to leave. We've had enough time to pour over the data of the event and to understand the protocols the Phantoms used that put us out here over five thousand lightyears from home." He held his hands out to his sides. "We know that we went through New Earth to get here. It was the only way our nav computer could reconcile our location. The evidence is there to support that what I'm proposing is not only possible but necessary. It's our only real option."

Noah looked away. His gaze went to the holoscreen for a few seconds. "What about the power core? We can't figure out why it's fluctuating."

"Can't we stay within a margin of safety?" Connor asked.

Noah gave a hollow chuckle. "I have no way to know what that is. They'll probably detect the moment we increase the output from the power core."

"Then we use enough power to go a short distance away. As long as we're not trapped inside this mountain or anywhere near this planet, it would be fine with me."

Noah rubbed his chin in thought, and Rhodes cleared his throat.

"There's a need for caution. Wouldn't it be better if we understood what would happen if using the I-Drive ended in failure?" Rhodes asked.

Noah blew out a breath. "I don't know. That's the problem. If we're wrong, we end up dead. We won't even feel it; we'll simply be gone. An even worse-case scenario is that we destroy this entire area. Beyond that, it could be what we're afraid had happened to New Earth and the entire Aczar planet would be destroyed because we took a huge chunk out of its crust."

Connor set his jaw. "Except that didn't happen."

Noah's shoulders slumped a little. "We *think* it didn't happen."

"No! It didn't happen! There isn't enough energy available in the power core to do that kind of damage. Remember what that Phantom said that started this whole thing?"

Noah raised his gaze toward Connor. "Move *through* space instead of *in* space."

Connor nodded. "This is it. We have all the pieces to do it. All we have to do is take that leap of faith," he said and eyed Noah for a long moment. "I can do it without you, but I'd rather you were there."

Noah blinked, his gaze sinking a little. Then he inhaled a

deep breath. "I'll do it," he said, and Connor arched an eyebrow. "Fine, we'll both do it."

"Uh, sir," Kincaid said. "That thing is glowing again."

Connor frowned and then looked at his wrist.

They are coming.

CHAPTER 31

Connor stared at the message for a long moment. "Phendran, is this you?"

Yes.

The reply was instant.

Connor chewed on his lower lip for a second. "Prove it."

You defied the will of the Phantoms and blazed a path for your species to follow. I've come to appreciate your stance on these issues. I've promised to help you, and it's a promise I intend to keep.

Connor gave the others a nod. "He's recounting a conversation we had. It has to be him."

Noah pursed his lips in thought. "Is he close by?"

Connor frowned. "Why?"

"Because he can help us with the power core."

"How would he help with the power core?" Rhodes asked.

"They have a more efficient use of power than we do. Their sources are smaller and pack a punch. That might give us the edge we need for this to work," Noah said.

Connor looked at the bracelet. "Did you hear that, Phendran?"

On our way to you. Begin your preparations and we will assist you.

"Okay, you heard him," Connor said. "We need to warn the others. Everyone needs to get to their stations."

They left the conference room, and Connor and Noah headed to the bridge. Rhodes followed them. Kincaid and Seger went to warn the others. Connor wanted them centrally located in case they had to fight off intruders.

They raced onto the bridge, and Noah went to a workstation.

Connor looked at Rhodes. "Don't you want to be with Cass?"

Rhodes blew out a long breath and glanced at the door. "Someone else is going to be with her. I'd rather help here if I can."

Connor gave him a knowing look. "Kincaid is a good man."

Rhodes gave him a tired smile. "Are any of them good enough for our daughters?"

Connor chuckled and then nodded. "Some are. Yes," he replied, thinking of Lauren.

Rhodes bobbed his head once.

Connor brought up the holoscreen that displayed the command interface and waited for Noah.

"Need a few minutes," Noah said.

He brought up the sensor feeds, which showed increased impact events.

"Sure, take all the time you need," Connor said with a bit of sarcasm.

"Is that what I think it is?" Rhodes asked.

"The mountain is being attacked," Connor said.

A video feed of the surrounding area showed several large

chunks of rock falling from the ceiling. Then, the destruction spread to other video feeds.

Noah muttered a curse under his breath.

"We can't wait for Phendran to get here," Connor said. "I'm going to divert power to the I-Drive."

Noah's hands flew through the interface. "Okay, yes, do it."

Connor navigated the systems menu and engaged the protocols to charge the I-Drive. The ship's computing core began pulling back power from non-critical systems. A governing AI managed the power flow as it balanced the needs of the computing core with other systems. Power began to funnel into the I-Drive.

"Need those coordinates," Connor said.

The protocols they used would only allow the I-Drive core to charge a finite amount until it had actual coordinates from the navigation system. It wasn't possible to exit n-space without them, and their failsafe systems wouldn't allow them to engage the I-Drive prematurely.

"Coordinates ready. Sending them to you," Noah said.

Something large and heavy landed on top of the ship. It must've happened nearby for them to hear the impact through the layers of battle steel. Connor looked at the video feed and saw multiple Aczar aircars flying toward them. Bright flashes from turrets he hadn't even known were there rose from raised platforms on the deck and began firing at the aircars. The aircars scrambled out of the way and some of them returned fire.

"Engines are online," Noah said.

The *Pathfinder* rose into the air and a countdown timer appeared on the main holoscreen. Connor retracted the landing gear.

"Untested protocols have been engaged," Noah said.

Emergency straps came out of the back of their chairs and secured them in place.

Connor watched the power to the I-Drive spike in a large draw. Then it burst beyond specks, and he looked at Noah in alarm.

"Damn it," he said. "I can't change anything now. The system is locked."

More of the mountain crashed on top of them, making Connor flinch. He wasn't sure what had happened to Phendran. Had he been in one of the aircars that had been destroyed?

Then the I-Drive engaged.

A gravitational field expanded around them, creating a bubble of space, bending it. To the Aczars racing toward them, it would appear that something had dragged the ship away before disappearing. The video feeds all went blank. Connor clenched his jaw, anticipating a destructive force that never seemed to arrive. What he did feel was a few moments of weightlessness and then the artificial gravity emitters came back online.

Connor released the breath he'd been holding and looked at Noah.

His friend blinked and looked as if he wasn't sure where he was.

The video feeds came back online, showing the "deep dark" outside the ship. Beyond that was a vast field of stars. Several of the video feeds became blocked by large, dark objects.

"Pieces of the mountain," Connor said. "They must've been caught inside the bubble."

Noah blew out a long breath that ended in a small grin. "It worked."

"Where the heck are we?" Rhodes asked, looking dumbfounded.

Connor frowned and looked at the NAV system. It hadn't given them their location yet.

Noah cleared his throat and began checking the systems. Almost a full minute went by, and he looked at Connor. "We're a hundred lightyears from the Aczars' homeworld."

Connor's mouth hung open a little. He knew what they'd been trying to do, and the shock of it prevented him from calculating how fast they'd traveled. He licked his lips and asked, "Is that what you were aiming for?"

Noah grinned and nodded his head a little. "Yeah, I was."

Connor blew out a long breath. "Oh, that's good."

Rhodes laughed and the rest joined in.

Several loud collisions sounded, followed by alerts on the main holoscreen.

"We need to move the ship away from here to get free of the debris we brought with us," Noah said and brought up the helm.

Rhodes looked at Connor, his eyes bright. "This means we can go home."

Connor smiled. "Damn right we can."

Noah flew the ship away from the debris field and several critical alerts burst onto the main holoscreen. At the same time, the artificial gravity field dipped and Connor grabbed onto the workstation to steady himself.

"The power core is unstable, and it's causing a cascade of systems failures," Noah said. He stared at the holoscreen but the data hadn't refreshed. "We have to get down there."

Connor tried to open a comlink to main engineering where Naya was stationed, but it wouldn't connect. "Let's go."

Rhodes looked uncertain.

"The computing core is frozen. Stay here in case we get back online," Connor said.

They left the bridge and ran the length of the ship through

corridors that were suddenly plunged into darkness, heading to main engineering. Emergency lighting came on, but it took a few seconds for the switchover. There were entire sections that had partial gravity in them, which meant that the issues were impacting critical support systems, including life support.

They raced down the corridor and saw flashing lights coming through the partially open door to the power core.

Connor palmed the door controls, and it opened the rest of the way. Naya Corman was on the floor, unconscious.

Connor hastened to her side and tried to wake her up. She wouldn't respond.

"Oh, my God," Noah gasped.

Connor looked up at him, and Noah stared inside the power core containment room.

Connor stood and turned toward the power core. Bright flashes of yellowish light made him blink. Something moved inside the core, and Connor squinted to get a better look at it.

It took several seconds for his eyes to adjust, but when they did, his heart stopped and his mouth went dry.

Salpheth was hovering inside the power core, and tendrils of energy were flowing from the core to Salpheth's body.

They both stared in shock. Salpheth was draining the power core, drawing it into himself. If they didn't stop him, they were as good as dead.

CHAPTER 32

Connor looked at Noah. "I thought he was gone."

Noah tore his eyes away from the power core. "So did I."

"He didn't follow us here, so he must've hidden himself somehow," Connor said.

Salpheth either hadn't noticed them or was ignoring them.

Noah blinked and looked away for a moment. "Has to be the core. There's no other explanation."

Connor frowned. "What about the core?"

"He must've hidden himself inside the core. They're beings of energy, aren't they? At least partially. What if before the I-Drive sent him away, part or all of him fled to the once place that could keep him here?"

Holoscreens flickered among a torrent of alerts, which paled in comparison to what was happening inside the core.

"Are you saying he somehow merged with our power core?" Connor asked.

Noah shook his head, then tipped it to the side as he considered his answer. "I don't think so. Maybe he inserted himself right next to it so they existed side by side," he said, closing his palms together. "This could explain the power fluctuations we've been seeing."

"And he did what? Just waited for us to use the I-Drive?"

Noah's eyes widened. "He wouldn't need the ship. If he can absorb or temporarily capture the energy in the power core, he wouldn't need the ship. He could just take the Infinity Drive, and there would be nothing we could do to stop him."

"Like hell he can," Connor said, marching toward the core. Then he spun toward the workstation.

"What are you doing?" Noah asked, catching up to him.

"He can't drain it if I purge the whole system. We can preserve what's left."

Connor brought up the control interface for the power core and began initiating a system purge.

"Connor, wait!"

Connor stopped what he was doing and looked at Noah.

His friend held up his hands in a placating gesture. "Just wait a second."

Connor flung his hand toward the core. "We don't have a lot of time."

"I know. I know. But there has to be another way," he said and dragged his hand through his hair.

Connor blinked, stunned. He shook his head and turned back to his holoscreen.

"Connor, no. Hear me out. Please!"

Scowling, he stared at Noah, losing patience.

"You're right. Purging the power core might rid us of Salpheth, but what if that's wrong?"

Connor's gaze narrowed dangerously. "You want to debate the moral implications of stopping Salpheth from killing us?"

Noah bit his lower lip. "Yes. Hear me out. The Aczar trapped him for who knows how long. The Phantoms left him behind and we don't even know why."

"It's because he's evil. That's why," Connor snarled.

"He's desperate. These are the acts of someone who thinks they have no other options," Noah said, his eyebrows raised. "Once upon a time, people thought the Ovarrow were evil."

Connor shook his head and turned back to the holoscreen, continuing to bring up the purge protocols.

"What if we trapped him instead?" Noah said.

Connor stopped what he was doing, his hands frozen, and he turned toward Noah.

"The Aczars did it for years."

Connor gestured toward the power core. "It's too dangerous to keep him in there, and there are no Aczars here to show us how they did it."

"You're right, we can't keep him in there. I spoke to Kholva about how they trapped Salpheth. It's an energy storage system. It isolates Salpheth inside it, preventing him from doing anything outside of it."

"We don't have an energy storage system," Connor said and turned back to the holoscreen.

"Trust me, Connor, please. There are so many reasons to do this. It's worth the risk. Unless you're okay with the Phantoms doing this to someone else?" Noah asked and paused for a moment. "Trust me, like I've trusted you all these years."

Connor winced. He'd known Noah for a very long time. Noah had been part of a core few who had always supported him, especially when no one else would.

Connor regarded him. "What if you're wrong?"

Noah stared at him. "What if I'm not?"

Almost every instinct demanded that he eliminate the threat. Salpheth would kill them, but Noah was right about one thing.

Salpheth represented an intelligence asset, and if they could control it, maybe it was worth the risk.

Connor stepped away from the console. “Go ahead.”

Noah swooped toward the holoscreen and went to work.

Connor lifted his gaze toward the power core. Salpheth remained focused on the core as well. Then, the purge began and Salpheth jerked away from it.

Connor turned toward Noah. “I thought you weren’t going to purge the core.”

Noah smiled and pressed the button to execute what he’d been setting up.

The ship’s main power core flashed a bright light, blinding them. Then the core closed as it was cut off from the fuel source. The purge protocols dumped all remaining energy out into space.

Salpheth was gone.

CHAPTER 33

Connor's mouth hung open as he stared at the empty power core. He turned toward Noah. "What did you do? I thought you didn't want to purge the core?"

Emergency lighting bathed the control room in a pale amber light.

"No, I had to do that, but I also did something else," Noah said.

Naya Corman let out a soft groan and they helped her sit up.

"Are you hurt?" Connor asked.

Naya frowned and then sighed. "I think I'm alright."

"Do you remember what happened?" Noah asked.

She blinked a few times, and then her eyes widened. "Salpheth!"

"It's okay. The danger has passed," Noah said.

Naya stared at them for a long moment, then sagged against the wall. "I just need a minute."

A glimmer of light came from the power core as the

restarting protocols engaged. A small yellowish globe came into being, spinning and growing. It stabilized in the middle.

"That's better," Noah said, lifting his chin toward the core. "It's stable now. It'll cycle up to whatever power is left."

Connor looked at the core for a moment and then at Noah, eyebrows raised. "Where is Salpheth?"

Noah grinned a little and gestured for Connor to follow him toward the door. "I'll show you."

He led them a short distance to the secondary power-core unit that was much smaller than the main. Waves of energy cascaded around a sphere, and floating inside of it was Salpheth's pale form.

The Phantom swooped to the edge of his cage and let out a silent roar, lunging toward them. He smacked against the barrier and was thrown back.

Noah arched an eyebrow. "I don't think he likes his new home."

"How did you do this?"

"It was pretty simple, really. Salpheth had two places he could go when the purge protocols were engaged. Either he'd leave the ship minus the Infinity Drive, or he'd retreat to the secondary power core. I changed the containment field for the core to trap him inside. We'll lose some redundancy for the main power core, but I thought the tradeoff was worth it."

Salpheth glowered at them menacingly.

"Can he hear us?"

Noah shook his head. "And thankfully we don't have to hear him if we don't want to. I'm sure he can guess what we're saying, though."

"And you cut off the secondary core from the rest of the ship?"

Noah smiled. "It's completely isolated. Basically, it's an energy field whose entire purpose is to continue to exist."

Connor considered it for a few moments. "What happens if we purge this one?"

"Then Salpheth would be jettisoned into space or wherever we happened to be. I don't think he'd survive very long."

"What makes you say that?"

"Because the Phantoms use ships themselves, or some kind of equivalent. Phendran said they wanted to ascend to become like the Phantoms, which means existing outside of n-space. But there has to be more to it than that. Then there's your encounter where they used some kind of construct to interact with you," Noah said and gave Salpheth an appraising look. "We're a lot closer to understanding that than we were before."

Salpheth moved within the sphere, causing a wake in the waves of energy coiling around the entire field. He looked as if he were checking it for weak points. Connor pressed his lips together, considering.

"We don't understand them that well," Connor said, "which means we need to be careful. I want the ability to purge this core at a moment's notice. No discussion. If there's a danger, we don't take any chances."

Noah didn't respond right away but eventually nodded.

"How do I talk to him?" Connor asked.

Noah went to the nearby workstation. "This should work. It's not a comlink. Your voice will transmit to the field, and it will operate as a speaker."

"Understood. Go ahead," Connor said. Noah gave a nod. "Salpheth, can you hear me?"

Salpheth's gaze darted toward Connor. "You will not survive this."

He ignored the threat. "Don't you want to return to your own kind?"

Salpheth became quiet and very still.

"There's a good chance our path will cross with the Phantoms again. Isn't that what you want?"

Connor waited a few moments for him to reply. Instead, Salpheth turned his back on him.

After a few minutes, Connor looked at Noah. "Turn it off."

Noah did. "He probably needs time."

"Well, he'll have plenty of that," Connor said and opened a comlink to Kincaid.

A short time later, they left the secondary power core. Kincaid would guard it for a while. Connor had left him instructions for monitoring the Phantom, as well as a way for him to purge the core should the need arise.

"Where are we going?" Noah asked.

"We're going home. Now. No more delays. Let's go back to the bridge. We know that the I-Drive works with the new protocols. There's no reason to stay out here any longer than absolutely necessary. I'm assuming we'll make the journey in stages, right?"

"We'll need to," Noah said.

They returned to the bridge and went to work.

Connor broadcast a quick message to the survivors, advising them that they were going to make another trek through hyperspace, bringing them closer to New Earth. He heard cheering coming back through the comlink. All of them were ready to go home. Connor couldn't wait to see Lenora, his daughter, and his grandchild. The thought of it made his chest swell with anticipation.

Noah couldn't stop smiling as he entered the first set of coordinates to the navigation system.

Connor monitored the main power core. Without Salpheth's

interference, it was operating normally. There were no fluctuations coming from the core, but they were down to about forty percent. Core degradation was still an issue, but for the first time, he felt like they were closer to getting home than they had been on this entire trip.

An alert appeared from the scanner array. Passive scans were running, and they'd detected something. Connor brought up the data window.

"It's nothing, just a small asteroid," Connor said.

Noah heaved a sigh. "That's random," he said and continued working. A few minutes later, he turned to Connor. "I'm ready."

"Are you sure? That was kind of quick," Connor said.

Noah blinked and then shook his head. "Yes, I'm sure. I said I was ready, and I meant it. Let's go home."

Connor's gaze sank to his holoscreen for a moment, and then he shook his head, smiling. "Take us home, Noah."

Power was diverted to the I-Drive as it spun up. They were using the protocols that had been put together based on what the Phantoms had done, as well as Noah's research. They'd already been proven, and Connor settled back into his chair.

A countdown appeared on the main holoscreen and was broadcast throughout the ship.

Connor thought about Salpheth. He'd been so close to getting what he'd wanted. What must the Phantom be thinking, being so close to being free, only to have it snatched from him?

The countdown came to zero and the I-Drive engaged.

CHAPTER 34

The ship entered hyperspace and Connor watched the data feeds update as they transitioned from n-space.

"Transition is good," Noah said, peering at his holoscreen. "Just waiting on telemetry data from the sensors."

Connor nodded and was about to give the all-clear signal to the others when everything jerked to the side and up, causing him to bite his tongue. He blinked and looked over at Noah. He was hunched over his workstation, dazed.

Klaxon alarms shrieked overhead and there was a huge power spike from the main core.

Connor was thrown back into his seat by a massive unseen force. His range of vision narrowed, becoming a long tunnel. Connor fought to remain conscious, but his vision was blurring. He must've blacked out, and he didn't know for how long. He stared at the main holoscreen. The I-Drive was still engaged, but it was drawing more power into it than it should've been able to. Data windows from the nav system came up as automated protocols were launched.

Connor gritted his teeth and reached toward his workstation, which took him several tries because the g-force was too much. He barely managed to bring up the override system that would allow him to abort. Then he transferred his authentication and brought the whole system down.

Connor stared at the main power core readings, hoping the computing core hadn't frozen again. If this didn't work, he didn't know what he could do to stop it.

One moment, the power core output had been dangerously high and then it cut down by half. It stabilized and went down again. The I-Drive disengaged, and he felt the enormous pressure leave his chest as the inertia dampeners were restored to full functionality. He sagged forward and gasped for breath.

Noah groaned and turned toward Connor. There was blood on the edge of his mouth and coming out of his nostrils. Connor's nose felt wet and he swiped at it with his sleeve. He had a bloody nose as well.

"You're bleeding," Noah said.

"So are you."

Noah frowned and raised his hand to his nose. "What happened?" he asked.

Connor retrieved the emergency med kit and grabbed a couple of trauma pads. He passed one to Noah and then held the other one to his nose for a few seconds until the bleeding stopped.

"I don't know. After we transitioned into hyperspace, things seemed to be fine, and then the ship jerked," Connor said and frowned for a second. "It was like when the event first occurred. Like we were hitting ripples."

Noah frowned and turned toward his workstation. He brought up a few data windows and then backed away. "Hyperspace ripples? Buildup of energy on the bubble, but that would mean…" He paused for a moment, fingers flying through the holo-interface. "The nav system can't figure out where we are."

Connor glanced at it. "Maybe it just needs more time."

Noah shook his head. "We're lost. I mean, really lost. Do you know how long you were unconscious?"

Connor tried to remember but couldn't and shook his head.

Noah's eyebrows pulled together, and he bit his lower lip, considering.

A comlink came from Kincaid. "General, I think you need to come down here."

"Is the prisoner still secure?" Connor asked.

"Yes, General, but he said he wants to talk to you. He's claiming that he's our only way home," Kincaid said doubtfully.

"We're on our way," Connor said.

He looked at Noah. "He must've done something to the nav system, maybe even our computing core."

Noah wiped the blood from the edge of his lip. "How? He never had access to it."

Connor shrugged. "He must've had some kind of access. All systems get their power from the core. He obviously intended to go somewhere. Some kind of override, maybe?"

Noah glanced back toward the bridge. "There was nothing in the nav system."

"Then he hid it," Connor snapped and held up a hand. "Sorry. I just really wanted to get home."

"It's fine."

Connor glanced at the main holoscreen for a second and then looked at Noah. "How far would we have to travel to scramble the NAV system's sense of direction?" Noah gave him an exasperated look, and Connor winced. "That far, huh?"

Without knowing how long they were in hyperspace or what

direction they'd gone, figuring out their location was going to be a challenge.

Noah nodded. "It'll take some time to figure out. Let's go question Salpheth."

They didn't speak much as they made their way to the secondary power core. A comlink from Seger pinged Connor.

"General, uh, you're not going to believe this but Phendran and three other Aczars are in the port airlock. They're requesting permission to come aboard. I think some of them are injured."

Connor blinked in surprise and stopped walking. He spun around, gesturing for Noah to come with him. "Permission granted. We're on our way."

"How the heck did Phendran get here?" Noah asked.

"He was on his way. He must've made it close enough to the ship to be caught in the bubble before we left the planet," Connor said.

"Yeah, but…" Noah considered it for a few moments. "They're lucky to be alive considering all the debris that came through as well."

They quickened their pace and were soon at the port airlock. Seger was helping bring them inside.

Phendran looked up at him. He wore a face shield that was partially transparent and looked as if he'd been banged up.

"Are you alright?" Connor asked.

"We will survive," Phendran said.

Connor glanced at the other Aczars. "We have a med bay on the ship. I'm not sure our equipment will be able to help you, but we'll do everything we can."

Phendran looked relieved, as if something he'd feared hadn't happened. "We are grateful for your help."

"How did you get here?"

"By stealth, in the same aircar we travelled in before. We had just reached your ship when suddenly we…" Phendran paused with a confused frown. "I'm not sure exactly what happened. Our ship was damaged, and based on what you told us of your ship's capabilities, we surmised that we must've journeyed with you."

"But your aircar isn't designed for space travel," Connor said.

"No, it's not. We knew that to assist you, we had to provide our own life support. We'd hoped to help you escape captivity and then we'd return home," Phendran said, looking hopeful.

Connor felt something heavy settle in his stomach. He was about to tell Phendran and the others that they were going to die. They didn't have the equipment to create an artificial atmosphere so they could survive.

Connor heaved a long sigh. "Phendran, there are some things you need to know," he said and proceeded to tell him what had happened, including the fact that they had Salpheth trapped.

The Aczar's facial expressions were difficult to read.

"Salpheth hid himself in your main power core. Interesting strategy on his part," Phendran said.

Connor glanced at Noah. "Yeah, we thought so, too. I don't think you completely understand the gravity of the situation. I don't know if we can keep you alive. We don't have the ability to reproduce your planet's atmosphere."

Phendran blinked and then looked at the others. "Your concern for our wellbeing is noted, but you needn't worry. We will adapt."

Connor's eyes widened. "How?"

"Our SRA will assist us. The process is possible. It helps to adapt to the atmosphere on Ichlos and other harsh environments. I'm confident that this will not be a problem for us based on our analysis of your EVA suits," Phendran said.

"That's unbelievable," Noah said.

Phendran nodded slowly. "I must warn you that Salpheth will attempt to deceive you with half-truths."

"He already has deceived us. We think he hid something in our computing core that overrode our NAV system," Connor said.

"And our power core is in bad shape," Noah said.

Phendran considered this for a few moments. "Then it is in our best interest to work together for the survival of all."

Connor smiled. "I couldn't have said it better myself."

He helped get the Aczar to the medbay, feeling detached from the situation, as if he were observing. They were thousands of lightyears from home, perhaps even more.

He stood outside the medbay while the others went inside. Soon after, Noah joined him.

"Phendran is building something that is supposed to help them," Noah said.

Connor nodded. "That's good."

Noah eyed him for a long moment. "It's finally hitting you, isn't it?"

Connor felt like his mind was racing, and he was only somewhat aware of where it was racing to. He leaned against the wall. "I guess so." He slowly shook his head and sighed. "I really thought we were going to make it home," he said and frowned. "This time."

A soft snort came from the back of Noah's throat. "Yeah, me too."

"We're lost."

"That's the simplest way to put it."

Connor looked down the corridor, not really seeing it. "Why would Salpheth want to come here?"

Noah folded his arms across his chest. "We stopped him

from getting wherever he wanted to go. Do you think he's going to tell us?"

He heaved a sigh. "If he doesn't, we'll have to figure it out."

"Easier said than done."

"Getting back home is going to be a lot harder than we thought."

Noah laughed, and it sounded only half bitter. "What an understatement, Connor."

He smiled tiredly. "It's what I do." He glanced at the med bay. "I bet Salpheth wasn't counting on us having any help from the Aczar."

Noah gave him a sidelong look. "You have a plan already?"

Connor pursed his lips. "Just a few thoughts. Come on. No rest for us."

Noah pushed himself away from the wall. "Or for anyone back home."

Connor was quiet for a few moments. This wasn't the first time he'd been cut off from everything he'd ever known, but he was sure this was beyond anything he'd ever anticipated. An image of his family came to his mind, and he held onto it, drawing strength from it. Somehow, he was going to make it home. They all would.

CHAPTER 35

Lenora could feel more than a few people glancing in her direction as Isaac Diaz—her son-in-law who she adored—finished giving the results of his investigation into Connor's disappearance.

Lauren's shoulders drew up tight as she watched. "Is that it?"

Isaac was hundreds of kilometers away from them at the site where the disappearance occurred. His likeness was projected above the holotank at her house.

"I'm afraid so, love. There isn't much more we can learn from the site. The ship and all aboard are gone. There is absolutely no evidence of an attack, so we've ruled that out as much as we can," Isaac replied.

Lenora cleared her throat, and the others in the room became quiet. "What about Kara's theory that this has something to do with the Infinity Drive?" She'd become very close friends with Noah's wife over the years, and the two regarded each other as sisters.

"She's understandably upset."

Lenora blew out a shallow breath, knowing Kara's lack of tolerance for inefficiency. "That's putting it mildly."

Isaac looked as if he'd been caught trying to soften the news. "Yeah, she's got a reputation for not putting up with nonsense. She's setting up shop here at the R&D facility and intends to recreate the conditions that led to the event. She said it'll help her figure out what happened to them. I'm hoping it'll help us find them."

Finding Connor and the others had been foremost in many people's minds since the event that had taken them away. There was no shortage of people who had assured Lenora that they would do everything possible to find them.

"Thank you for the update, Isaac. Safe travels for your return home," Lenora said.

She left the room, giving her daughter time to say goodbye to her husband, and her guests gave her some space to collect her thoughts. A slight flutter swooped around in her stomach, feeling much like a butterfly taking flight. She caressed her middle. Connor had disappeared before she'd found out.

She went out into the gardens and walked the path Connor had made for her. Everywhere she looked were reminders of him. Sometimes, they caused an ache in her chest because she missed him so much. God, she really loved that man. Though they'd had a lifetime together, it was nowhere near enough time for her. She needed him back.

It wasn't long before Lauren sought her out.

Lenora's daughter gave her an appraising look. "How come you look so calm?"

"I am calm."

She had to be, and it was as simple as that.

"No, you're not. You can't be. Not now. Now with…"

Lenora gave her daughter a reassuring smile. "Lauren, I knew marrying your father came with the risks that marrying men who have dangerous occupations brings. Over that time, I've had to face the very real possibility that one day your father won't come home. But every single time, your father has defied those odds. Where other people fail, he doesn't. It's an enduring truth that I believe. No matter where your father is, he loves us and is doing everything he can to get back to us as fast as he can." She reached out to take her daughter's hand. "You can't lose faith. I know I never have, and I pray for your father every day."

She watched as Lauren's eyes became misty and felt hers doing the same. Mother and daughter hugged.

"But where did he go? What happened to him? How do we get him back?" Lauren asked. A frightened look came over her. "What if—"

"Don't do that," Lenora warned, shaking her head. "If you play the 'what if' game, you'll drive yourself crazy. Trust me. Just remember, there are a lot of people who love your father. We will find him. Make no mistake about that. But it won't work if we can't keep it together."

Lauren wiped her eyes and nodded. "You're right, Mom. So, when are we going?"

Lenora smiled and arched a delicate eyebrow.

"We're going to the R&D facility, right?" Lauren said.

"Transport is already on its way here. Pack light. I guess we'll surprise Isaac."

Lenora didn't know what she was going to do once she got there. The work being done at the R&D facility was outside her expertise, but she hadn't been married to one Connor Gates for all those years without picking up a few skills here and there.

AUTHOR NOTE

Thank you for reading, *Pathfinder* - Book 17 in the First Colony series. This is the first of a multi-part story that will take a couple of books to tell, the scope of which will expand beyond Connor and the wayward Pathfinder. If you've read the entire series, I hope that by now I've built up enough trust with you to feel assured that telling the story this way will be satisfying and, hopefully, rewarding to you as the reader. I realize that ending the story this way can be frustrating for some. They want Connor, Noah, and the others home safe. That remains to be seen. I know it's awful of me to do that and I'm sorry. Please don't hate me. I sincerely hope that you're excited to read the next fun filled ride to learn what happens next. The scope of the story is increasing and couldn't be contained in one book, perhaps three books, possibly more. It will depend on you and your support, which I really appreciate. That's the long and short of it. If you enjoyed the book, please consider leaving a review. They are so helpful with discoverability and send a powerful message that this author is worth your valuable time.

Thanks again for reading.

~Ken

If you're looking for another series to read consider reading the Federation Chronicles. Learn more by visiting:

https://kenlozito.com/federation-chronicles/

ABOUT THE AUTHOR

I've written multiple science fiction and fantasy series. Books have been my way to escape everyday life since I was a teenager to my current ripe old(?) age. What started out as a love of stories has turned into a full-blown passion for writing them.

Overall, I'm just a fan of really good stories regardless of genre. I love the heroic tales, redemption stories, the last stand, or just a good old fashion adventure. Those are the types of stories I like to write. Stories with rich and interesting characters and then I put them into dangerous and sometimes morally gray situations.

My ultimate intent for writing stories is to provide fun escapism for readers. I write stories that I would like to read, and I hope you enjoy them as well.

If you have questions or comments about any of my works I would love to hear from you, even if it's only to drop by to say hello at KenLozito.com

Thanks again for reading ***First Colony - Pathfinder***

Don't be shy about emails, I love getting them, and try to respond to everyone.

ALSO BY KEN LOZITO

First Colony Series

Genesis

Nemesis

Legacy

Sanctuary

Discovery

Emergence

Vigilance

Fracture

Harbinger

Insurgent

Invasion

Impulse

Infinity

Expedition Earth

Fallen Earth

Resurgence

Pathfinder

Space Raiders Series

Space Raiders

Space Raiders - Forgotten Empire

Space Raiders - Dark Menace

Federation Chronicles

Acheron Inheritance

Acheron Salvation

Acheron Redemption

Acheron Rising (Prequel Novella)

Ascension Series

Star Shroud

Star Divide

Star Alliance

Infinity's Edge

Rising Force

Ascension

Safanarion Order Series

Road to Shandara

Echoes of a Gloried Past

Amidst the Rising Shadows

Heir of Shandara

If you would like to be notified when my next book is released visit kenlozito.com

Made in United States
Troutdale, OR
10/26/2024